Caught in the Pot

Thank you to anyone who purchased, read, or reviewed this first book of mine.

And to my family who thought it was cool I wrote a book, instead of a weird waste of time.

And to Andrew who let me use his laptop to write after I kicked mine off the bed and destroyed it.

Ink
Tilly
Salt
Tilly
Junk
Tilly
Rope
Tilly
Blood
Tilly

There is a small coastal town with a population of just under 3,000 people.

Averaging over one per day, it has one of the highest rates of opiate overdose in the country.

It is also the hub for the area's largest export.

INK

His fingertips pinched the sewing needle as he held it in front of his eyes, examining the tip for imperfections. Of course, this needle was like every other needle he had ever used but he felt proud of the special care he took. He took his time with every detail because it was the only thing in his life he was good at. It was his way of savoring the feeling, and he wanted to make it last. He sat on his scratched and faded coffee table that sat too low to the couch painted with mysteriously darker patches of stains forgotten and tired seams now allowing the guts of the cushions to press through. Directly in front of him sat a kid of about fifteen waiting for him patiently. This kid was not patient in the sense that he was being polite with the process, but in a way that indicated he did not, and never really did, have a place to be.

The two of them sat close, facing each other in the silence of the basement suite. The loudest sound in the room was the occasional burning drag the kid took from his cigarette. Smoke floated above them both and slowly disappeared around the blades of the unmoving ceiling fan, transient, much like the one whose lips blew it out. An unnatural yellow light seeped pathetically into the living room from the connected kitchen. It was a dim and dingy space. The small television sat black and turned off, as it always did. The brightest light in the room came from the kid's cigarette.

He took his eyes away from the needle and reached for the shaving razor next to him. He sat barefoot, wearing black jeans and a white t-shirt with ink stains all over it. He took his time, sitting in confident silence imbued within him because of this ink on his shirt. It was his camouflage, hiding away any person he was outside of these moments with strangers who waited on his couch. This ink on his shirt was why they were there at all and the shirt represented that and hid him just the same. Deep down, this was probably the reason he himself was covered in small, black tattoos, most done by his own hand: maybe to cover himself up, or maybe to try and change who he was. It didn't really matter why. He never thought about it because he didn't care about it; it was what it was.

"Okay. Take off your hoodie." The kid took his sweatshirt off without any hesitation or awkwardness.

"And where do you want it?"

"Here, I guess." The kid pointed to the top of his forearm, seemingly at random. It was impossible not to notice the purple track patch on the inside of his arm, evidence of the overuse and infection from drug use. This hoodie-hidden secret, now exposed, didn't seem to bother either of them. He had seen this many times before, and if the kid felt any shame for it, he did not show it. He just stared back at him with two unapologetically hollow eyes.

He took the kid's arm and the razor and shaved what little arm air there was on the young skin. He placed the blade back in the exact spot he had grabbed it from initially. The other items he would need sat idly waiting, placed neatly in order of when to use them. The kid took his arm back without looking at the now smooth patch. "It's going to be eighty dollars for this."
"I only have sixty."

He closed his eyes and with a quick nod and wave of his fingers, he took the cash from the kid.

Picking the needle back up, he examined the tip once again out of habit, as if something had changed in the last few seconds since he had last looked. In his other hand now was a generic blue lighter, picked up at some station with the plastic now beginning to peel. He sparked the flame and placed the end of the sharp needle directly into it.

This was the moment when the air in the room always changed. It never mattered if sitting on the couch was a fifteen year old junkie or a thirty five year old man already covered in tattoos; when a flame wrapped around a needle that was about to enter your skin, danger became present and caution replaced the stillness. The flame disappeared and he opened a near empty bottle of cheap vodka. He tilted the bottom carefully until the alcohol was dangerously close to the lip and almost spilling over. He dipped the

needle inside, quickly and carefully, disinfecting it. He righted the bottle, allowing the liquid inside to fall back into its rightful place at the bottom just before handing it over to the kid. The alcohol wasn't for the pain or the nerves. This kid was clearly no stranger to needles and he was not nervous. The vodka was an agreement, an offering, a symbolic gesture that he was not there to judge vices and that he was no stranger to them. The kid, having finished what was left, discarded his cigarette butt and handed it back to him.
"Thanks."

With the now sterile needle, he took appraisal of the waiting items beside him. This was everything he would need for the next hour or so to do what he did best. Like a surgeon and their scalpel, a welder and their torch, or a painter and their brush, every move he would make from now until it was finished was done with intent and poise.

It was time to begin.

Every time he picked up the classic yellow pencil it reminded him of his years in elementary school. He had been to so many different ones in just as many moves, it wasn't so much a memory of another lifetime, but another life completely. Any feelings of lost nostalgia it created lived alongside a comfort that he had found a better use for the pencil. He wedged the dull end of the sewing needle between the metal casing that held the eraser and the eraser itself, a bayonet for his writing tool. Just like the pencil never wrote, the needle never did any sewing. He took a roll of thin, white thread and taped the end of it near the end of the pencil. He then wrapped it around and around the needle, like a growing snowball, until just the very tip of the needle was visible. He pulled the string with care and caution to make sure it was tight and would not unwravel. He poured some of his ink into a shot glass that he had disinfected earlier -- not that it mattered to the kid whether or not it was clean -- but it mattered to him. He dunked the string-wrapped, needle-tipped pencil into the ink and let it sit. He stared at it. There was nothing to see -- the ink was thick and black -- but it was his method. He knew that beneath the surface, the ink was slowly seeping its way into each layer of the string, soaking it. It would hold all of the ink he would need, only dripping and leaking toward the edge of the needle, an

unbeating heart of black. Lifting it out carefully to make sure no excess drips fell, he examined it closely before looking at the kid. "Ready?"
"Yeah."

He shifted his weight to crouch closer over the kid's arm like any expert that dealt in care and detail would. His eyes hovered above the kid's arm, examining it like a cartographer might a map. He checked the needle quickly to see the smallest drop of ink waiting, hanging from the edge. He pressed the fine tip of the needle into the thin skin of the kid, depressing as far as it would allow before it broke through, plucking it back out instantly. A small ink dot now appeared on his skin that would be there forever. For every person he tattooed, after the very first poke, he unconsciously gave a quick glance to meet their eyes. His pause communicated that this was their chance to stop, and their silence was the unspoken official agreement to continue. The vacant and indifferent look from the kid was all he needed to know. The thread was doing what it was designed to do and had already replaced the metal tip with more ink. It was the last time he would look away. He stuck the skin again. And again. And again.

CHAPTER 2

Kane, happily awoken as he always was by the clanging of sea bells and the excited squawking of birds ready for the scraps from the catches of the day, immediately began making instant coffee. The locals called the sound the seagulls made "mewing," which sounded too soft of a word for the irritating orchestra of the gulls. He would stick to calling it squawking. The bells, just as loud but much more pleasing, were signifying the plethora of boats of all sorts that were starting to head out for a day of fishing, hauling, gassing, catching, and trapping. Kane ran the tap, cupping water into his hand and feeding it directly into his mouth before filling the electric kettle and flicking the lever down.

Nothing about this small town felt like home to Kane, but none of the inevitably temporary "situations" ever really did. Home is where the heart is and a house is not a home -- he had never known a thing about the first sentiment, and only ever knew the latter to be true. He had arrived in Maine six months ago and the sense of belonging had never decided to arrive with him. With each move, he had always hoped to feel that way, but really, he only became more familiar with each location, a knowledge of the landscape rather than a kinship to a community. He moved from place to place, town to town, job to job, for the exact opposite reason. He only ever grew bored of it. He'd never had trouble making friends when he was younger, but he found in adulthood it was difficult for him to be bothered. Boredom had a way of making Kane feel an imminent claustrophobia, enough to force him out before that became his reality. It was his way of taking control, making it his own decision to leave rather than being beat once again by a failed agreement he had made with himself, that this new place would be different, that this place might be home. To avoid this recurring feeling of failing himself, he always talked himself out of the current town and into the next one, without even knowing where the next one might be. By the time he figured that part out, he had already talked himself into believing it. They were all just random dots on a map he followed to connect with the hopes to reveal some larger picture. When he had arrived here in Sachem five months ago, he had had a feeling things would be different, but those always expected inclinations were quietly subdued when he slowly started to realize that he may have been wrong once again.

Kane would live in a place for six months, maybe more, and then be eager to depart once again, leaving no lasting impression on anyone. Nobody ever left an impression on him either. He typically jumped towns fairly far from the one before it. Kane left for no apparent reason so that the next town had no choice but to feel new to him, otherwise it would feel inauthentic. It would be as if he had never left. With each new town he came closer to the realization that he was probably going to run out of different types of places and there would be no borders wide enough for him to not feel smothered. For now, he could only keep trying, nomadically chasing the idea of having a home and a life. Kane liked who he was, he just didn't like the world around him.

Four towns and two years ago, he was doing a bit of part-time work in the Atoghonny National Park. He had been surprised to get the job, but they needed the help. It paid well and he liked working in the forest. He was part of a three-man crew that would cover a small, designated area of the park and find diseased trees previously identified by a similar type of crew with a red "X" in spray paint. He was just there to spot the falling tree and help carry the cut segments to the truck. He was new and was not tasked with the responsibility of a chainsaw. He didn't want it anyway. His favourite moments were the ten or so seconds of the tree falling. The deafening and invasive sound of the chainsaw, making him feel tight with guilt, an unwanted imposter ripping through the decrepit, rotted wood. And then, the blade would pass through the trunk and cease its noise, stilling the forest again as if they were just faceless subjects in a photograph. The tree slowly and quietly tipped, the forest an audience in silent awe as the tree fell toward the ground where it would crack and splinter and reverberate powerfully in a final death rattle. It forced Kane to feel the chaos and the quiet. Soon enough, the two other guys he worked with asked him to have a beer after work. Kane went, as he had learned it was always better to spend a few hours on a Friday night over a few beers, than for the length of a work week after turning down their welcoming request. They were nice guys. Kane even acknowledged to himself that one might feel uncommonly lucky to work with them out here in the trees, but it just felt forced. He had been in this position before, and it wasn't until he finished his second beer that he knew it was time. Monday came and Kane, sitting next to his two modest bags of clothes and personal belongings, was already headed Northeast.

It wasn't the case that all it took for Kane to be pushed away from a job, or a place, was any type of personal interaction. He actually wished he had friends he was close to, or people in his life that he loved. It wasn't as if he was making his way to some Northern forest to live off of the land, away from all of the insufferable people going from A to B, A being birth and college and B being career and death. No, he respected those decisions and often wished it was how he felt. He just wasn't wired that way. He liked normal things -- going to movies, restaurants, keeping up with sports -- he was just doing them alone. He was very lonely and he felt it deeply, and he was becoming very good at being that way. He had a few friends from high school he still kept in touch with, but that fake checking in felt worse than having the relationships drift away altogether. People grew apart and Kane felt more comfort in that than most people. So he texted back when texted, and he answered phone calls when they came, but when things would slip away, he never reached out to pull them back.

His family was in the same place he'd grown up in. He loved them very much; they were a small family which made them tight. They didn't have expectations for him to settle down anywhere and they accepted his traveling nature. He thought they even loved him more for it. He wasn't just the mold of a person who did what he was "meant" to be doing. Then again, they would probably welcome any decision he made, as long as he was the one in control of it. They checked in often to see how, and where, he was. He missed them and he felt at home when he was there, but it was a fleeting comfort. It was his childhood home and he was now twenty-two years old. It felt strange that his life was a search to create something he seemed to have just grown out of. If he had any idea what he was searching for, then maybe he could better look out for it. He was unknowingly wandering throughout his own life, hoping to stumble upon something that seemed to come so easy to other people. Kane didn't know if other people were forcing it, but he hoped not. He knew he never could.

After a full day's ride, hitting several towns scattered down the line of the highway, the bus had taken Kane further west. Without ever having any source of income and or promise of a place to stay, he still never arrived in a state of panic or worry. The first night he would always stay in a cheap motel and then figure something out the following day. He had nothing but time and he was resourceful. He lived modestly and selfishly, and although he never had enough money for it not to matter, it was enough to continue this way of life without a fear of continuing on terms other than his own. Once he knew exactly what town he was actually in, he would seek out the bus terminal attendant and ask for directions. Everyone he met remained faceless, all of their unique looks and traits blending into one swirling and ultimately fading memory. But the bus attendants he talked to always stood out to him and he remembered most. Maybe it was because they were always the first interaction he had in every new possible home for him. With every "Hello there!" came a snap recollection of each of their faces in each of the towns he had lived in the past four years. He said thank you and was gone, gone like the other faces and places he had momentarily remembered.

Kane had found a rundown place to stay just off the highway and immediately looked for the first restaurant that had both WIFI and offered all day breakfast. He had learned that in many small towns this was often impossible. He was lucky and found a diner rather quickly where he ate and searched through jobs and available short-term leases. He saw nothing worthwhile and was too starving and exhausted from his journey to absorb any of the information he was seeing anyway. He happily pushed these worries to the back of his mind for tomorrow. He still did not feel worried and knew that he wouldn't become so. If there was nothing when he arrived, then there would be opportunity elsewhere. And that is what happened. He spent two more days in his brief hotel home, earnestly looking at a way to settle down. He managed to find a room in an apartment for a suspiciously cheap price. That would have suited him just fine, but there was no work. There were postings online for the local grocery and convenience stores, a ticket taker at the theatre, and, of course, the odd serving gig, but he never entertained the idea of applying, and never did. These jobs were not beneath him, but he wanted -- or needed -- to work as alone as possible. Totally alone was a hard thing to find, but surrounded by people would quickly expose himself to himself. The repetitive facade in hoping that the next place he arrived in would be the one he would call home could be just at the next stop and was consistently ignored or forgotten. If he gave himself an honest try and six months, he could keep believing in it. If he had decided to take one of those jobs, he would be gone in a week, feeling discouraged and empty. Even if they had nothing in common, every town felt exactly the same to him anyway. It was a contract with himself that he must live cheap and work with the ability to keep to himself. Kane ended his search by setting his phone screen side down on the table. His clichéd classic eggs-any-style breakfast would arrive soon anyway. He would rather think about where to go next in the morning, get back on the bus, and try again at another town. Which is exactly what he did.

The bus carried Kane south. There was really no other direction for him to take. He had no interest in going back the way he'd come, and north would quickly run out. He crossed another imaginary line, and although he could not see the ocean, he knew it was nearby. Of course, a child's knowledge of geography was the dead giveaway, but it was more than that. It was the salt in the air and the way the birds called out to it and not the blue above. When you are raised next to the ocean, perceptive or not, you feel its familiarity forever. It was a generational knowing that you had returned to the edge of the land where waves crash and cliffs withstood. It was knowing that at these edges, for centuries, the promise of dreams and new life could be granted or destroyed. Kane was just as sensitive to it when he was nowhere near the ocean and he could see it in its people. It had been years since he had seen it, the longest he had gone in his lifetime. He felt eager to see it again, a feeling he rarely had anymore, and that made him that much more excited. The road signs that told him what each little town was also reminded him constantly of two things: he was now in (and "Welcomed into") the Down east District of the region, and this was where you would find fresh lobster.

Kane's familiarity to the ocean was with the Pacific Ocean, warmer and more peaceful than here at the Atlantic. Back home the waters were filled with luxury fishing vessels, recreational boats, cruise ships from time to time, and people swimming and surfing when the weather permitted. The Pacific Ocean was a beautiful visual force in the grey of winter, and in the summer, the water and its beaches became the electric current of excitement running through the coastline. He had never fully experienced the East Coast, but he had always envisioned the Atlantic side as a clashing mismatch to the Pacific, like two twins raised in vastly different homes. The Atlantic was colder and nastier. Rather than signs informing of a "Lifeguard on Duty" there would be "No Swimming - Dangerous Cliffs" in their place. That hadn't really mattered to Kane sitting on that bus after leaving a town with no prospect of staying, and it wasn't just for his surprising longing to again see the ocean. He knew that these were going to be small, salt of the earth communities that relied on that choppy water as a way of life. These roadway signs continued to remind every car on the road that seafood, especially lobster, doubled as this area's key tourist attraction and way of life. There was going to be work, and the type of work that demanded you kept your head down, but also paid incredibly well. This was an assumption of course, but Kane closed his eyes in his belief in it, and fell asleep. Often when in between situations, Kane's desire to call each new place home made him nervous. It was the realization of the nearby ocean, promise of money, a possible home and a fresh start that allowed him to relax.

When he opened his eyes, he felt the slow winding of the bus and the only thing he could see out of the window was the ocean. He was overwhelmed by the sight of it. It was the suddenness of seeing the enormity of the ocean that struck Kane. It wasn't necessarily that he had forgotten how beautiful the sight of it was, even now at sunset sitting one hundred feet above it. The ocean had always affected him that way, no matter how often he was around it. What struck Kane most in this moment was the crushing weight of nostalgia. Nostalgia was something he rarely felt anymore. By design he kept most baggage of the past in the past, but this was inescapable. Kane was lonely and he knew it most when he felt this way. Nostalgia was a haunting of good memories and held little comfort when one longed for better new ones. He felt like he was having nostalgia for the feeling of having nostalgia itself and for the first time since he'd left home, Kane really believed things were about to get better. His shoulders were tight, his heart was beating quickly, and a tear fell from his eye, another part of himself not felt since before leaving home.

There may have been towns just like it while Kane had been asleep, or possibly more suitable further along the road, but it was the next town that he knew this was where he would be getting off. Here, it was ocean on one side and thick forests on the other. The sign was small and partially covered by those overhanging branches of pine, and Kane read of this new town, the town that, for the first time, might not be like all of the ones before it. "Welcome to Sachem! Settled in 1763. Shiretown of Downeast District, Higher County. Population of 2,500. Home of Lobsters and Lighthouses."

The bus rounded the cliffside corner and he saw Sachem sitting there, waiting. The road they were on travelled directly downward, with the only other visible road a mile or two across the cove, up and leaving the town. Sachem sat, existing hidden in its own world, likely as it had since 1763 and eons before that. Fishing had created this town and fishing was what sustained it and he appreciated the ancient function of that. The sun was almost down now and he had seen no boats out on the water. He knew he would find work and he would stay here for as long as he could. A small, tight-knit community like this meant he could lay low but also that he may need to leave in fast fashion, as he had in so many other previous places. Now armed with the name of the town, he was already searching online for vacancies and postings with all of the possible opportunities running chaotically optimistic through his head. He had looked forward to stepping off the bus to speak with another bus attendant to ask if there was still a place he could grab something to eat and stay for the night. He knew that there would be. There always was.

The lever for the electric kettle snapped upright as the water boiled and steam escaped. Kane himself snapped out of this daydream hold of doubts and worries about his situation and made himself a cup of coffee. As he drank, still standing over the sink, he continued to dwell on why six months ago he felt like it would be different. He has fooled himself before, but this time he was so certain, and his mistake worried him. His work was fine, but the hours were dependent on weather, making pay inconsistent. He would need to figure something out because despite this town and his unknown purpose in it, now stale, he had a budding feeling that he might still want to stay. Kane gave his mug a rinse and set to get ready for the day. He had the day off work, but plans later in the day. No, this town of Sachem didn't feel like home to him, but she was starting to.

CHAPTER 3

Kane flicked the lights off in his suite, stepped outside, and locked the door. He had found this modest basement unit near the bus terminal the night he arrived, on a large message board filled with notices of town meetings, a lost dog, a couple cookouts, and the like. It was the only listed property for rent, so he'd called the listed number immediately with crossed fingers. He didn't know what he would find online, and this suite was furnished with a bed, a couch, and a few smaller amenities. A woman answered, Brenda, and she asked him a few questions - what he was looking for, his price range, his job -- of which he had none -- and finished by asking him if he had a place to stay that night. When he said not yet, she told him he could crash there and that they could talk about it in the morning. She sounded welcoming, but not desperate for a tenant either. Whether it was small-town hospitality or he'd just gotten very lucky, he arrived graciously and paid a cash deposit and first month's rent in the morning, no paperwork. Brenda had sounded 30 on the phone, looked about 40, and was probably closer to 60. EVen though her hair was fully grey and her hands and face wore wrinkles, she had the youth of someone used to fighting, fighting for what you want because you knew who you were, and fighting time as it came just the same. The unit was small, made smaller with no windows, but, like the ad said, there was a bed and a couch; it was all he needed. The once white carpet of the living room ran into the adjoining kitchen's linoleum, both slightly browned and warped from time. The rent was cheap and anything else he needed, like the electric kettle, was small and inexpensive. He had his phone, laptop, clothes, and his small black pack with the things he used to tattoo.

Tattooing was a side business that travelled as well as he did, and it helped him earn a few extra bucks. In a town with no tattoo parlours, filled with fisherman that made enough in an hour to pay for an entire tattoo, he imagined it might mean better business. He had done a few a week for the first couple months since arriving, just a couple of the people he worked with and their odd referral. That well seemed to have dried up and he would have to look for other ways to find people interested in getting pieces by him.

The tattooing Kane did was simple. Classic stick and poke, small images, always in black. He was covered in them, which was often the trigger for people to ask him about them, leading to interest in them, leading to Kane giving out more tattoos. The extra fifty or sixty bucks he would pull in for each tattoo wasn't really why he did it. It definitely helped, especially when hopping from place to place, but he did it because he loved doing it. He took a well of ink and a sharp end and created beautifully crafted art that people would wear forever. Most of it was skulls and hearts, of course, but no matter what it was, he took pride in creating and elevating his simple style. Often, people refused to believe that his work was not done with a machine. They couldn't imagine that stick and poke could result in these detailed illustrations. It was this simplicity that allowed for the delicate and refined look of his efforts. It took much longer, and patience was required from him and the client, but this traditional approach is what made him a master of his craft. A clunky, buzzing tattoo gun served a purpose, but it wasn't Kanes. He had had an affinity for drawing in high school and it had been his depression that made him no longer care about it. He would resort to cutting sometimes, and he found that the release of pain by a razor was the same as a needle injecting ink into his skin. He was able and proud to turn his self-harm into a therapeutic process. Maybe it was his cure. Maybe it was just an emotional re-direction of sickness. Either way, his depression had lessened with age, maybe through puberty, or maybe when the pressures of school life faded. Or maybe he was just used to everything. In any case, his love for self-tattooing stayed with him and he had become exceptionally adept at it. Kane was covered in these tattoos, evidence of how skilled he was, and on other parts of his body, how unskilled he used to be. He appreciated both. He had fantasies of working in a shop in a professional setting and, maybe one day, even being recognized for his pieces, but his antisocial leanings always prevented him from ever pursuing it in any real way.

Kane wasn't ashamed of his tattoos, but he never liked them to be present for a first impression. As he left his place, he zipped up his hoodie, assuring himself that each one was covered. The air was bitingly cold anyway. This close to the water, this early in the morning, the cold was easily enough to painfully tighten the skin on your face. It worried him for the actual coming cold with the changing season. He had arrived at the tail end of winter and found an uncomfortable amount of those days unbearably bitter. There was one night in particular when an ice storm had approached, sweeping freezing rain over the town and solidifying the air in a thick frigidity. His basement was always plenty warm and his blankets he had deemed worthy until then. In an act of desperation, he'd put on at least three of his sweaters and a pair of sweatpants under his jeans. This made him bulky and ridiculously immobile when he rolled the third pair of socks over his feet. Swearing and mumbling, watching the white breath escape his lungs, he'd been sure they were now in some sort of state of emergency. In the morning, after taking off all of the extra nighttime attire with some difficulty, he asked Brenda if she had been okay throughout the night. Brenda just laughed at his feeble, inexperience of what was necessary in the weather conditions that could roll through a coastal town on the Atlantic. She told him what he would need to buy for future such occasions that would be the norm in the middle of the cold season. He bought new bedding, a new jacket, and a floor heater. He didn't mind -- if anything, it helped him feel acclimated to the town, like he was investing in a future there. Whatever the winter decided to bring, he'd like to think he was now fully prepared -- in his head and his closet -- but concerned he still remained.

Sachem was peaceful in the afternoon. He had never gone to the docks as all of the ships were leaving. They left far too early, but he could hear it sometimes, even from his tucked away basement paradise two miles away. He could hear the loud slamming of crates, the echoing of mass shouting, and all of the other impact blows that he could only guess what had created them -- instruments of a lobster fishing morning sunrise. He could hear the hints of engines sparking to life, one after the other, sporadically, a fleet of animals waking up from their sleep. No, mid-week at noon, all of the ships were out to sea and none would return for hours.

Kane walked down his street, between the rows of houses, toward the ocean. He had a long walk before him and wanted an ocean view for as long as possible. Each house was small, humble, none like the one beside it, which actually made them seem similar in the non-suburban way you would certainly find in most neighborhoods in any big city. One house would be off white, paint chipping and peeling, and the next could be bright red because last year it had had a fresh coat of paint put on. Homes were practical structures, and the necessity to repair them as they needed healing created a mosaic of color and form. He wondered if at one time all of these houses had looked more or less the same. Here, craftsmen and builders were not necessarily available, or they would be expensive, requiring everyone, or at least a neighbour with the offering of a case of beer, to be the fixer-upper. These homes had to withstand gale force winds, hail, rain, salt, and the hard squeezing of the freeze and gentle pull from the sun. Most of these homes were one story, each one built as needed over time, likely by a descendant relative. There was pride in the patches, in every board of wood in the siding, and in the different colored shingles on the roof. Here, there was no remodeling or kitchen renovations, no mansions with the better view sitting above the rest of them. Each home was a family heirloom, every patch a ritual, a memory to their family that had lived before.

The streets had small kids riding their bikes or playing street hockey. There were no parents keeping an eye on them here. It was clearly a close-knit, safe community. Fights over tree leaves hanging in another's backyard or yelling at fast cars with children playing nearby would not happen here. There were not many people in the town, and even fewer when all of the fishermen were out, which he guessed was somewhere close to half. During Kane's first few weeks, Sachem appeared like a ghost town. There was nobody walking along the sidewalks of the streets. The often-empty General Store and the local bar, The Trap, were always deserted during the day, as were most other businesses. The call of a gull and the crashing of the waves on the seawall was so lonesome and loud that the lack of any inhabitants was eerily clear. It was on the weekends he saw the town come to life, families enjoying the fruits of a hard-worked week and cherishing time together missed. People walking by, holding hands, eating ice cream, on their own or in a group, would notice him. Kane imagined in this small community they knew he was a fresh arrival and admired him as an object of curiosity, although this might have all been in his head. The Trap was always busy at night. He had been a handful of times to grab an easy bite and found it was mainly fishermen at varying levels of drunk, and young girls who made do without being in the city. The bar, like the town, was a community where each person interacted or kept to themselves, a welcoming ecosystem. Sachem was indeed a town of ghosts, but not a typical one, where residents were nowhere to be found. A ghost is a relic of the soul that lasts far longer than it might have meant to as time passes. This town, of working to fix and to feed and to enjoy with the ones whom you loved most, was a town of the past, carrying the soul of what it had always been.

Kane reached the edge of the town, the heart of the community -- the wharf. Even with the docks empty and bells lazily and lightly dinging in the breeze, the hum of the spot felt alive, like the inexplicable energy of a cleaned-up car crash. Every sunrise and every sunset, hundreds of boats and people gathered here, preparing and unloading the day's work. He had seen them come in one night. It had been a disciplined anarchy. The first few boats had glided into the shallow waters of the cove with the occasional yell of anticipation to get fast to work. Massive cages filled with lobsters were being slammed from the large fishing vessels and onto smaller skiffs, before propelling the crew and day's haul to shore. It seemed impossible to Kane that these small boats could hold up that much weight, but they gently pushed forward, bumping into the docks with ease. Each member of the crew clearly had a specific task, but it was impossible to tell what and how they were coordinating. Years of repetition and the passing of genetic code had given them the efficiency of a NASCAR pit crew, throwing and tying ropes, lifting cages, running, yelling, and more. Faces were stern and determined. This trained pandemonium that one wouldn't expect from lobster fishing boats was amplified by the hundred or so boats arriving at similar times. There was no coordinator of traffic; they policed themselves. There was clearly a right of way, first-come-first-go system, but to Kane, it just appeared as a frenzied mash of boats like ants to get to dock and finish for the day. Arriving, they yelled at each other, ribbing and joking about one's manhood or less than impressive catch, and they smiled, but that determination never left their eyes. Kane imagined in awe the mental and physical toll that would take on a person day after day. He would love to see them organize and head out at dawn sometime. It was far more demanding than the work he was doing required.

Four options existed for anyone in the town of Sachem for work, providing you didn't have a connection to one of the seven businesses. Option one was working in the forestry industry, and, even though he had enjoyed that job, he aimed to take on something new. To fall back into forestry would be a forced admittance that he had never had a reason to leave in the first place. He saw there was plenty of work available and felt relieved that there was that to fall back to if the other two didn't work out. Brenda had told him about the other two options when his answer was a smiling, "What is there?" when she'd asked him what he planned to do for work. The second was blueberry picking, a seasonal job with perfect timing, beginning soon after he arrived. Apparently, this meant working two or three fields a week, with long hours making up for the low wages. Kane liked the idea of this, working different locations, isolated work, even eating a few blueberries here and there. The last option was more adventurous than the previous two, which was one of many reasons he chose to pursue it. It was out on the ocean -- shallow snorkel diving was required in small teams of four. He loved being in the water and it had been so long, plus he doubted his companions could get on his nerves from five feet below the ocean surface. This work would require Kane to get a license, which put him off at first, until he realized it took about ten minutes and all the responsibility essentially fell onto the boss anyway. Brenda told him that three to four days a week, small groups would boat out to shallow areas in the cove to snorkel and scavenge the bed floor for scallops. There was a law in Maine that each person was only allowed a certain quota of scallops per day, and per week. Kane was a hard worker and discovered he could get paid the same amount in four hours for working his ass off, as opposed to six or seven, so his decision was an easy one. Brenda told him all he had to do was go down to the docks and seek out an application at one of the two scallop outfits. The way she understood it, they were both always willing to hire and offered similar values. Kane went into the first Oceanside scallop office he saw, applied, and was told he could start Wednesday if he could get his license application in on Monday. His first day had been that Wednesday.

Training for scallop diving had been very basic. On his first day, his boat captain of the day (it was always different) had him swimming and exploring the ocean floor, identifying the life that lived below, acquainting Kane with the waters. The captain had said it was to respect the ocean and to literally and figuratively get his feet wet. Kane figured it was just to prove he could swim and handle a snorkel. Within two weeks, he was indeed finishing his quotas fast, often signing out when the boat was in for lunch at 1:00 p.m. Diving felt easy and he was good at it, so much so that the shadier captains would actually spread out his haul to the other divers so that he could keep working, in turn making his day longer. Kane never said anything to anyone. He didn't want to cause trouble, and it was only a couple of the captains that operated this way. Plus, his coworkers might hear about his complaints and feel ashamed, or even hold resentment. He had come across a handful of other people that worked in the same way as himself, but it was rare. The others weren't slackers, they just weren't as good -- too young, or weren't racing to get finished like he was. It was another part of the job he liked -- the boat crews were not only small, but always changing. There were fourteen boats and about 150 people to be dispersed over all of the shifts. As the months passed, this large and accessible pool of people would prove to be a great resource for tattoo clients. At his busiest, he was doing three per week, the most he had ever done. He never felt like anyone would get too attached or feel they had to become friends. Kane spent most mornings in the water, snorkeling facedown, a net in his right hand for scooping scallops, and a net bag in his left to store them. It was the strangest odd job he had embarked on during his travels.

Kane never considered lobster fishing as a fourth option. Not only did he assume he wasn't suited for it, but the idea of asking for a place on one of the boats and then earning his keep seemed far too intimidating. Once, out of curiosity, he had asked Brenda about the options available to him for work on a lobster trapping boat. She had a small laugh to herself. It was clearly not meant to embarrass or annoy him, and it didn't. He could tell in her small chuckle that it simply conveyed the high level of difficulty involved, and the idea of an inexperienced person even thinking about the work, let alone stepping foot onto a ship manned by the trapping virtuosos of Maine, was laughably absurd. Kane had asked her as a passing "what if?" and the second he'd asked and seen her reaction, he laughed at himself and joined in the foolishness of the idea. He thanked her for the help and nothing more was said about lobster fishing.

Now, having walked through the outskirts of Sachem, with fewer homes here and there, spaced apart by the limitations of the land, he found himself to be quite nervous. The road was steep and long up the hill, the entire town below and behind him. This vantage point of the cove and the odd fishing boat sitting idle in the bay, unused or in need of repair, was new to him. It was the same leaving road across the cove he had seen when he'd first entered Sachem from the other side. The wind was strong high up here off the water. He could see past the corners of the bay and into the open ocean. There were boats everywhere, tiny and barely visible. The waves from the edges of the horizon built toward him, smashing powerfully to play a distant, soft sound. It was hypnotic. Anything man made was respectfully quieted by the soft sounds of hushed nature. There were no distant sirens, no jackhammers, no countless sets of tires passing infinitely by at eighty miles per hour. This town had no white noise and he closed his eyes and listened before continuing on. The moment was shortly appreciated before he continued on his once-again anxious walk, thinking of the simplicity of this new town, and wondered, in the many reasons to leave, if this might be the one to stay. Kane's nerves rattled harder as he walked up this long road for the first time, to see her house for the first time, and to meet her mother, also a first for him.

CHAPTER 4

Tilly had invited him over for dinner the week prior. "It's the blue house with no driveway. There's a broken red car out front sitting on the freshly mowed grass. If you can't find it, call me. But you'll find it." And with that information, and an address that meant nothing on these backroads anyway, Tilly had kissed him and left. He saw the car, a red and rusted Chevy Impala from the early 80s. The tires, one of them flat, were surrounded by high, uncut grass in tangled tufts one might walk through in forgotten fields. It must have been quite the car in its day. Making itself known in bright blue was now the house. It had taken him a little over an hour to walk here, and now, steps away from the front door, he wished he had walked slower. His heartbeat was quick and he found it difficult to breathe normally. There were just two small windows to the house. They may have seen him already, meaning he was too close to back out now. One foot in front of the other led him to the door in a heightened state of worry over absolutely nothing. She was a wonderful person, and the way she spoke about her mom, he knew she would be too. He had been nervous enough when he'd hung out with Tilly the first few times, and this was like their first date all over again, but with an audience of two. Hell, he was still nervous around Tilly when it was only the two of them. Did she know he was covered in tattoos? He was glad they were covered and hoped they wouldn't be brought up. He felt like he was about to be the butt of an inside joke. Despite all this, he hadn't seen her for a week, and he was now raising his hand to knock on the front door. He was terrified, but equally as excited to see her.

Thinking back to when Kane had met Tilly, the exact moment was questionable. Does a meeting mean the time they were fully aware of one another, trading observations, enough to feel they knew the other? Or does an official meeting require the exchange of names and an acknowledgment of the understanding of the information? Kane wondered what he would say when Tilly's mother inevitably asked the "and how did you two meet again?" question later that night. It felt to Kane like their moment of meeting had been from one hundred yards away.

Kane had noticed something on the rocks just off the shore the morning before, and he returned even earlier the next day with his sharpened graphite pencil and folded sketchbook. He sat on the seawall, legs hanging over the edge, and observed the scene that had drawn him back to capture it. With the water a murky black and the sky itself an ocean of grey, it made conditions for sketching perfect for Kane. The tidal waters were drawn far now, revealing the ordinarily hidden bedrock beneath. A line of distinction was proof of how high the water had been only a couple of hours ago. On one side, accidental pools of water had gathered across the stretched beach, attracting excited gulls to investigate the improved food choices. Rocks were still dark with wetness, exposed to the air before the safe return of cover. Clams, mussels, and oysters covered rocks sitting heavy in the floor of mud. The water was a carpet, pulled back, showing a hidden world brimming with hidden life. On the other side of this line, it was dried out and dusty, the odd empty beer can wedged into the rocks that were painted with an astonishing amount of fresh and crusted bird shit. All of the boats were long and far out at sea, but one remained, planted on the rocks, leaning slightly. Two women and one man were scraping away at the barnacles and grime buildup on the hull of the boat. It looked like exhausting work, and as these three chiselled and chipped, wiping sweat from their faces, they did so with a patient pride. This was a part of their duty and it needed to be done before they could get back to work. This boat sat alone, waiting sadly, looking unnatural. The tide rolled away and there was nothing this boat could do but wait for it to return as it always did. Kane related to it. He drew it because he thought it too alluring not to. He put graphite to paper and began outlining his image. Kane's style was simplistic, but he still took his time. He used very little shading, keeping the images small and dark, boldened by the pieces of his subject that he saw most in himself. It was during his examinations he noticed a person, a brunette girl, far away sitting on the seawall bench with her own sketchbook. She was at least a hundred yards away from him, but he knew she was drawing by the way she was hunched over her pages, the way her head went up and down, and her obvious focus. Kane watched her, amused by this improbable chance encounter. How funny to think someone else had come to the water in the morning to draw, and to imagine she was even drawing the same boat as he was. Fate was not something he particularly believed in, but that would be something, two people feeling compelled to visit the same area to construct their own interpretations of the same seemingly ordinary boat and the task of cleaning it. He would never know anyway. Suddenly, her body language told Kane she had stopped her drawings and she looked over toward Kane. He quickly retreated back to his image and started drawing again, thinking about her now and his invasions and not of the stranded ship. He looked back at her, still looking in his direction. She sat too far for him to tell with his eyes, but he knew. She went back to drawing and he did the same. When he dared to look up again, she was gone.

The next day, Kane had decided to return to sketch. He had finished the boat but saw other things that called him back. A lone tree growing from the water, a lowered dock flattened to the ocean floor with the tide out, an eagle resting on a rock waiting to see a fish to snag from the water; he found himself inspired. The cove was foggy in the morning and he felt like he floated alone in this quiet time of the town. Walking toward yesterday's position, from far away, with headphones in and loud, he noticed someone was now close and walking toward him. Startled, he looked up and saw an impossibly pretty girl with long, brown hair and olive skin passing him, grinning, mouthing words he could not hear. It made him stop as she passed by with a casual grace, uncaring whether he had heard her or not. He took his headphones out and looked at her quizzically.

"I'm sorry?"

He noticed now she was carrying a full booklet of shuffled and messy yellow pages. She stopped and laughed, realizing that, of course, he hadn't heard her.

"I was saying the boat isn't there anymore."

"The boat?"

"Yeah, weirdo. The boat we were drawing yesterday. It isn't there anymore. Must be back on the water."

Kane just stood there, silent and looking baffled.

"Okay, well...hope you find something else to draw." She smiled at him. She was not flirting with him, but the nature of who she was had an effect on Kane beyond flirtation. The mysterious being from yesterday, born from coincidence, was now in front of him and confirming his wildest assumptions that he had created in his heart as he, and apparently her as well, had drawn the same boat stuck to shore. Kane forgot about any plan to draw that day. He ran after her moments after she had left. Instinct had thankfully taken over before any lack of courage could find its way into his brain.

"Hey, sorry," he said to her, panting slightly. She looked back at him with adoring interest. "You were drawing that boat yesterday too? How did you know I was?"

She continued walking, now with him, smiling affectionately at this boy whose innocent eagerness she found refreshingly sweet.

"That boat yesterday was so perfect. What else would you have been drawing?"

She really had been enamoured by the same boat. With each word, he felt flattened by her casual charisma, and he wondered to himself if she had that effect on everyone who met her. He wondered if he was special, or if wonderful coincidences followed her, the way that luck might follow a gambler. It made no difference. He was lucky enough to be the one to currently share it with her.

"Can I see what you drew?" he asked her. She humbly paused and hummed as she thought of her answer, but her smile had given her away. She was excited to share her work with him, and in return, see what he had done. They sat together on the next park bench. They joked with each other and praised the other's work while playing down their own. He had told her her work was much better and much more interesting than his was. He wasn't lying. His boat was simple and detailed, as if it was a metallic carving rather than a drawing on paper. She had taken up the entire page, capturing the boat perfectly, but also the rocks, the water, the dock in the near distance, and the tree line and ocean, both close behind and far away. Her ability to capture the attitude in all three workers was remarkable. There was a motion to her world in this still. She had a genuine gift and she thought he was being overly nice, but said thank you all the same. He told her he was proud of his work but he never drew anything that he couldn't tattoo on skin. It just didn't appeal to him. It always came back to that. So she asked about his tattoo work, and they talked for an hour, understanding the most intimate aspect of the other's art from the first moment they had ever spoken. As the fog lifted, and the town began to wake up, they left their waterside bench and went for coffee. Talk of art turned into talk of life and they left each other, both beaming, with plans to see the other again in a few days' time.

After many hangouts and conversations just as lovely as the first, he was there, knocking at her door. The calm before the storm, the silence after the knock, and then, the beat of footsteps from somewhere within the house coming closer. The turn of the knob paralyzed him and he took a deep breath in hopes of settling his nerves, a reflex he wasn't even aware he was doing. The door opened with a fury at their feet. Tilly's dog, a small runt of a thing, was scrambling to see who was at the door, like all dogs seem to do. She gently kicked and scooted the dog back, who must have given up because it didn't return. She stood straight up now, taking a deep breath and running her hand through her hair to fix it. With the flash of her smile, and a deep breath of relief from him, she stuck her tongue out at him playfully. The screen door still separated them. She looked beautiful.

"Hey there," he said, calmer now, forgetting how nervous he had been, now thrust into the situation and thrust back to her.

She stared back at him, waiting, before putting her shoes on and stepping outside. Expecting to have been invited inside, Kane looked back at her, puzzled. "I thought we were…"

"Come on, weirdo."

She led them back to the road he had walked in on, now heading further out of town. He hadn't been this far on this side of the cove before. The south side of the outskirts of town was nothing but forest and ocean, separated only by the highway. Here, on the north side, there were more open fields that led to the high cliffs over the ocean. They were much higher than the town and now far enough away that they couldn't even see down the hill. The town was no longer there. There were no houses and no road. It was only them. He had a faint idea where they were going.

"I thought I was going in to meet your mom."

"You will," she said, assured. "We aren't going far."

Kane didn't press any further. Franky, he was pleased about the postponement, a momentary relief. As he spoke mainly about the oddities and discoveries of his new hometown, she talked about winters in Sachem, her last boyfriend (Robbie Markum in grade four), and the probability of her childhood dog Arlo being telepathic. She was a goofball and listening to her speak was as much fun as he had had in years. Mid-sentence, without pausing or acknowledging the gesture, she took his hand in her own and held it as they walked. He smiled to himself as she spoke. This felt too nice and too new not to appreciate that this was the first time they had done so. They had been seeing each other now for close to three months. They had kissed before, held hands, and had sex, but now at her home instead of his, walking hand in hand, it was becoming apparent to both of them that this was more than a summer fling or curious crush. They had both been hoping it meant more, but this was affirmation to each other, and they privately rejoiced to themselves. With the sun falling into the water, so did he, falling into her every word and every way of being, and he did so with the ease of the slowly hiding sun. Whatever longing he had been searching for, whatever sadness he was trying to cure, he never felt it with her. Now that she seemed to be a part in his life, he wanted that feeling to stay. He wanted to stay. He wanted to keep listening to her speak.

"I live so close, I used to come here all the time." They were walking toward the edge of the cliff, where she was peering over, checking for something down below. She let go of his hand, took several excited leaps along the cliff face, just close enough to momentarily terrify him, and sat down on the ground.

"There it is."

Kane stepped beside her, standing tall, looking out over the cliff. The sky was dimmed, half the setting sun still visible, still peaking from the ocean, changing the entire sky to pinks and yellows, clouds no longer white but reflecting and making different colours, a dramatic oil painting across the silent ocean down below. Below them, standing triumphantly red, white and tall in this breathtaking scene of nature, waves crashing all around it futilely, as if trying to bring it crumbling into the sea, was a lighthouse.

"Sit down," she ordered, sweetly. He surrendered.

They sat together on the grass, next to the cliff and above the lighthouse, witness to the sun's continued dip below the sea line. They shifted themselves to find comfort on the hard ground, squirming slowly into each other as they spoke longingly of where they wanted to be in life and where they had come from. They'd had these conversations before, but each time came with more honesty, more willingness to let the other in. Doubt and indecision had a way of creating barriers even to yourself, and letting each other in, one moment at a time, was a way to let those walls crumble. As they understood each other, it was an allowance to understand yourself. Kane sat back, holding himself up as Tilly sunk her head into his chest. They were both talking, listening, and looking out over the ocean.

Tilly had been here since she was little. Her mom and her father had moved to Sachem when she was only two years old. Her father had needed more money than what was coming in so they'd looked for any small town to start their family. He worked in logging for two years before he told Tilly's mom, Jessica, that he was moving away and that he would be moving alone. Her dad was never really home, and he drank a little too much, but her mom had still never expected this. She'd begged him to stay, not out of love, but for help with Tilly. He said he would pay her child support and by the end of the week he was gone without telling Jessica where to. Tilly said that it was so she didn't follow him and that she probably would have. Tilly didn't hate her dad. He had been unhappy and getting more so so he left. He'd kept his promise and always paid the child support. After a year of anonymous return addresses, the cheques started to have a return address. Tilly thought it was so she could reach out, but she never tested it. She never saw her dad because she didn't care to, and she imagined that was why he never asked. He never remarried. When Tilly was twelve, she and her mom had gone to his funeral, because she had asked to go. The service was in Texas. She didn't know anyone there and she hadn't cried. She just never had a dad. She loved her mom and she loved her childhood with her. Tilly was nineteen years old and desperately wanting to move to the city -- a city, any city. Kane hoped to himself that he would go with her. She wanted to work somewhere easy and go to school. Post-secondary school was not something most of the kids from the thirty or so graduating class of Sachem High ever considered, but she always had. She mentioned art school and laughed it off, but Kane could tell she was serious about it. Tilly wasn't scared to leave -- her courageous spirit was aching to. She was afraid to abandon her best friend, her mom. She didn't like to talk about that part of her plan because she didn't like to think about it. She couldn't think of a way to go and it ruined all of her plans, leaving her helpless. So she spoke about these plans as dreams and nothing more, and Kane didn't press her on the matter. It wasn't the time.

"Why don't you come up here anymore?"

Kane could tell she knew her answer immediately by the way she didn't think about her answer. She took her time with the question, likely to ensure to him her answer was truthful, and to leave no room to discuss the matter further of why she felt unable to leave.

"I felt claustrophobic." He knew exactly what she meant, and she knew he understood, but in the open spaces they rested in, she elaborated further. "You can see for miles up here. Nothing but trees and water and land. I feel locked in by it."

"You can still feel locked in when you are surrounded by places to go. Trust me. To someone else, this is the very edge of the world."

"Not to me."

"I know." Their embrace felt tighter in their understanding of one another. Kane knew he shouldn't press the issue, but he had never done so while including himself in any potential plans. "Let's get out of here then."

"You just got here," she laughed.

"I came here to get away. Not to...drop anchor." Kane could feel her eyes rolling at his lame attempt at nautical humor.

"Maybe."

Tilly jumped up abruptly, leaping, playfully to her and haphazardly to him, towards the face of the cliff.

"Get away from the edge!" he shouted playfully with a genuinely concerned smile. She didn't budge, standing defiantly, looking out over the water, as if for a sign to leave it all behind, a signal of permission. Kane was stricken by this perfect person that made the falling heavens of a fiery sunset behind her disappear along with the well of his doubts. He wanted to put his arms around her, but with her on the verge of falling over, he called out instead.

"Come on, Lighthouse girl. Let's go."

She turned her head, long hair waving behind her. She was no longer searching. She looked at him like she had found it.

"Lighthouse girl?" Turning her back to the dangers below, she stepped into Kane, pulling him closer and looking up at him. "Lighthouses are a warning to sailors, you know? It is a sign saying that you are too close. Keep away! Danger!"

They both laughed, still looking into each other's eyes. Smiling, she waited in return for his joke back at her. His laugh quieted and only a half-smile returned.

"Lighthouses are a call to home. Where they stand, that's where home is."

Tilly looked up at Kane in adoration, him admiring her back. She pulled him closer still until there was no space between them, and no space around them. There is no ocean, no trees, no falling sun, and no fears. They stood in the absence of everything else, and, like it was the first time they had ever done so, they kissed.

The two of them arrived back at the house, late for dinner, but her mother, Jessica, never mentioned it. Kane, now riding a high of the confirmation of returned feelings, was more at ease. Tilly herself was in high spirits and it made her mom happy to see it. This loving happiness was a new and unique experience to each of the three at the table, a formed wake that rippled through and rocked them all. They ate, laughed, asked questions, and navigated conversations to get to know the other and expose themselves. Kane asked about the car out front and said that maybe he could take a look at getting it started again. Tilly called the dog over to prove his telepathic ability to a laughing Kane and an eye rolling Jessica. He expected Tilly's mom to be a nice, quirky woman who adored her daughter, but she had a vibrant youthfulness -- which made sense. She had Tilly at a young age. She didn't try to impress or quiz or alleviate like some mother's might have done -- she smiled easily, admiring the scene with a charm you might see detailed on a postcard from a cafe in Paris. She had flowing red hair that probably looked just like it had when she gave birth to Tilly, and eyes just as brown, but now with the distinguished evidence of crow's feet at the edges, something Kane couldn't help but think was attractive. Jessica asked Kane about his own hometown with genuine interest and her own experiences visiting the West Coast. There was a natural settling in between them, not dissimilar to old friends reuniting, but without the burden -- or gift -- of time spent. It was dark and Kane had a long walk home. The time had come in the night for him to leave. Jessica protested and said he shouldn't be walking at the late hour, but did so knowing she had no alternative offer. Tilly walked him outside, apologizing for hauling him out there and losing track of time.

"Don't be sorry, weirdo," he said. She smiled and kissed his cheek goodbye and it would be all he thought of on the way home.

It was close to midnight when he got home, still feeling light from the loveliness of the night. Kane poured himself a cup of water from the tap before collapsing onto the couch. He closed his eyes, wishing Tilly was there with him. He wondered how that might ever work with her living with her mom. She had stayed over a few nights after telling her mom she was staying at her friend's house. Wherever he was coming from, whatever dreams he was having, waking up to her beside him was where he wanted to be. But if she were to move away from her mom it would not be in this shitty basement suite. It would be in another city, in a nice apartment, maybe for art school. Would Kane be welcomed along? Would he want to be? He made enough money to live selfishly and the necessity for needing more made him nervous. The way he felt towards Tilly was unquestionable. Questions arose with the promise of love and Kane could not help analyzing and rationalizing any of the different scenarios and fractures that could weaken any idea of his future. He thought of her giggle as she repeated herself that day on the seawall, the first time they had spoken. He thought of her silhouette against the most spectacular sunset he had not cared about. He remembered the kiss on his cheek and the way she called him weirdo. She had told him she recognized him in herself and how unique that was. How strange that was. How unique it had been they had met under the exact same circumstances and to run into each other again, and to then get along so well. It felt so beautifully weird to her, so what else was there to call him? He was her weirdo. These fears he had were so easily defeated by the wonder of Tilly that it cured him in that very moment, and it meant security for the next time he might have concerns. He would only need to think of her.

She was all that he wanted and that would be the answer to any question.

Kane reached for the black bag that rested at his feet. He carefully emptied the contents one by one onto the table before taking off his shirt. He shifted down to the floor from the couch and picked up the sewing needle and the lighter. His torso was covered in tattoos, more ink than skin. They were small and black, a collective piece now. He looked for space on his body; he only needed a few inches for this. He never really took note of any of his tattoos. The small tree on his ribs, above a horseshoe. There was a heart on his left shoulder, and on the other, a skull. A candle, a harp, a knife, a house, a cassette tape, a pair of boxing gloves -- he was covered in these black-stained artifacts. He found a patch of skin on his chest, realizing it was on his heart and thanking chance that it was not yet covered. He poked his skin with the needle, the first spot of ink. He often felt depressed after a tattoo. Some felt this way because of the adrenaline dump from sitting through a willing pain. More commonly for Kane, it was simply just a strange feeling to change yourself permanently. He loved every tattoo that he had, but for a brief moment, it was like he was different, giving pieces of himself away. He poked himself again, determined and motivated to etch this feeling into himself. This tattoo would not make him feel sad. He poked himself again, knowing it would never be one to ever simply blend in with the rest.

CHAPTER 5

October came and marked the eighth month Kane had been in Sachem. This date was significant to him because it had been the longest he had stayed anywhere without finding an excuse to pack his bags, and it also told him winter was approaching. He had been warned, mainly by Brenda and several of his bosses, how cold it was surely going to get. He knew it would be bad, even worse than he probably imagined, but there was nothing to be done about it. It was on its way. Deep down, Kane assumed that winter would be an excuse to push him out to the next town, further south with warmer sun. Maybe subconsciously Kane had given up on this experiment and was circling the country and assumed he would fail and return home, dizzy and even more lost than when he'd left. With each move, this seemed more likely. But now, he was still here, in the blue dark of the morning and in three layers of clothing just for his short walk to work, the work that he liked less with each passing day into the calendar. The thought of him jumping into the ocean, as the air bit his skin and coated his breath so thick it reflected the yellow in the street lights above, seemed inconceivable. Today was the coldest it had been in Kane's time there and he wondered how he was going to manage the changes, in season and in the day's work. At least those on the lobster boats weren't actually ever *in* the water. How much worse could it be? He had left jobs and towns for much less, and arriving to work, seeing all of the other crazy people arriving for the day, he knew why. Every 1000 doubts he had about this job and the cold, he had 1001 thoughts of the alternative without her. Those thoughts would hopefully produce enough fire in his heart to keep him from catching frostbite.

Kane stepped into the small shop that was filled with other scallop divers. There was usually nobody inside the shop; people would causally prepare for the day on the curb out front, on the docks, or on the grassy area across the street. Friends would joke and play before the day's work, while others, like Kane, would wait while drinking coffee. Today there must have been thirty people jammed into the office, like the scallops they would catch and toss into a bucket. People were getting ready inside, a few newcomers adding to the cluster, but most just realizing their bad luck of arriving late and getting ready in the cold outside. Cursing the cold and laughing at the absurdity of their jobs was the only conversation. "We still work when it's this cold?" some anonymous boy asked sheepishly. Those that were not too bitter laughed at the question. Many people, including Kane, undoubtedly were happy the question had been asked. The laughter was enough of an answer; it spoke to the naivety of the new workers, and the attitude to think this slight October chill was enough to halt the day. "The ocean doesn't freeze, kid. The scallops don't mind it either."

Thankfully, in extreme temperatures such as this, there was more to the get up than the standard wetsuit and flippers during the winter. Once everyone was dressed and ready to load onto the boats, the captains handed out specialty gloves and face covers for more protection when in the water. While they did this, the boss was giving a speech about how there would be hand warmers on the boat and more breaks because too much time in the water was now a health risk. Because of this, quotas would fill slower and therefore early days off would be ruled out from now on. Kane assumed today was the day for the speech because they clearly had far fewer people show up for work today than usual. This was more of a promising plea than a motivation. The boss ended by saying luckily there was bound to be more work as certain people that couldn't handle it would surely quit. The inability to handle the work, no early days, and more days of work than his usual four made Kane acutely distressed. Reality was setting in and if it wasn't for Tilly, he would already be walking home to pack. Instead, he was stepping onto a boat, carrying a pair of flippers and a fucking snorkel.

A slight tease of morning sunlight appeared, lighting the cove and bringing no heat with it. The boat smashed into the top of every wave. The harshness of the air and the wind made monsters of each wave and the boat plodded through, pathetically battling them. The air was painful, the fingers of winter pinching and twisting every exposed area on Kane's skin. He was fumbling around with his flippers, fingers and feet so numb they acted slower than his brain ordered them to. The five discomforted others on the boat were having a similar struggle. Jumping into that black water seemed impossible. He wondered if it were possible for the water to be as cold as the air hitting his face without being frozen solid. He needed the sun to bring any heat it could and break this morning freeze. He had only been on the boat for forty-five minutes.

The guttural churn of the engine cut and the captain called for a handful of crew members to watch the rope before hurling the heavy anchor into the rough and dark waters, disappearing immediately despite being at a probable depth of six to ten feet. The apprehension on the boat was now as much in the air as the cold was. There was a feeling of unanimous solidarity on the boat until the point came where everyone was just sitting, no more adjusting face masks or shoving hand warmers into their wetsuits. The boat just awkwardly swayed in the silence after the howling ride out. Even the captain looked hesitant.

"I know this sucks, but I promise, once you get swimming and the sun comes out, it feels like any other day."

Kane and the others looked at one another, shifting eyes in awkward glances. Nothing was said. They were postponing the inevitable. If there was a time to back out, it would have been on the shore. There seemed to be a collective understanding -- they would need to get through today, and if then they decided it was awful enough, they could simply end their career of scallop diving. Kane stood up, partly to get it over with, and partly to end the silence. The others stood with him. All of them put their snorkels into their mouths and looked at each other, shrugging and chuckling through their masks. Kane thought of the two more days of this bone chilling hell until he had his next day off, and of the plans he had made with Tilly. And then he thought of Tilly. And then he jumped in the water.

Kane sat next to his fellow boat companions on the wooden bench that ran along the wall in the office. The only sound Kane could hear was of his own chattering teeth like a jackhammer pounding concrete. Even in his near frostbitten state, he felt self-conscious about it, but nobody else seemed to be faring any better than he was. They were probably hearing the same sound emanating from their own rattling jaws. Funny how as the warmer it got, the more painful it became. He was too cold and wet to check his phone for the time, but he imagined it was close to 4:00 p.m., four hours longer and twenty degrees lower than usual. Ten hours on the freezing water, above and below the surface, and his muscles ached from clenching and shivering. The warmth of the room was helping to warm his skin, but it was also waking up his numbed nerve endings and the agony in his extremities was so excruciating he could barely hold onto the hand warmers he'd snagged from the boat. He remained sitting there, trying to breathe onto his hands, face down and wincing, waiting for the pain to slow and pass enough to be able to take his wetsuit off and change into warm clothes. It seemed like such a quick and easy thing, but there was no will to do so. He just wasn't able. Strange that this would now seem to be the worst part of the day. The shock of jumping into the water had taken his breath away and the shock had never really given air to his lungs. Snorkeling had been almost impossible. When he'd surfaced to take a break on the boat, the bite of the air seemed even colder. He never got used to the cold out there; each time he went under or came up, it seemed to get worse, fighting the growing power of the elemental. If the sun did warm the cove today, it had come too late for Kane to notice. He looked up to see if the others were changed already. They all sat there, cringing, rubbing the hurt out of their knuckles. The hooks and cubbies above their heads were still overflowing with shoes, backpacks, and coats. They must have been one of the first boats in. They felt so slow out there today. As he had done on the boat, Kane stood first to take his wetsuit off, showing the others again that it was time. It would be better to just get it over with, get dressed warm before all the others arrived, and get home. They did so very slowly, sore from the gnawing of the constant cutting chill, making strange acrobatic twists of their bodies to escape the pains of simple movements.

The walk between the scallop office and Kane's home was typically a breezy twenty minutes long, provided he wasn't wandering and sketching little things along the way. Tonight he went straight there and it took him forty minutes. Every joint felt like they had been wrung and twisted for hours. It was more than muscle soreness. There was that, too, of course, but it was his knees, knuckles, and ankles that were in agony. Swimming and sitting in the cold had done it, but now shuffling home, he felt the effects, even after he had warmed a little and the burning sensation had left his skin. One of the young girls that had been on his boat had begun to say goodbye as she signed out and left, and her words slurred. "Goodbuh." Her face had numbed over from the cold, and Kane walked home saying arbitrary test words to himself, making sure it wasn't happening to him. "Hello...hello...mouth...my mouth...." He felt bad thinking about her. She had looked scared.

The inevitable visiting of winter, or the unbearable day of work, gave the town an ominous feeling, a flexing air that frightened him. During summer, the breeze was a sign of the glimmer of the warm air, waving flowers and lifting spirits. Colorful clothes drying on line would flap harmlessly in every other backyard. Now, in the twilight of both the day and the season, the breeze haunts the town. It is too cold here for lively possibilities. Every parent and child were stuck kidnapped inside their own homes. The wind moaned loudly through the streets, smashing aggressively into houses and fences, tearing into every opening, masking any noises that might be threatening. The wind pierced Kane's ears. It was deafening. A fear of the dark was a fear of the unknown, and this inability to hear conjured the same feeling that someone might be lurking around the next corner, right behind him, stalking him. Loose screen doors banged against the side of frames, knocking helplessly. It was too cold to be outside, giving the town that usually felt peaceful a quiet, ghostly feeling. Traffic lights continuously turned green, yellow, and red for nobody. Stumble and stagger as quickly as he could manage was all he could do. He wanted to move faster, but his body would not allow it. He wanted to check his phone, but he couldn't further expose his fingertips. He wanted to stop checking what was behind him, but he couldn't shake the feeling something was closing in on him. Turning down his alley, he finally saw his door, and while he was too disturbed to feel excited or relieved, he did grit his teeth and flex his muscles in achievement, thankful that the eerie odyssey was over.

Kane hadn't eaten anything since breakfast, but he wasn't hungry, likely from the state of shock. He took off his jacket and crawled into bed and under the sheets like a burrowing animal escaping an early spring frost. He would get up to make something easy to eat once he'd warmed up. It felt as if that might never happen. He wondered, jokingly, if the marrow in your bones could freeze solid. He sat in a survivalist fetal position, his hands were held together, tucked between his thighs, knees sat high into his chest, compacting himself as much as his limbs would allow. His feet were curling into one another, covering as much surface area as possible. He wasn't being overly dramatic, he just wanted to be warm again. He wanted the pain to go away. He hoped it would be gone by the morning, and that was when the wave of worry clouded his mind, knowing he would have to do this again tomorrow. The worry at least took his mind off some of the pain. Kane started thinking of excuses not to go already, but he knew he would. Available jobs in this town were limited and if he quit, it meant he would have to leave her. He could not help his mind from running wild with alternative measures to dying a slow death of prolonged hypothermia, jumping into the shallow, freezing waters of the salty Atlantic so restaurants across the country could charge obscene amounts for bottom feeding creatures. Payment for a day of scallop diving was for a filled quota and not hours worked. Kane was set to earn the same amount of money, for far more working hours, each one sure to be more agonizing than the one before. Jobs were limited and a discussion with Tilly about their future seemed premature. He needed to do some searching, but tonight, his mind was not in the right place for it. He was battling exhaustion and could feel himself losing, drifting to sleep. He hoped a long sleep would be enough to cure his ails enough to get through the morning. He would eat a large breakfast. The light in the living room was still on. With some effort, he reached into the piled contents of his clothes on his floor and grabbed his phone to set his alarm. It was only 7:25 p.m. There was a missed text from Tilly. *"How was work, weirdo?"* Kane smiled and closed his eyes, sinking into the pillow, finally feeling warmth for the first time that day.

CHAPTER 6

"If it was really that bad, what are you going to do?" Tilly asked Kane, concerned, sitting on his couch while he stood in the kitchen waiting for the water to come to a boil. His day off had come after another equally hellish day at work. But Tilly was here now and he was happy. If he had any hope that he might get used to the current conditions on the boat, they were squashed yesterday. Exhaling slowly, trying not to make a laborious effort of the simple task of grabbing two mugs from the cupboards, Kane replied, smiling. "It wasn't great." And then set the two cups for coffee on the counter and leaned against it. He looked back at her watching him, concerned and grinning, waiting for an answer. He showed no sign of worry to her, and she saw right through him. Kane stuck his tongue out at her; she remained grinning and rolled her eyes at him just as the water in the kettle began to boil.

"I have no sugar, sorry," Kane said.

"I forgive you," Tilly replied.

Kane had done enough whining in his own head. He didn't want to spend the escaping time with her talking about the cold or the scallops or how he was so fatigued and sore he had struggled to get out of bed this morning. If it were up to him, the topic would never have been brought up at all. He would have happily come up with an alternative and just as soon tell her when it was a reality. It wasn't like he wanted to keep his work life or plans from her, he just knew he could deal with it on his own. He had always been like that. What good could it serve to whine to Tilly, have her worry, and have it dominate their conversation like it was about to?

The two days at work had flattened him. One the second day of work, he had the benefit of knowing what to expect, but the third had the downside of his being more physically and emotionally weakened than the rest. He hadn't eaten enough and that made him sick on the boat. His joints and the tips of his fingers were still pockets of pain that reminded him with every movement, and returning to the source only gave the cold more time to work it's indifferent way back into them. His chance to heal had passed and he imagined that any form of getting used to it was just another way to say "permanent damage." Sitting on the boat, breathing hot breath into his knuckles, he thought maybe if he stopped and just gave into the cold, they would finally go fully numb. Instinct would not allow it. When he woke, soreness had forced him to lurch more than once just to sit up in bed. Exhaustion had given him hollow bags under his eyes. When he limped into the bathroom, he knew he couldn't hide this from Tilly when she arrived. He had to put his hands on the wall just to carefully get his legs over the two-foot-tall walls of the bathtub. He was in rough shape and Tilly had indeed noticed it immediately.

"Here you go," he said, handing her both coffees. He sat stiffly beside her and grabbed his cup back from her. They both took a sip. It was too hot to drink and Tilly set hers on the coffee table to cool. Kane let his rest on the arm of the couch, holding it in his hand. He didn't want to have to reach for it again. He put his other arm around her and poked her left cheek with his tongue. She smiled, looked into his eyes before closing them, and kissed him quickly on the lips. Even as they kissed each other, or in the moments that would follow when she rested her head on his chest, he was still thinking about her eyes. Every time she would kiss him, she would look at him like that. Or maybe it just wasn't enough time to allow himself to stop thinking of them, like a flash of light so bright that it stays in your sight even as you close your eyelids. Her brown eyes were not marbled like most, but flecked with gold, flakes sitting on the surface of the auburn pools. In these eyes, he could tell something was wrong. She was worried and Kane was ignoring it. They had been seeing each other for months, but there hadn't really been a test yet. They had been enjoying getting to know each other, but now Kane realized he would be failing her if he bottled this up. Small habits of concern ignored lead to painful habits, and Kane could see this even with his limited experience in romance.

"I don't know what I'm going to do about it." he said as Tilly grabbed his hand, relieved and engaged. "Hoping I just get used to it, I guess."

"You think you can do that?"

"I don't really have an option." The few options they chose not to address hung in the room with them, as obvious and fleeting as the steam escaping their coffee's. The silence waited for them to speak over the possibility of moving. "It's as bad as it will get anyway though, right?" he said wryly, choosing humor over a possible difficult discussion. She laughed back, aware and appreciative. Like always, they understood each other.

"For sure! It doesn't get any colder than this here." They both laughed.

"I will figure something else out. These things always have a way of working out."

"They have worked out for you because you have moved away."

"I just haven't stayed anywhere long enough. Haven't given it a chance. I haven't had a reason to."

"But you do now?"

"I do now."

Kane kissed her again and reached now to set his coffee down. He winced and let out an over-the-top, high pitched wail as he did so. He did this to make it fun. If he had winced and taken a deep breath instead, the severity of his situation would have been too apparent, too worrisome. Even if Tilly knew this was an act, she laughed along with him. Tilly hadn't gotten angry with him for withholding, and Kane didn't become self-conscious when she asked about his pains. They both navigated this understanding of each other so perfectly that it built a trust to allow the other to blossom their feelings as it became comfortable to them, without judgment or impatience, and they did so while laughing. Kane grabbed her hips, ignoring the travelling pains this caused from his hands to his thighs, and placed her on her back on the couch. He held himself above her with his arm and kissed her hard. He kissed her with all of the appreciative force of a young man realizing for the first time that he was in love. He wasn't ready to say "I love you" yet. Even if he was, those three words wouldn't be enough to explain how he felt about her. Words would always fail him, so for now, the kiss would have to do.

As they exited Kane's place, he couldn't believe this was the same town as the past two days. It was still freezing cold, the wind still trembled, and the stamped shadow of a grey winter remained, but it was again a quiet fishing town. Of course, he knew this nightmarish world couldn't exist with Tilly at his side, holding his hand, and without the promise of willingly jumping into frigid waters, but it stunned him all the same. It reminded him the world was not going to, and never would, change for him. He would need to adapt. Today, he just wanted to be with her, who was now goofing around, half dancing and half strolling in front of him.

Tilly needed to make a few stops to pick up some things, which gave Kane a reason to run errands of his own. They did this without a thought or appointment once a week, effectively serving as their "date night." There was no theatre in Sachem they could go to. Even if there was, they probably wouldn't go. Sometimes they would watch a movie on his laptop, but they wouldn't make it very far. They would either talk through it, laugh over it, or end up shutting it off completely and having sex, admittedly all preferable options for both Kane and Tilly. They had gone for the odd beer at The Trap together, more so for the people watching, with Tilly giving Kane the scoop on all the bar patrons. She laughed hysterically the entire time. Kane still didn't know if it was because of the look of astonishment on his face or because she was making them up as she went. He suspected it was both. He really doubted that the real John Jacob Jingleheimer Schmidt had been born in Sachem and that "that man, over there, at the bar with the beard" was his great-great-great grandson and that he never had to work because he was the only living heir to the Jingleheimer fortune, all of it accumulated royalties from the jingle. He was rarely seen in public and had become an alcoholic recluse, living in his enormous cabin off in the woods all by himself. "When he was young, whenever he went out, the people would always shout" and it was around then in the story when she would break into fits of laughter, very impressed with herself.

Most days like this, they just wandered Sachem with loose plans and an aimless direction. It was nice for both of them that they felt as comfortable with one another in the openness of the world. There was a new vulnerability to it. They enjoyed leaving the safety of intimacy in bed and in each other's arms. They took turns choosing a spot where the two could sit together, with a pack of beers, and draw. If Kane chose a spot in the forest, she would choose next, maybe on a bench downtown surrounded by buildings, or at the edge of a dock. They would draw whatever they desired and showed the other when they were finished. Kane always finished first so he would draw a few things. His were simple and detailed objects, and hers a beautiful capturing of a scene. Sometimes an object he would choose would find its way into one of her works. When he first saw her drawing, his eyes would widen and his jaw would drop and he would fawn and wax poetic over it for five straight minutes, amazed, meaning every word. She would simply look at it, taking it in her own hand, and say, "that's nice." She never meant it passively or sarcastically. Her eyes fell softly on him, showing him that it was nice he cared about these things. She told him she appreciated the way he saw the world and that he cared to share with her. It made him feel seen. That sharing of a moment created an allowance to think of the other when they saw beauty in between the lines of life. When something stood out for any reason to them, there was now a tangible way to share it, and a curiosity to see how the other might interpret it. Each time they did this, drawing a slice of the world together, they would save it, keeping them in a shoebox underneath Kane's bed.

The days of free time and errands never felt wasted or like chores. They were just marks on a map, chapters marking their day as they wandered and did whatever they wanted, whether it was drawing, or having a picnic, or lifting rocks on the beach to see the life scuttling underneath, or looking at each title with a careful silence at the bookstore, sometimes buying them to read somewhere, sometimes not. Lying in bed, or spread on the floor, they would listen to music, asking each other questions and then answering their own. What is your favorite color? If you could see anyone in concert, who would it be? Are you afraid of anything? Do you believe in ghosts? Do you want kids one day? It was these days, hopping from place to place, with Tilly skipping and smiling, the questions were often goofier and lighter. Would you rather travel to Jupiter for a day in a spaceship, or cruise the ocean super fast in a submarine with really good headlights? What was your favorite Halloween costume when you were a kid? What is your favorite cereal? And each question would lead to an argument and then to laughter, but always getting to know one another, discovering love and happiness in a simple fishing village that you wouldn't be able to find on most maps.

There was only one store in town to buy groceries and other essentials. Kane picked up extra hand warmers for work and Epsom salts for the recovery afterward. He also bought energy bars for the boat, all needed items he had learned the hard way these past few days. Tilly bought nothing. Kane didn't feel like going into the office to pick up his cheque for the week. He would be back in a few days and wanted to avoid the ground zero of his suffering as long as possible. Tilly stopped by the local gardening shop she worked at part-time, Green Fingers. They talked with her co-worker for a few minutes, and even though she was always there, she enjoyed visiting. She paused on the way out to look at a few of the shrubs and flowers with Kane, even though she saw them all of the time. It was wonderfully obvious she enjoyed her job.

Next door, at the art supplies store, smelling of dried watercolor palettes and fresh paper, she grabbed more sketching paper. Kane decided to get more India ink for tattooing. He still had some left, and although he hadn't tattooed anyone recently, he decided to in case of emergency. Maybe a part of him just wanted the subject to be breached. They both left the store with each of their art supplies in plastic bags, Tilly smiling with excitement and already reaching into hers.

"Look at what else I bought." She pulled out a colorful piece of cardboard with different colors individually encased in plastic and two small paint brushes. In large bubble letters next to a cartoon image of a tiger, it read "FACE PAINT." "Just in time for Halloween!" She laughed as Kane inspected the purchase.

"No way," he responded, amused but standing his ground.

"Halloween is in a couple weeks!"

"And I doubt that'll be enough time for you to talk me into that."

"You're getting whiskers at least."

"Oh yeah?"

"You'd make a cute cat."

Kane just smiled at her silly persistence. He reached into his own bag and took out the small bottle of India ink. He held it in front of his face, head cocked, and thinking deeply, Tilly already shaking her head and pulling away from him, both of them smiling now.

"If you get to use your new purchase on me…"

"Definitely not."

"Then it's only fair I get to use mine on you!"

"Mine washes off!"

They laughed, bickering with each other in a good-natured way, walking nowhere in particular, all of the day's tasks now completed. Kane had never really been one for Halloween since he was a kid, and Tilly had no tattoos. The two laughed at the absurdity of each prospect, knowing in the back of their minds the other was likely going to convince them to change it, and it thrilled them both. They felt awakened. Tilly mentioned to Kane that for Halloween, she would need to work the desk at Green Fingers, handing out candy, as most businesses did in the small town. She asked him to join her and he said of course, even if saying he had plans elsewhere might get him out of face painting.

In this, the beginning of winter, time was the only way to tell the sun was soon to set. There was no following of the sun across the sky, no rise and fall, no waking or dimming, and definitely no blue sky turning a fiery red before allowing the bright white of the moon to take its place. No, it was the same dull shade until all at once the black of night swallowed the grey. To the disappointment of Kane, Tilly would be going home tonight. The day's adventures were finished and they could both feel their time coming to an end. She would need to leave soon.

"I'm going to walk you home."

"No, it's too far."

"That doesn't matter."

They were downtown, already walking in the direction of her house, down this main street with two traffic lights and only one turn before touching the water to quickly head straight up and out of sight. Tilly turned left, not necessarily away from home, but an odd choice.

"Where are you going?"

"You can walk me to the bottom of the hill, but that's close enough. Thank you though."

"Okay," Kane said smiling, not daring to argue.

"You would freeze to death on the way home anyway."

Kane continued smiling. "Where are we going though?"

"I'll buy you a beer at The Trap first. Keep you warm."

"I appreciate that," he laughed.

The Trap was only a few streets down. It was both dinner time and the immediate place many fishermen would rush to the second they arrived on shore. He hoped they would get a spot at the bar; it was the best vantage point for Tilly to tell her stories. She was still hopping on light feet a few steps in front of him. It always made him smile to see it. He loved her for it. It wasn't skipping, and it was dancing either. It was just walking with easy abandon, a delicate freedom that started wherever she began. There were the occasional pauses in her step, a cute step back on her heels or her toes, her eyes focused on what her feet were doing, or looking at the world around her, maybe a smile thrown behind her directed at Kane. It was a constant of joyful movement and because it came from her, it was natural. The only attention she ever drew from it was her given magnetism. To see her walking straight forward, hands placed in her pockets, would be like seeing rain falling upward. Kane almost walked into her when she came to an abrupt stop at the corner of the street, and he smiled, grabbing her as he did it. He was leaning in to kiss her when he saw what she was looking at and then the sobering look on her face. It was just as disturbing to see her face without a smile, as it was to see this woman kneeling over a crumpled and still body on the street beside a truck that dinged repeatedly with the door hanging open. Standing directly over this kneeling woman was an older man looking gravely at the scene. They both wore jeans and tucked in white collared shirts, as if in unofficial uniform, there on business, lanyards hanging around their necks. Their poise in the distress gave them a control over the situation. Kane guessed they were both around sixty years old. Behind the truck was an agitated young man, thin and jittery, pacing helplessly, clearly waiting for a hopeful outcome. On the street, behind the truck that still dinged, was an older, decommissioned-looking ambulance. The lights and sirens were both off, and there were no apparent EMTs anywhere, but Kane knew it was here for this. Tilly covered her mouth in horror as enough time had passed to fully express the severity of the situation. No signs of life came from the body on the ground, looking about the same age as them, early twenties, as the anxious young man paced with a face already stricken with the coming misery. There was nothing to say. Kane grabbed Tilly harder. To be looking was an invasion of privacy, but to leave felt like an immoral indifference to this person's life. Tilly grabbed him harder in return.

"Come on," the woman kneeling said with determination, willing life into this kid. "Work!" she added. Kane wondered why they weren't doing more. Why were people just waiting? Why was he not being rushed to a doctor, or the hospital, even if the nearest was fifty miles away? She had in her hand what seemed to be a small plastic bag, and she handed it up to the man standing beside her.

"Is he going to die?" the wiry young man pleaded, no longer pacing. The question hung in the air, all of them now waiting to see what that answer would be. Nobody moved. Ten seconds went by. What had happened here? Tilly's chest had stopped moving. She was holding her breath, with eyes wide in horror. Another ten seconds went by. Kane realized he wasn't breathing either. The determined eyes of the woman never left his face. She did not look away. She did not give up. It wasn't hope. It was need, because to look any different, to stand up, to say anything meant that this person was never going to breathe again. The first movement of this group of strangers was the hand of the taller man reaching to the back of his apparent partner, a sign of permission to let it go, a comforting expression that this was not her fault and no longer her fight. Scaring everyone, when his hand touched her, as if it was a defibrillator, the boy's eyes snapped wide, swallowing a loud gasp of air into his lungs. Tilly, startled, amplified by Kane himself jumping, let out a small, choked scream. The worried and watching young man screamed, "FUCK!" in a disturbed sense of relief and sat down on the sidewalk, tears in his eyes, hands together in a thankful prayer glued to his forehead. The repeated "ding ding ding ding…" of the open driver's side door of the truck continued. Had it been going this entire time?

"Come on," Kane said. They walked down the street, toward Tilly's house now, forgetting all about any previous plan of beers and fun.

"Holy fuck," Tilly sighed, still catching her breath, tired from the stress of the scene. Kane looked behind him, the quiet aftermath of near death now unfolding. The two paramedic types attending to the revived human being, now sitting half up, coughing. The worried friend waited closer to his friend. He waited for the moment he could talk to him, or hug him, or cry with him. He waited patiently for his turn, like a racer in the starting blocks before the gun.

"Yeah," Kane replied to Tilly, looking at her now, taking a hold of her hand. "Holy fuck."

CHAPTER 7

Kane thought it strange to have never noticed it before. He laid in bed, on his side, staring at nothing, still sore with nowhere to be, lost in thought. His sweet evening had been confused in a disturbing collision after stumbling upon an unbeating heart of a young man. What had happened to that poor guy? Why were those two trying to help him with such calm and without panicked expediency? And who were they? They seemed formal, and there had been an ambulance, but they were not certified EMT's. That much was clear. And why did the anguished friend sit waiting as if measuring his own culpability? There did not seem to be any witnesses to some dangerous crime, and no talk of suspects. No, he'd just sat there, the way a witness might sit at a confession table, not guilty, but too late to make any difference. Kane had walked away in a frozen confusion, while Tilly had walked somberly, losing her natural rhythmic step. When she'd told him, it had made perfect sense, and not just the scene, but many things he had seen living in Sachem.

"Drugs," she had said to him and also herself, walking home, both forgetting The Trap entirely. "Overdose." Kane heard her and said nothing. He didn't doubt it. He didn't combat it. He understood it. He knew she was right. She said these words with a conviction of history because she had seen it before. It was not a guess; it was a memory. His silence assured her that he believed her and was processing the recent events with the new information. When she spoke, she didn't stop and Kane never interrupted. It was a flood of information that expanded Kane's knowledge of Sachem and also of Tilly's concerns with it. She had never mentioned it before, but the night was a catalyst, prompting her to rehash all of it, a therapy Kane was pleased to idly listen to.

Sachem was a small town with a big drug problem. The high school she had gone to was small, and apart from a little weed, she'd never really noticed anything. She still didn't notice anything, except for nights like this one when there was a lifeless body on the sidewalk, or in a bathroom, or in the backseat of a car, or in the gossip of the town, quickly spoken and quickly forgotten. Every overdose in town was a persistent reminder of the problem. It wasn't swept under the rug to be forgotten. It was ignored. Apparently, much of the workforce in Sachem viewed opiates as a necessity. They needed it to go on. This led to other drugs, other habits, other ways of reaching the high, and, of course, inspiring others to do so. Teenagers, men and women, boyfriends and girlfriends, captains of ships, foremen of logging crews, street cleaners; the drug came where it was needed and leaked its infection, bleeding into everywhere else anyhow. Heroin went into the blood and hit every capillary and blood vessel rushing through the body and the brain. It infected the population of people in the same way. Kane could detect the contempt in Tilly's voice as she versed him in the state of Sachem. She had no friends addicted to it, no family members had died from it, but she hated it all the same. It was always a present threat, always offered, and always available. Everyone knew of another that had once been just like them who was hooked. "Did you hear about so and so?" was commonplace conversation. Most of these overdoses happened inside, in bedrooms and living rooms, leading to many deaths, with small mournings. That was why he hadn't noticed it. To any outsider, this was a hiding monster that hadn't yet shown its fangs from their closet, or its glowing eyes from under the bed. Like many small towns like it, Sachem was a hollow morgue, filled with people living under the rules of an addiction that killed at will, trapped by the slamming of the waves and a desperate fear that blocked them from escaping. A shudder leapt down his spine that he was sure Tilly could feel.

Kane knew drugs flowed through every community in the country. He knew what they could do to people and what it could turn them into. He wasn't that innocent. It was the ignorance of not seeing it that bothered him, a slithering feeling in his upset heart. He had been here the better part of a year. He didn't really talk to people, but still, he should have known. He thought of the two Samaritans that had helped resurrect the boy with no name. The bag she had handed to him with a drug kit to resuscitate him. That explained the stillness in the chaos; they were waiting and hoping for the Narcan to work. Kane's only question after processing what Tilly had told him was who those two were.

"They are volunteer responders," she told him. There are no nearby hospitals, and no real budget for ambulances or emergency healthcare workers in Sachem, so the town relied on a handful of experienced retirees and good Samaritans for things like this. It made sense, as frustratingly tragic as it was. Fewer resources, less help, and fewer ways to combat addictions. This meant more deaths than necessary. The desire to leave felt stronger to Kane than it had before, no matter how sore or cold he was after a day of scallop diving. He had put his arm around Tilly's waist, and she'd thrown hers on top of his shoulders. Kane finished walking her home, both of them still reeling, but enjoying the last few moments with each other before she walked inside and Kane returned, walking into this freshly gutted town below.

Kane sat up in bed, restless and awake. It was 3:30 a.m. He rubbed and pressed his eyes, both to wake up and force the burrowing thoughts of the night from his head. It hadn't been the time to bring up leaving Sachem with Tilly. He didn't know when the right time would be, but it would need to happen. Anxiety was just urgent worry. No room was left to focus on the idea of going back to a job he feared, or the oncoming winter, or the expanding detachment from the town he lived in. They tunnelled quickly around and inside his brain, reaching every corner of his thoughts, impossible to focus on just one. He closed his eyes and took a deep breath, each swirling problem hanging in mid-air, floating back and forth to the ground, like thrown leaves. They now sat there for Kane to pick each one up and look at them, dealing with every one of them, taking his time. The town and winter were the same issue. Conditions were not ideal and he would like to leave both. Winter, he could handle anywhere, but not where the only available means of work meant being captured by it, held hostage by the money and the torment it inflicted. The only solution was to move away, something he would have done months prior had it not been for Tilly. She wanted to leave, but felt she couldn't, and he couldn't without her. So, he would need to make the best of living here and maybe one day, she would pursue the life she so faintly expressed she wanted elsewhere.

You got paid by the quota on a day scallop diving. He had typically worked three or four days a week up until now. Days were short because he worked hard and he would pull in $100 for the day's work. This was more than enough for what he needed. Now, with the extended breaks on the boat, he was hitting that $100 for an eight-or nine-hour day, and each minute was far worse than it had been in the summer. His boss had said with people leaving, they may need people up to six days a week. Kane would be making the same amount of money, for double the hours, in far worse conditions, and with more shifts expected. That wouldn't just be torturous, it would be stupid. Beyond that, for the first time ever, he was thinking of settling in afterward. If, and hopefully when, they did leave Sachem one day, he wouldn't mind looking for a decent place with Tilly. No more basement suites and extra rooms across the hall from strangers. They could make it their own habitat. They could purchase a comfy couch to curl up on during rainy days, not before checking the bookcase in the hall for a book to lie flat on their chests. Tilly could scatter tall plants that took up corners and small ones with reaching arms to fill space. Just like it was in her paintings, the flourishes of her mind would be seen in their lives. Maybe he could get an apprenticeship at a tattoo shop. These were all ideas that had crossed his mind before, but they had become exciting when Tilly had come into his life and solidified under the pressure of these circumstances. He understood and respected her perceived obligation and decision to have stayed this long. They had not been dating long and she didn't owe him anything. She had been up front from the beginning, but Kane also felt excited about the possibility of settling into a real life. That felt new to him. She must have known she couldn't live here forever, and Kane was sure her mom couldn't let her either. Maybe Kane would look into a logging job again. He would surely see less of Tilly but that was a responsibility of life, a necessary sacrifice.

Kane felt relieved. The tornado in his head of doubts, fears, and confusion that swirled inside his head had lifted, calming the winds and revealing a soft sunlight. Tornados didn't simply tire themselves out. A low, cooling air must intervene to interrupt their violent circulations. He had waited out the storm. His mind felt clear. He felt lighter. The room felt quieter. Nothing had changed, but he knew what was and what was not in his control. He had two things he needed to do. One required little effort for him and had no pressing timeline. He had to be patient. The second was to find a new job or suffer the one he had now. Thankfully, if the former did not work out, he had the latter, as unappealing as that might be. Kane checked his phone. 3:48 a.m. He sat in the quiet, waiting to see if his mind conjured any other anxieties that he would need to conquer. There would be no better time than now. No problems emerged, but an idea did, an idea that he thought may lead to something, but probably would not. Either way, he felt awake, refreshed by his alleviated thoughts, and the confidence of nothing to lose.

Kane brewed the coffee below boiling so that he could quickly down it, which was what he did. He threw his jacket over his sweater, ready to step into the blackness of early morning, happy it wasn't to change into a wetsuit. He carried himself with an energy, an optimism that fortune might reveal itself to him very shortly. This promise of opportunity was there because Kane was willing it there, and even he could see that. He was alone and he didn't care. This probably wouldn't work out anyway. He opened the door and noticed his sketchbook resting on the kitchen counter, the corners curling upward as if reaching out to be taken with him. Graphite smudges and fingerprints were pressed onto the cover and spine, the same graphite that stained the tips of his fingers and was embedded in the beds of his nails. Kane almost went back for it, but he stepped out and shut the door, leaving it behind. When those pages were open he wanted no distractions to capture the purest meaning of a moment. Where he was going, and what he was going for, required him to absorb information. This exploration of self by looking elsewhere was one of fascination and although he felt reluctant to admit it to himself, it was also a research expedition. To simply admire a scene and learn nothing would be a failure.

When Kane arrived, at roughly 4:30 a.m., with no sign of the sun or the moon, hundreds of lobster fishermen were already hauling cages across the dock, smoking cigarettes, clipping their rubber overalls tight, and loading their boats with the gear for the day.

CHAPTER 8

Kane had seen the fury of the crews before, working around each other in a uniformed chaos, like bees in a hive or ants on a hill. Their faces had looked tired, awaiting the peace of home and sleep, the sun setting or already disappeared, a dimming candle to put them to sleep. Despite the fatigue they must all be feeling, they never wavered, never rested, and never seemed to complain. They moved quickly and efficiently. This morning, Kane saw for the first time this process as they were set to go out. All of them moved the same way, but their faces were fixated, determined, a vitality that must have replenished itself each night and was sustained by habit. This was a force of disciplined fishermen. They did not joke around or ask questions. There was the occasional calling yell for attention or to orchestrate themselves, but they were silent in their focus. It was still very loud. It was not painful on the ears, but a powerfully heavy buzz could be felt from the hundreds of moving feet and hands, working with nature and their equipment. The waves incessantly clashed with the land. The tones created from the bottom of boots scraping the rocks underneath. The off and on drum beat anytime someone walked across the dock. Gear was being put down, picked up, slid there and pushed here. A seagull cried and a captain would whistle for his crew. It was the layered track of a song and only Kane could hear it. This was the cry of the Valkyrie. Every clam covered rock, the foam forming at the crest of each wave, every plank of wood on the dock, and the hardened faces of fishermen glowed yellow under the stale glowing light of the electric lanterns above. Even the smoke from their cigarettes glowed yellow, as did the vaporous steam that billowed from all of their mouths, proof of their hard work as well as the freezing air. They worked in shadow.

Kane sat on a bench on the street that followed the ocean all the way around, a divider between sea and town. There were no houses or other buildings here, a cove within the cove, where the wharf sat. This quayside spot didn't look like much in its state of emptiness during the day. It was a skeleton of what was taking place now. While Sachem slept, the normally deserted rocky beach was now covered in empty cages and ropes, a messy junkyard. Kane refused to believe this happened every morning. There seemed to be no organization or designation to any items on the beach. Cages were clustered all over, hap hazardously on the uneven surface, tilting and tipping over. Ropes lay coiled beside them, or laid down awaiting to be bundled. Filling any gaps between cages was random clutter, back from repairs, new, or whatever the case. Kane saw several anchors of all sizes, some with two and some with three prongs curling out from the middle. There were life jackets, toolboxes, oars, deflated and inflated Zodiac boats, coolers, large red jerry cans assumingly filled with gasoline, pairs of rubber overalls and rain jackets slung across any one of these items of debris, and more. People kept grabbing items, hauling them into their arms or going end to end with someone and carrying it from the detritus, maneuvering the peril of the rocks underneath with ease and onto the docks, making organized sections. As fast as items were removed, more were added from the large shed with a sheltered rooftop and minimal walls or from their trucks parked on the street that Kane currently sat on. These hurried tradesmen walked in front of him and beside him, paying him little notice. There were a few others who watched, an elderly woman walking her small dog taking quick and tiny steps, a few passerby taking in the morning, just the early riser types that were taken in by the spectacle of it just as he himself was. The docks were usually an empty wooden web, stretching out onto the water, splitting different directions, a floating system of wooden pathways. Organized piles now lined the docks, the massive empty lobster cages taking up the most room, and any carriers of items for future piles sidestepping each one with grace. Like a wave that formed and built, higher until it crested and crashed, the mass of labour here did the same. Much of the work started on the roads with the unloading of the trucks, down to organize and unload onto the rocks, leading to the docks, and now people began to load their piles from the dock onto small skiffs. As they did so, these smaller boats would fire up their small engines, taking them a few hundred yards away to the larger fishing vessels. It did not seem to matter who got their first in the morning, who was faster, or who had a level of seniority, they all worked with ease around each other, evolving and gelling together. It was chaos theory.

As skiffs departed, more room on the docks was created, meaning fewer bodies to work around and productivity only seemed to increase until multiple skiffs were on the water, the docks were full, and the beach was back to bare rock, so astonishingly sudden that Kane wondered if he had even remembered the mess correctly. The action was further from him now, on the docks and boats departing for other boats to head out for ten, twelve, sixteen hours before returning in the same dark as when they had left. The sun was beginning to rise now, already filtering out the harsh orange glare of the lights on the wharf. Different engines, small or large, were being ripped violently to life, one by one pushing the boat away from Sachem, a building applause before making their leave. Kane saw everything now. He watched one woman in a panic, running down the dock as the others waited, appearing as if she had forgotten something. About twenty docked skiffs loaded and were checking the last of their duties before joining the twenty or so that were already on the water, headed for their large fishing boats. The ships comfortably held the crews of four to eight people. The front half of each boat held the driver, roofed and windowed. They stood tall, cables holding ladders and water bobs, and of course, the ones already stocked and started were packed with empty cages, some five high, making them stand taller than even the boat, about fifteen feet. All of the boats had names on them. Some he could read and some he couldn't, depending on how far away they were or how large the print. He saw *Rock Bottom* waiting to be boarded. There was *Miss Fortune*, *Chasin Tail*, and *Lobster Mobster*. Kane smiled. They were all a fun play on words, nautical puns, and plays on familiar phrases. He thought about what he might name a boat if he ever had one. Maybe *Free Tilly*. He looked at his phone to see the time. It was 5:20 a.m. Kane would not have believed that in the disarray of the shore when he'd arrived, that all of the ships would now be being loaded or on their way out in forty-five minutes' time. Nobody was on land anymore. Most of the boats now were peacefully gliding toward deeper waters, to their traps and the appearing sun out in the horizon. Many of the boats were no longer visible anymore at all. The sun now shone its light on the town. The docks were empty once again, not a single item left behind. It was as if nobody had been there in years.

With nothing else to do, Kane walked home. Maybe he would grab another cup of coffee, even though he felt awake. He was awake with a troubled mind, too troubled to fall back asleep to draw. He had gone there to investigate a possibility and it wasn't that he'd found the wrong answer, but he hadn't found one at all. If anything, he'd raised more. He wondered if he was being stupid. He certainly was being naive. Kane always remembered a poster from his elementary school days at times like this, and he hated it. It was the "You miss 100% of the shots you don't take" quote attributed to Gretzky or Jordan or probably both and every athlete and corny motivational speaker that had ever spoken to a gullible crowd. Of course, you missed it if you didn't try, but sometimes maybe passing was the right play. Maybe stalling a few more seconds would be more beneficial. It was always more complicated than that. Despite his disdain for the quote and the fifteen or so years that had passed, he always remembered it. He walked home, wondering if he should take the shot. Maybe more investigation would help calm his worries and answer his questions. Maybe Brenda could help, or maybe she would just chuckle at him like she had before. He wouldn't blame her for it.

Brenda didn't laugh at him. Kane stood on the steps that led up to the porch she frequently and currently sat on, drinking tea as she did most mornings, revelling in her freedom to do so in retirement. Before he posed the ridiculous idea, Kane had made some offhand small talk as he often would when he saw her. He liked her and she liked him. He was nervous to ask her about the likelihood of him finding work on a lobster fishing boat. To even think he might be able to work on a lobster boat with no experience, ignorant to the physical demands of the job, would certainly seem foolish to her. Kane's question this time wasn't him just bringing it up for the first time, he'd sought her out and that was obvious. She examined Kane, allowing the soaked tea bag to rest on the lip of the mug, leaking brown liquid down the side. Kane just let her think, careful not to show desperation, ready to explain his motives and ability.

"It's extremely difficult work Kane. People's heads get messed up out there. So do their lives."

"I know."

Kane had worked hard his entire life. He'd grown up just below middle class and worked his entire life. He had been nervous before every new job, but willing and with a chip on his shoulder he was always liked by his bosses and more than capable. He knew this would be the hardest job he had ever had, much harder than scallop diving. But he would be above water, and he would make much more money. If there was any boat willing to train him he was confident he would pick it up fast. He would lie about wanting to build himself a career in it. He would be in over his head and nervous every day, but if he could survive the first month, he would stay as long as he needed to make enough money and have enough time to go by that maybe he and Tilly could start new. Whatever the future brought him, he wanted it with her, and he wanted to set himself up to be in the best position he could be in. He didn't want fate to sneak up on them only to be treading water. He would rather drown in the waters of the sea than the ocean of lost time.

"I won't let that happen. Maybe nobody will take me on, and maybe I won't be able to pick it up. But the work won't be so hard it takes me out. I'll deal with it. I have to."

Kane hoped she could sense the conviction in his words. Brenda had lived here her entire life. Like everyone here, she knew everyone here. She was kind and she was fair and he was happy it was her he could ask, whatever the outcome might be.

"I'll ask around for you."

Her looking into it was all he needed. That was her yes. That was her approval of him giving it a go because she believed his words. It was her saying yes to going out on a limb for him and recommending him if there was room in a crew. This was his confirmation hearing and he had gotten her blessing.

"Thank you." He thanked her for thinking well enough of him to stick her neck out. He thanked her for the possibility of a new life she may have just granted him. They continued to talk about things, the weather, the extra work with minimal pay of scallop diving, when she would see Tilly again, and the deer that no longer visited her front lawn as they had in years past. He asked her if there was anything she might want from the store. She told him a carton of milk and he said no problem with a smile as he declined the money she offered for it. He had the day off. He owed her much more than six dollars of milk. Anyway, now he could pop quickly into the local gardening shop to pay a girl a visit.

CHAPTER 9

Lying underneath the decrepit chassis of Tilly's mom's Chevy, Kane's arms fell to rest, painfully burning. He had been scraping and scrubbing vigorously at the carriage underneath with brushes and cutlery ill-designed for this type of work. Both arms were already so tired from work that he could only keep at this for moments at a time. He used a couple of butter knives to chisel rust from the frame joints, then brushed it, rust falling away onto the browned grass beside him until the entire thing could be washed and oiled. This had been his project for a month now, even though scallop diving was now overwhelming and he felt weaker than when he had decided to start working on the car. Despite this, he still liked doing it, and wanted to get this cleaning over and done with before the imminent dumping of snow. He could labor over the engine in the snow, but he didn't want to be down here on the ground. The snow would soon build walls around the frame and he would have to dig himself in, lying in the dark on frozen ground, a browned outline of a dead car like the chalk outline of a person dead just like it. Another winter's rust and he may not be able to chisel it away anyway.

Jessica insisted there was no point. The car would never drive again, but Kane had wanted to do it, even if she was probably right. He wondered how long this car might sit here otherwise. It had been her ex-husband's car, and then the family car, and a dead battery and flat tire later, it was nobody's. She explained to him that they walked everywhere anyway, and when the battery had died they just left it for so long that when they went to check it again, they realized the tire was flat with no spare. They could have fixed it that day with a hundred bucks and a few hours, but they left it for another time. "Next week," they had said. As they had gotten used to it, the gas gelled, another tire had gone flat, and the growing grass took its hold on it. It was still a great car when they left it for dead. When Tilly's dad left, he left it there, reminding the both of them of him; it was just a monument to his presence and of the time gone by. Either he was in too big of a hurry to leave or he didn't care about it anymore, both were heartbreaking to Jessica at the time. Tears welled in Jessica's eyes when she told Kane about the explanation for the red relic of a car. He wanted to fix it for her. He didn't care if she never turned it on, drove it into town every day, or pushed it over the cliff, he just wanted to do it.

Kane's dad had taught him what he knew about cars, which wasn't much, but enough to figure things out for himself. His dad, Dave, worked in telecommunications, sales or marketing or both sort of maybe. Checking the oil and fluids of the engine was easy enough, and when the time came to clean the oil filter or change a tire, that became easy too. Along the way, a few things his dad couldn't teach him had come up, so they'd looked into it together. Coolant was leaking and the timing belt was wearing thin and they'd asked a mechanic how they would go about fixing it. His dad wasn't asking for an explanation, he was asking for directions, and Kane had known it. More needed to be learned, but they knew where to start. Kane remembered his dad winking at him as they walked out of the auto body shop. The few simple obstacles they learned to fix for themselves, the more they learned about the bigger picture of the car. Working on this car, Kane could see that his dad had never taught him a thing about engines or automobile mechanics. He taught him how to approach a problem and to care enough to take pride in self-sufficiency.

Working on the car was also just another reason to be with Tilly. She would always lay out on a green and torn folding lawn chair, play music over her beach speaker, and read her book. He suspected the speaker was more for him than it was for her. Occasionally, she would call out to him to ask something like if he'd ever seen Bigfoot as a kid growing up in the West or what his thoughts on the explanation of the Fermi Paradox was. She was smart and she was a weirdo. She would lay back with a tall iced drink, reading through her large sunglasses as if poolside in Cancun even though it was chilly and windy, sitting bundled in a winter jacket instead of a bikini. Not today though. Kane worked alone, which did make it feel less like a charming favour and more like work. When she was there, even when they weren't talking, it still felt lovely. Jessica was making a late lunch that he would soon go in for and Tilly was getting ready for the night. Today was October 31st. She wouldn't tell him what she was dressing up as, only that she was hoping he would allow her to apply cat whiskers to his cheeks. He had told her maybe with a wry smile, when of course the answer was yes. This was Kane's first day off in six days and he had had to request it. He was struggling through it, essentially given the choice to commit to them or cut back to one or two shifts a week. He really never had a choice. It had been three weeks since he had spoken with Brenda about lobster fishing. Three weeks seemed like enough time to let that idea go and come to terms with his situation. Today, he was just thankful to be finishing up the bottom of this car, which was once caked over in metallic plaque. Now, you could see definition in the metal frame. It was important to literally work from the ground up. He was thankful to feel comfortable at the family home of the girl he was in love with, and have those she cared about embrace him. He was thankful to be hanging out with Tilly all night, and excited to see who she will be. When she'd kissed him as he was wedging himself under the car, before she ran excitedly inside, she had told him she would be staying over tonight. He was thankful for that too. He forced his weakened arms up again, one final push and he would finish this, the hardest part, for good. And then his phone rang.

With his hands covered in greasy gunk, Kane carefully opened the door using his feet and his elbows. Jessica heard him and rushed over to help, handing him a small, red towel. He leaned against the wall, physically drained, taking his shoes off and wiping each finger with the now-blackened towel.

"How's it going out there?"

"It's coming along quickly actually. But next is the engine. I can clean, not sure if I can repair."

She was standing in the kitchen, calling out to him at the doorway, focused on chopping vegetables for the night's dinner, and speaking with him with her back turned.

"Either way I can't thank you enough, whether it ever runs again or not."

"It's a fun project. There's people that would pay for the chance to fix a beautiful car like that."

"Maybe I should start charging you then." Kane could see her smile in her jesting suggestion. There was still no sign of Tilly. She was either still getting ready or allowing suspense to build before her big reveal. He sat at the kitchen table, still holding the towel Jessica had given him. His hands were stained and he would wash them when dinner was ready. He didn't want to make her feel like he wasn't comfortable in the room alone with her. She was multitasking, back and forth around the island from the stovetop to the open fridge. She smiled at Kane sitting there. He hoped the smile was a subconscious recognition that he was at ease around her, even in silence. And he *was* at ease around her. He realized it had been so long since he had last seen someone cooking. He missed it. Until now, he never thought of it as a simple pleasure. Like everyone's, her kitchen was unique. Her stove was gas and old, but sturdy in the way that made you wish they were still made like that. It was placed between cupboards and a countertop with a hanging spice rack and a half full knife set. The salt and pepper, mounded in bowls and not in mills like he had known in his parents' kitchen. A mortar and pestle, a sign of enjoyed cooking, propped up a spatula and a whisk. It was the way she liked it, an eclectic mess that wasn't clutter, but her fingerprint on the room in the home that had the most life. Her hands worked around the kitchen from memory, quickly slicing or opening and scraping something into a pan. The sink was filled with soapy water and she would give each a flash scrub, cleaning as she cooked. Her skill wasn't frantic, but she moved fast. She was enjoying herself.

"Scallops okay for dinner, Kane?" she asked, heading back to the pot of boiling water on the stove. His heart dropped. He was very hungry. He had probably caught the ones she planned to cook.

"Of course. Do you need any help?"

She turned again and looked at him with raised eyebrows. He assumed she was communicating back to him "of course I do not need any help" in her friendly way. He was sort of right.

"I'm not making scallops, you git. I'm making spaghetti." They both laughed.

"Okay!" Tilly called from another room. "I'm all dressed up."

Her mom stopped stirring her pot and turned, pausing the kitchen activity completely.

"Let's see it then." She gave Kane a little eye roll, calling attention to the goofiness her daughter had for the dramatic flair.

"It's nothing crazy. It's pretty simple really. But it is genius and I hope you both can guess it."

"Just get out here already, you maniac," Kane called back at her, now smirking at her mom, sharing in their understanding of the nature of her.

Tilly did not answer back. They both waited in the kitchen, listening to the first of her footsteps before appearing. Was she going to be completely unrecognizable? How obscure and deep was she diving into irrelevant pop culture? Kane didn't know if she would be a lion, the *Home Alone*-like screaming person from the Munch painting, or the fourth-place contestant from season eight of *Survivor*. He imagined Jessica's guesses were just as random. Tilly appeared, now standing in the doorframe, smiling and already laughing, presumably at her own goofy genius. Once Tilly was done buckling over laughing, spinning for show, and hiding from initial embarrassment, Kane and Jessica could see her Halloween costume in full. It was a disheveled look. A black suit, white dress shirt underneath, untucked, and a red floral tie slung around her neck. Sitting on her head was a wig that appeared to be the flowing brown hair of a male. She was also wearing perfectly round glasses with no frames. Kane thought she looked extremely cute. He also had absolutely no idea who she was trying to be.

"Well..." Tilly posed, waiting for guesses. "Amazing idea, right?"

"Ummm..." Jessica delayed, amused. Kane was relieved she also had no idea. Tilly's smile started to fade. She looked at Kane who had the same puzzled look on his face and the smile was gone.

"Neither of you know?!" She threw her arms up and stood there with her arms at her side, acting angry, only making it that much funnier. Her smile didn't return, but she was in on the joke. "I need one guess at least. This idea was so perfect and it is going so under-appreciated." She stepped from out of the doorframe and sat next to Kane at the table, not before poking Kane's nose and sticking her tongue out at him. Jessica was plating the food now, and she took the first guess.

"One of the *Men in Black*?"

"Mom, do I look like Tommy Lee Jones or Will Smith?"

Kane was laughing harder now. Jessica placed the food down at the table, Kane thanking her through chuckles.

"Well, I don't know Till! You could be anyone!"

"The *Men in Black* are famously very put together. Do I look like I am ready to fight aliens? Am I wearing dark sunglasses?"

All afternoon, Kane had been under a car, Jessica had been making this meal, and Tilly had been preparing her costume. For the first time, they were now all together, sitting at the table and Kane felt the bond only felt over food and laughter. He hadn't felt a sense of home since he had left, but he felt it now. The red sauce pasta, of course, tasted like home, too, especially not having had an honest home cooked meal for months. It was perfect. Kane began to thank Jessica when Tilly interrupted him first.

"And what is your guess then?"

Tilly chewed on her food, swivelling in Kane's direction to stare at him, waiting for his answer. Kane took another bite and chewed slowly, biding his time. He tried to get inside her brain and think of what she could be going for. He knew he wasn't going to get it, he just wanted his answer to be interesting.

"You are…" he started, still chewing, thinking, letting the moment hang. "Alan Arkin on his way home from work in the movie *Glengarry Glen Ross*?"

Jessica laughed loudly in delight at the absurd specificity of his guess, and also, he assumed, on the happiness of how well he knew and understood her daughter. Tilly just looked at him with a contorted face as if he had insulted her beyond all apology.

"What? No, weirdo. Guys, I am Hugh Grant as Charles. From *Four Weddings and a Funeral*? Best Picture nominated rom-com from the '94 Oscars? Specifically, in the opening scene when he is late for the wedding."

Kane was already laughing and now only continued to do so, shaking his head, both to indicate he should have known, and in many ways, that he had been right all along. Jessica smiled at her with love, smiling at the two of them, enjoying one another. Kane noticed it. He felt accepted. Some mothers would warn their daughter against seeing a person like Kane. No real job, unclear future, and covered in tattoos. Jessica had never done that. She never forced Tilly to make a living for herself and find someone worthwhile, forcing her to move away, rebel, even leave with Kane somewhere, accidentally solving all of his current troubles. She just saw that Tilly was happy. This alternative never crossed Kane's mind, other than to appreciate how wonderful a mother Tilly had because of it.

They sat around the table like that, eating, laughing, and poking fun at each other. Kane thanked Jessica for dinner. Tilly reminded him he was getting whiskers. Kane nodded in agreement. He forgot about the phone call he'd received just an hour earlier. They left the house, with Tilly stepping lightly in excitement as she always did, and Kane admiring her, being drawn toward her, as he always was.

Fog hung over the streets, bending between the buildings and looming even more massively from above. One would think this would make Halloween that much more terrifying, but it didn't. Halloween was a happy time, at least in Sachem. Tiny little ghouls and superheroes ran around excited, followed closely by their adoring parents. The sun was setting, giving kid's that forgotten summer energy one would get on a warm, windless night, knowing they were allowed to be out even with bedtimes drawing near. Kane and Tilly sat at a foldable table at the front of the gardening shop with the door propped open. Small groups walked in and out, faces full of excited smiles, young and frightened eyes, all covered in masks and makeup. Loud calls of "Trick or treat!" could be heard echoing down the street following each audible knock on the door and ringing of a doorbell. Tilly was unsurprisingly inspired by every costumed child that walked in, asking them who they were supposed to be, or taking guesses while smiling over their shoulders at their adoring parents. She was better at this than he was, but he was loving every moment of it, and he hoped she knew that. He presumed that she did. He did have cat whiskers after all.

The sun was down now, most of the families now home or on their way home. They still saw the occasional trick or treaters, but now it was mostly annoying teenagers that were too old and had nothing better to do. Kane couldn't really blame themselves. It was almost time to head home. Tilly agreed, but wanted to stay a little while longer. A six-year-old Hannibal Lecter had just come in and she didn't want to miss out on anything. Kane couldn't blame her and he needed to talk to her anyway.

"So, when I was working on the car earlier, Brenda called me." This was clearly an opening statement for more news and Tilly waited for it. "I never told you this, not to keep it from you, but in case it didn't work out and I figured it wouldn't anyway…"

"Weirdo, what is it?"

Kane felt nervous now. He hadn't deceived Tilly, but now on the brink of a new reality he knew she wouldn't approve. She had told him about the dangers: dangers of the water, of the work, and of the type of person that typically desired it. He was nervous for himself too. It didn't matter that he had thought this up, or inquired about it to his upstairs landlord, or gotten news that he would be given a shot. But it meant something now. Telling Tilly made it real.

"She got me onto a boat."

"A boat?" she asked. She knew what he meant.

"A lobster boat."

"I didn't know you wanted to be on one."

Kane spent the next few minutes over-explaining himself, nervously quick, about his current unhappiness and doubts, and of the opportunities he had carefully thought over that being on a lobster fishing boat could make possible. His body was getting destroyed from scallop diving, and had little money to show for it.

"Trick or treat!" The conversation halted awkwardly as a princess and a cowgirl came in holding out lumpy pillowcases.

Kane continued that if he could handle it, he would make in a day or two what he was making in a week scallop diving. Tilly listened to him, uninterrupting, understanding that he was right and disappointed for the same reasons.

"Trick or treat!" yelled a ghost, a mummy, and a vampire.

Tilly had already mentioned before in passing that drugs were particularly bad on lobster boat crews. The cruel demands of the job made drugs an acceptable solution to common workplace ailments. Nobody in Sachem was getting high, they were getting better. Kane promised he would quit at the first sign of any trouble. He never believed she suspected him of being the type of degenerate person to turn to drugs like so many people in town, but she would worry his life would be in the hands of people that were. Two skeleton parents waited with their skeleton dog on a leash as their little young skeleton stepped to them, shyly, quietly saying "Trick or Treat" while looking at the floor. Tilly listened to every word Kane had to say, her delighted smile returning with every new kid. Kane was unsure which points he still had to address. The streets were fairly empty now. A light in the hardware store turned off. A group of teenagers, smoking and drinking from paper bags were walking toward the beach, into the darkness. It was quiet. It was just the two of them now.

"Hey weirdo…" she started saying, looking at him, now grabbing his hand to ease the nerves he was hiding so poorly. "Congratulations." She kissed him. "I'm still going to worry and tell you to be careful more than you think I need to."

Kane laughed away the relief that had built inside of him. "That's okay."

"When do you start?"

"I think next week. That's what it sounded like."

Tilly nodded, realizing in that moment, as he was as well, that these were now the last of the days they had together before overworked hours and fewer freedoms to lay around together to draw and waste the day. They had both treated time like an unlimited commodity when it was really a depleting resource.

"We have a lot of candy left. Let's go eat all of it."

He kissed her now. She stuck her tongue out at him. They both pushed their chairs away and stood up, her locking the front door and him grabbing the half-full box of mini chocolate bars.

Kane sat with his legs spread across the floor, surrounded by torn open wrappers. Tilly lay on the couch above him, arm slung across his chest. She was still wearing her dress shirt and glasses, the suit and tie thrown into the corner of the room. They were unwinding, enjoying each other in silence, occasionally opening yet another a new chocolate bar despite being uncomfortably full. John Carpenter's *The Thing* played on Kane's laptop, sitting on the floor, neither of them paying any real attention to it. Kane was enjoying Halloween and the distant screams and tense moments of silence from laptop speakers that felt like a tradition in the making. Tilly poked his cheek. Kane reached for a piece of candy that was halfway to being underneath the couch entirely and forgotten forever. His hand went in for it when he also uncovered his tattoo bag and quickly flipped to his knees holding it out excitedly in front of him and her. She laughed and shook her head.

"No way."

"Look at my cheeks!" he said, now remembering his six whiskers and feeling thankful he didn't wash them off. She just kept laughing and shaking her head. He didn't expect her to get her first tattoo right now. He was just playing with her, having fun, driving a lively energy in the room. She ignored his plea with a smile and closed her tired eyes. Kane began unloading each tattooing tool anyway, one by one, placing them on the table, ignoring her, smiling, and making a show of it. "So, what are you thinking of getting?"

"Ummm. Give me a Jack-o'-lantern."

"Where?"

"Right here, please." She pointed to her cheek, dimpled from her smile. Kane left the tattoo kit and sat on the couch beside her, leaning in and falsely inspecting her cheek.

"Okay yeah, I think I can make that work." He poked her cheek with his tongue and rolled his eyes, leaving their shared smile and sitting back down on the ground, back to the movie, playing the martyr.

Tilly let her arm fall back across him. Kane playfully bit it before unwrapping another chocolate. The moment was calming now, the laughter quieting, smiles fading back to faces of content and the slowing pace of their excited hearts. The movie played on. They enjoyed it that way for some time before Tilly sat upright to eye the tip of the needle he had taken from his bag and put on the table.

"What were you thinking of giving me?"

"Whatever you asked for."

"Okay." She started unbuttoning her dress shirt. "Let's do it." She pulled her arms out of the sleeves and took it off, tossing it aside. Kane was already laughing it away.

"Yeah, right."

"You are starting a new job. You'll be tired and whining about it all the time. This might be our last chance."

"Are you serious?"

"I want it right here." She pointed to a spot right under her left breast. "As small as you can do it."

"And what is it we are doing?"

"I want a lighthouse from you."

Kane closed his eyes for a brief moment, smiling, as if she had unlocked a secret that he had been keeping. Tilly returned his smile with a curious one back.

"What?"

"Nothing." He jumped up eagerly from the floor to wash his hands. He came back and kissed her softly on her lips. "You sure?"

"Like you said, you do have whiskers after all."

The skin plucked as the metal tip entered and retreated from her skin. Kane looked into her eyes one final time, her infinitely inviting eyes. Her deeply brown irises were covered in those golden flakes, a well of everything that she was, and right now, she was vulnerable and trusting, her face telling Kane that it was more than okay. He felt her love even through her adorably dorky Hugh Grant glasses. It is what she desperately wanted. He stared back in reassurance. If this was not love, then nothing was.

"Are you ready?"

She nodded. Kane pressed the needle into her skin a second time.

The tattoo was halfway finished, the small black rocks and the base of a lighthouse. All that was left was the remainder of the cylindrical tower and its lantern. Tilly had not seen it yet, she only looked at Kane. This was the first time she had seen him work, and she was enamoured. It was also her first tattoo, and Kane considered the possibility that she wanted to be surprised.

"Why did you give me a little smile when I asked for a lighthouse?" she asked him. "Is that like, a totally cliché white girl's first tattoo or something?"

Kane smiled wide, but without taking his eyes off of his work, nor did he pause from it.

"No," he said quietly and honestly. "It's our thing. I feel included, I guess."

"Maybe I just like lighthouses."

"Maybe." Kane kept working.

Kane was finishing the lines going up the lighthouse as straight as he could. This lighthouse would be about an inch and a half tall. He would shade in the sides lightly and add the round lamp on top with a bit more ink and Tilly would have her first tattoo. There were a few beads of both ink and blood building on her skin, holding on by the tension of her skin. If this was hurting her, she showed no sign of it.

"Almost finished," he clarified, in case it did hurt. She only just stuck her tongue out at him.

"Does it hurt?" She stuck her tongue out again. Kane laughed and stopped for a moment, the first time he had done so since he had begun. "That night you took me to the lighthouse was the best day I've had here." If he was truly being honest, he would have said it was one of the best day's he can remember at all.

"Me too, weirdo."

"And so when you asked for a lighthouse I knew it meant alot to you too. And you mean so much to me. And whatever worry you have about me and this new job, trust me that I am doing it for the right reasons. And any future worries, just tell me. Okay?"

"Okay." She stared back at him, looking relieved to hear these words she possibly didn't know she needed.

"Also --" Kane started to stand and pull his shirt off over his head. He stood above her in bare feet wearing dark jeans, torso covered in tattoos, and whiskers on his cheeks. She looked him over curiously. He watched her, waiting, as if he was the clue and the answer to why he had stopped, as if it was written on him. And, of course, that is where the answer lay. Kane pointed to his heart. Tilly's mouth dropped in disbelief. She grabbed him by the hand and pulled him in for a closer look. On his heart was a small, darkly shaded lighthouse. It was simple, standing above a foundation of rocks, two dots for windows going up the side. Now she checked her own unfinished lighthouse. It was the same one and Kane now felt worried that even though she had asked for a lighthouse, maybe withholding that this would be a matching tattoo would be a betrayal.

"You had a lighthouse already?" she asked him quietly, still looking at her own, now with two ink streaks running down the side of her body, and more drops of blood than before.

"I gave it to myself the night you took me there." He sat back down, helplessly waiting for her reaction.

"I can't believe we decided the same thing." She seemed disoriented, either deciding how to unleash her anger at Kane, or her love. Kane just sat, much more worried than hopeful. Tilly sank off the couch and onto the floor with Kane. The blue in his eyes and the brown in hers crashed into each other like waves before their lips did the same. She kissed so hard that Kane had no choice but to kiss her with equal force. Passion like this was always an instinctual push and pull, moments of desire while the other displayed patience, needing the other person now and the teasing to make the other wait. Kane bit her lower lip, and she took a handful of his hair and pulled him back, lingering and savouring it before she lunged for more, slipping her tongue into his mouth so that he could stop and make her wait, flipping her onto her back, now looking down at her.

"Are you ready?" he asked. She nodded.

It always happened that way with them. They took each other's clothes off and had sex in the spilling kitchen light on the carpet of his living room floor. Kane, with whiskers on his cheeks, and Tilly, with glasses and a wig that Kane threw across the room causing them to smile through their kiss. Tilly grabbed his face, as if to make sure he stayed real in this moment, this boy who loved her and who she loved back. Kane's hands explored her body, feeling every bit of her with a tightness, telling her how much he loved the way she felt, how he didn't want to let her go, and how much he loved her in that moment and always. In these explorations, his fingertips streaked blood and ink across her torso and breasts.

"The tattoo…" Kane began to say. Tilly was kissing his neck, and now bit his cheek. They were both breathing loudly now, moving together, bodies reacting stronger to the feeling they were giving one another.

"Finish it later," she said, smiling for a second before they both closed their eyes, giving in completely, stopping time and leaving just the two of them, her wearing nothing but glasses and a fresh tattoo, and him with nothing but whiskers on his cheeks.

TILLY

Tilly loved the moments after, when their tangled bodies rested, intertwined, coming down from the high of sex, allowing their hearts and breaths to slow together. Silence didn't exist then. It was not an awkward or a comfortable one. It was simply them. Tonight, they would lie like that on the floor until one of them kissed the other, and they would both rise, maybe to wash their face or brush their teeth, and get into bed, cuddling closely all over again. Everything that couldn't be put into words had already been expressed, so they would lie together falling asleep. Tilly always stayed up later. It was a shame to sleep through this feeling. She supposed there would be a time when they would say "I love you" in the moments like these, but not just yet, even though she very much did.

She traced the slight bumps of the fresh tattoo on her skin. It was a thrill to know it was there, and that he put it on her forever. The light was still on in the kitchen and she could see the lighthouse on his own chest. Hers wasn't finished yet, but it would soon be the same as his. Things had moved so quickly with Kane, but it didn't scare her. That was the thrill. She loved everything about him, from the first time she'd seen him drawing the same boat she was. Everything in life is cyclical. Birth, death, seasons, people, moods, relationships, tides; everything in motion. That poor boat had been stranded and helpless, but it needed to be. Its crew had tended to it and sacrificed the time and money and now it was on the water and serving its purpose. It was where it should be. And some day, it would need to be repaired or cleaned again. She saw the beauty in the cycles of that boat, and she had seen her own situation in it. It had compelled her to revisit the shore with her paints and paper. It had looked so achingly close to the water. Was the next tide the one that would set it free? She had never written in a journal. She had this. And then she saw him.

Tilly felt that way because she was aimless. Bored was one thing, but being aimless was a way to let that wasteful boredom live longer. She knew what she wanted to do, but couldn't do it. She could not leave her mom behind and meeting Kane had only made that need to leave Sachem deepen. As time went by, and their relationship continued to get stronger, two things had made themselves much more apparent. The first was that Kane only became more understanding with her obligation to stay. The second was Kane had been so good to her that it made her want to leave with him that much more. Kane was not a pushover. She had never demanded anything of him, and he had never told her "whatever you want, we do." He was his own stranded ship, which was probably why he had also drawn it, and she was drawn to him. No, he was great to her, but also funny, sarcastic, and not afraid to make fun of her. He disagreed with her on things and challenged her. She was still going to believe in ghosts, but maybe he had a point and they had landed on the moon. She loved the way his mind worked and how he expressed it, and it came out in his art. He was much better than she was. She could recreate a scene in impeccable detail, but he was interpreting the object. He had this way of giving life to everything on the page. He saw the same beauty in a stone as he did a mountain. His works of charcoal could be thousands of years old. When she drew, her eyes and brain did the work. When Kane drew, it was his hands and his heart. She was careful, as if imagining a ruler was lying on the paper, and Kane worked the pencil in a quick fury, like a chef over an open flame. He saw the beauty in her and loved her for it in the same furious way.

It was this obsessive passion that made Tilly worry. He happened to be a great artist, but he would be good at anything he put his mind to. It was why he worked so hard. He was often done quickly, but it was because he wasn't able to live without intent. He never saw it that way because he didn't care, and why would he? He hated it and the money wasn't great. But lobster fishing was going to be full time, physically demanding, and the money was incredible. Kane was smart, but she'd grown up in this town. She saw what it did to people. Kane would never turn to drugs like so many others, but the thought of him being around it was worrying enough. What if they were high and responsible for him? It happened all the time, and she was unsure if Kane knew that. More than anything she was proud of him for taking it on, and selfishly, she was happy it was partly for her, or for them and their future. Before Kane had told her the news of his new job, she had planned to tell him something as well, but now she decided to wait. It may never happen, and with Kane starting a new job, she didn't feel it was fair to build hopes up for an unclear timeline. If the time came, she would tell him. Tilly had been taken aback when her mom had told her about her plans to move west. Deep down, it was what Tilly desperately wanted, but hearing it come from her, she felt slighted. She had stayed for her and now she just left? But she hugged her mom, and in the embrace, realized instantly that was ridiculous. And then she felt relieved and then felt guilty for that too.

"You can't stay here forever. I can't stay here, and I have the land I can sell. I'll be okay."

"Where are you thinking of going?"

"I don't exactly know yet. The idea of talking about it with you always seemed so much more fun than me thinking about it."

And that was all they had really said about it. She knew more conversations were coming, whether she or her mom brought it up, but either way, it meant there was an open door to leave, someday soon. It was clear that neither of them wanted to remain planted in an exploration of domesticated ennui. She couldn't wait to tell Kane, but for now, she would let him settle into work.

As was the likelihood of moving, or the fears for Kane's wellbeing at work, they were all out of her control and they were now just possibilities. There was no point in arguing over spilt milk while it was sitting safely in the bottle. She was in love, and he loved her, and they would say it to each other soon and have more drawings, adventures, and sex on floors like they had tonight. She was still drifting in that wonderful hour after sex. She folded her arm over Kane and tucked her face into his side to sleep. She felt owing to nobody. She was excited for herself. She was happy for her mother. She was in love with her boyfriend. With her eyes closed, seconds before she drifted to sleep in a panicked nightmare that would wake her up and that she would not tell Kane about in the morning, she couldn't help but consider that having him on those lobster boats was a very bad idea, and that she was absolutely powerless to it now.

SALT

His arms were burning. It must have been the last one of the day. He couldn't remember how many were left. He never did. If he knew when they were finished, it might make him quit anyway. Forgetting allowed him to continue without measure. He bent over the boat as far as his searing lower back would allow. He grabbed the thick rope with his gloved hand and heaved as hard as he could with all of his might. With his core still flexed, he dipped down again, straining himself even more, grabbing with his right hand and rowing back to generate as much momentum as he possibly could. He did this back and forth, pulling the rope that appeared to be infinite, descending deep into the water, disappearing into the murk. He never remembered how many pulls it would take him either, for the same reason he let the remaining number of traps left to slip from his memory. He was not exactly new but he was still the new guy. This was his task alone.

"Okay!" a crewman yelled quickly, like a gunshot releasing a lineup of anxious runners. He had heard this simple word shouted like this all day every day, signalling the last few moments he would need to hold the rope steady with both arms. The rope and his arms stretched taut, the slow twisting could be heard and of course, this was not his arms but it disturbed him every time all the same. Two crew members stepped carefully behind him and grabbed the rope from the deck, careful to avoid any tangles, especially at his own feet. He could not see them working, but he remembered from training what it was they needed to do. With this excess tail of the rope, they fed it into the large wench that would grab it and let go for nothing. At that point, the captain would press a button and the cage would appear in a mere minute. For now, he could only hold on with both hands gripping hard, turning red, exerting every ounce of effort he still had left at the end of the day, waiting for the second call, the go ahead for him to let go. He could not let go of this rope before that. If he ever made that mistake, all of that rope they had in their hands would fly back into the water, tugging at their palms before it sent the cage with it straight into the deep. Nobody was pushing him out of the way and pulling the rope themselves, and hadn't done so for a few days. He must be improving.

"Okay!" the same crewman called just as loudly, but lacking the urgency of the first call. This was the moment the two metal wheels successfully grabbed the rope and the moment he could finally let go. He breathed hard, his heart was racing, and he was seeing stars dance and dissolve everywhere he looked. The pain was so sharp inside his skin it took some time dull as he played it off as if he was totally fine. Working hard was the only way to stay on this boat and to stay away from embarrassment. One of them chuckled and slapped him on the back as his breath slowly came back. Without the air in his lungs to laugh back with him, he just raised his eyebrows and nodded along, half smiling in exhaustion.
The small engine in the crank whirred as it slowly but effortlessly continued to pull the rope. He prepared himself again. The pain his fingers were about to feel always took his mind off the fire feeling in his biceps and shoulders. He and another waited quietly, staring at the rippling water line where the rope met the water. In this moment, tired and weak, after hours and days of looking down at this rope, down became his up. It happened every now and then, only in brief flashes of long glances, that he believed he could grab the rope and begin to climb it, up into the water and away from here. The moment would leave his mind and the cage would appear. Darkened in the deep, the image confused by ripples in the water, it came into view like an apparition, an underwater mirage. Closer to the surface now, the rising mosh of black lobsters inside formed into view like a smoky apparition. Sometimes there were none and other times the cage was exploding at the seams with them, pinchers poking out the side, chaotically walking and swimming over each other in feeble scrambles to find escape. This trap was about half full, a good haul. The wheel of rope was now building on the machine, raising the moving black and red swarm of

shells, eyes, claws, and tails until it finally broke the surface of the ocean, knocked by a wave before floating in the air, hanging, swaying, seawater rushing and spilling out each side, a short lived dome of falling water, splattering loudly in a rush until just bubbles and foam remained. The rope above, in its fixed point on the pulley, was as close to the boat as it could get. A crewmember extended the large metal hook to bring it close enough so they and another could grab it with their gloves and haul it in. Thick, protective gloves protected them against any possibility of a claw crushing a finger clean off the hand. It still hurt when they tried. That, and holding something that likely weighed about 200lbs by its thin metal wire frame. Two of them hauled it in with a third crewmember shuffling in to help set it down. Both of them took their gloves off. His skin looked bloated and translucent, light blue from the cold. Two deep indented lines ran perfectly straight along his fingers and one along his palm from carrying the cage. Half of the day's work consisted of setting and dropping traps, the other half was bringing them up. The number changed at times depending on things like repairs or catches of the day. They would not drop a trap that needed fixing and they wouldn't bring one in that had no lobsters in it. He guessed this was the fifteenth trap they had brought up that day.

He watched the lobsters fight over nothing and for everything. They were helpless but they couldn't know. He wondered if they were afraid in their struggle for survival or if it was purely instinctual. Their blank beady eyes told him nothing. Their tiny movements were quick, struggling, but none of them really moved at all. This was a fight against each other now and it was a standstill. They were a blurring image created by the clicking of claws and shell on shell tapping one another sporadically. Each time he heard it, he found it unsettling. He thought of desperate people, submerged in their own versions of water and hell, trapped and fighting against one another against the cage, making the same gnashing sounds he could hear now.

Sitting on the bench that ran along the side of the ship, he waited. Two of the crewmen reached into the mess of creatures, quickly measuring them, throwing some into the water, and keeping others. The dreadful writhing sound of this deformity in nature lessened with each lobster and he was grateful for it. He watched the ones to keep have green elastic bands wrapped around their weapon-like pincers and dropped into separate cages, called pots. He carefully observed so that he could one day know how to do it if he was ever called upon to do so. Training on the boat had been terrifying, a trial by salt water, and he wanted to be prepared. It also took his mind off of the pain he was experiencing, now that he was sitting still with the very useful adrenaline wearing away. He could feel every muscle hardening already, lactic acid seeping in every tissue fibre, coating his entire body that was already sore from the day before. His fingers were bleeding today, but only a little. The worst was his lower back. Many fishermen wore a back brace and he had been meaning to get one. Anything to help this pain. Out here, he felt stuck in it. At least at home with his neck on fire he could cringe. He could buckle over or fall to the floor without the worry of being seen. Out here you had to push through. Sometimes he could see the old scallop diving crews he used to work on and felt foolish for ever thinking that was difficult work. It was nothing compared to this. But he would be making almost $350 for today. That was a week out there, fucking around blindly searching for scallops. He thought of a hot bath and how good that would feel. He doubted he could stay awake long enough to draw one anyway. Through his Grundéns waders, he could feel that the flesh of his feet had become mushy and itchy. His shoulders slumped in exhaustion. His breathing was finally even. Again, he could feel the cold whip of the wind on his face. It burned his cheeks and made his eyes water. The last lobster was banded and they shut the trap door to set it and get ready to drop it back in the water for retrieval early next week. He sat strangely upright with his jaw slightly higher than comfortable. It was the constant search to find and hold whatever position he could that brought him the least agony. The pot splashed and the rope sucked down following it, the other side attached to a buoy, their beacon. The captain steered the boat now, changing their direction. With each wave that hit the side of the boat now, waves of pain rippled through as an extension. He winced every time, but held back cries.

"Six more!" the captain announced, pushing the throttle of the ship forward.

CHAPTER 11

Snow now covered Sachem as it was beginning to decorate itself with Christmas ornaments. When the first flakes fell gently to the ground, the town seemed frozen in a serene scene, as if they were trapped inside a snow globe, just shaken. Each snowflake pirouetted alongside the others like dancers on a stage, and as a similar audience in awe, each citizen had watched with calm eyes as kids stuck out their tongues and made balls of it in their hands to throw at one another. The freeze of winter came quickly, shattering the novelty of the first fall, as Kane was sure happened every year. The snow and the cold and the grey now had its firm hold on Sachem. Kane wouldn't say this inevitable shift in season made him depressed exactly, but an obviously joyful current of the town was now hardened in ice, waiting to be thawed. His wellbeing was now much worse off than summer, and he was seeing Tilly less and working more often. It was hard to tell what was personal and what was the effect of his surroundings. Looking out his front door, the bright signs lined with lights of green and red to be turned on after dark would be a much-needed rejuvenation for the spirit of Sachem. The top of each light post was hung with a white snowflake to hang from the top, or a reindeer, or the familiar bearded face of Santa. The roads were sheeted in packed-down snow from the cars brave enough to drive on it. The sidewalks were all freshly shoveled as they always were, proof every Sachem citizen had experience and a duty and they stood ready for it. The trees surrounding the town stood tall and green still, one of the few signs of colour left to see, other than the scum and algae on the hulls of boats and rocks as the tide was out. In the cold, even the fog looked denser, as if it had distinct lines that you could draw without any shading at all. It was an intertwining mass of grey that hung ominously over the water always, occasionally stretching itself to peer and peek into the lives of Sachem, a breathing beast. Kane could not decide if the decorations would give new life to the community, or be a sad comparison of what was, like a child that needed a coat over their Halloween costume, or when he would go into the city with his family and see prostitutes wearing high heels one size too big or

84

coated in flaky and stale makeup. Dark times could remind one of dark thoughts. But he was making real money now, and it was worth it. Today was different, and the inescapability of those sad feelings that made him see the town that way were only curiosities. It was Saturday and that meant he had the day off and that meant he was going to see Tilly soon.

Kane looked around his apartment. He needed to do something about it. It wasn't cluttered and messy; he would need to actually live in it to reach that state. To him, and he feared to her, this was worse than messy. His apartment was completely devoid of any comfortable living at all. He's been too sore from work to do anything, three weeks ago Tilly had been busy with work, and the past two weekends, they had spent either at her home or outside. They had been meaning to look at the car's engine and do some final drawings together before the true cold rolled in, but he was too tired and it was already too cold. It was too late now. He was exhausted and sore from work, awoke at five in the morning for no other reason than habit from the job. He would lie in bed, dozing off here and there, but he never really could get back to sleep as hard as he tried, or as fiercely as he craved it. First, he made himself coffee, grabbing the grounds, the kettle, and the press so that he could drink this haze from his mind. These were the only things in his kitchen, in his entire place, that he ever really changed at all. His tattoo kit remained on the carpet floor beside a leg of the coffee table. It had stayed there, untouched, since he'd given Tilly her still-unfinished lighthouse. His fridge was completely empty, save for half-empty bottles of both ketchup and mustard, a vanilla yogurt that was surely needing to be thrown away, and a bag of half-dried and wrinkled carrots in the crisper. They had been in the fridge when Tilly had been here last, no more and no less. He had been buying pathetic, plastic wrapped, plastic tasting pre-made foods for the week every Sunday. He was too tired to make anything anymore, for dinner at home or lunch the next day at work. Tilly would surely notice and take it as a sign of despair, or uncaring, or the unacceptable terms Kane had made with himself under these new circumstances. There were no new accessories in his place, no plants, no new furniture, and no kitchenware that he would definitely need if he were doing any cooking, or relaxing, or living at all. These were all things she would notice. The things she would not notice is that he had gone through almost no clothes or laundry in a month. He only needed his work gear, which he washed twice a week. This mundane task was so laborious and taxing on him when he needed to just lie down and get to sleep that he was soon to clean his work clothes only once per week. Tilly wouldn't notice the level of garbage and its contents in the can remaining almost exactly the same as when she had last seen it. In his bedroom, he would wash the sheets so that she couldn't detect the repulsive smell he was sure was there. He couldn't tell anymore. It was in his pores now. Every night, dripping in sweat and fresh off a lobster boat, splashed with dirty seawater, dotted with the shit of birds he wiped on his waist when his fingers would get covered because everything at sea seemed covered in it. He was sure his bed reeked and sat thick in the arid room, so he would take care of that first. The bin in the bathroom was full of discarded toilet paper rolls. The toothpaste was a little emptier. One of the five bulbs on the mirror was burnt out. The shampoo bottles had hardly been touched. He saw in the mirror his sunken face, realizing the bags under his barely open eyes had built dark cushions that stained his face. He had a dark and patchy stubble that looked pathetic to him. Seeing it longer than it had been in years, taking in his reflection with concern for the first time in a while, it caused him to pause. He hadn't even noticed. He was a poltergeist in his own home, roaming in and out, never fully being there, occasionally affecting the objects inside. There was nothing new because he didn't need it or had no time for it, and nothing was cleaned because he used nothing. All of this seemed temporary anyway. Why force a living when you were busy making money to begin one elsewhere? This was now just a place to sleep and store his things, waiting for all of this to pay off.

His growing savings account was earning more on the boats than it ever had before. The most money he had earned before this was a summer job he'd had out of high school for the City of Seattle. It was easy; ten hours a day, doing casual grounds maintenance. He would mulch municipal gardens, plant trees, weed whack long grass around a schoolyard fence, and things like that. In five months, he had managed to save up thirteen thousand dollars. He had been on the boats for just over a month and made half of that amount already. So he had enough to start elsewhere, and the longer it took, the more money he would have. Seeing no downside to it, Kane was perfectly fine with this lifestyle, and Tilly was the respite. As long as his body could take it, of course. And that reminded him to go into the bathroom and hide the clear orange capsules inside the wrapped and white pharmacy label with the words OXYCONTIN written in bold, as if not only to identify its contents, but to serve as a warning signal. With every spot Kane thought of to hide these pills, his imagination came up with ways of Tilly stumbling across it. These had been prescribed to him. He didn't feel he was doing anything necessarily wrong, but thought better to avoid it altogether. Without these, he could no longer function. Kane decided to secure them in his small, black tattoo kit bag and, instead of hiding it, kept it clearly visible on the coffee table. She would never pull down that zipper and peer inside. It was a diary to him. He had never expressed this to her in the slightest, but he knew she understood that. She knew the way he thought, just as he knew the way she did. So that wass where he hid it from Tilly, just before heading into the bedroom to rip the musty sheets from his mattress, but not before placing one of the small golden pills into his mouth and swallowing it dry.

On his first day at work, a Monday at the wharf, Kane had looked across the sprawl of moving bodies and was terrified. He was already nervous -- as he had been for days leading to this moment -- but was now just nervous he would have no way of finding the crew. A regrettable internal voice he tried to fight was the hope that he wouldn't. Brenda had given him the number of the captain of the ship, and Kane had made the call. The voice on the other end of the line was powerfully calm, a rushing river seen from far away. It was the voice of a man with the experience of being in charge of both his crew and his words, and he explained with a tranquil simplicity. Kane was told to come down to the water at five in the morning, sharp. His name was Sam, he would be wearing a red cap, and they would be getting ready near the high shore east of the dock. Afraid of showing his ignorance too early, Kane simply said thank you for the opportunity and that he would find him. There was no direction on what to bring, what he should wear, or what to expect, just the click at the end of the call. So Kane stepped onto the slippery bed of rocks and set out to find the right red cap, of which he saw many. The tide had only started going out half an hour ago and there was already a prickly frost covering the rocks. It was freezing cold. The breaths of hundreds of throats plumed in every direction directly above the heads of fishermen. He heard no complaining. In the hustle of frenzied preparation, he searched while doing his best to stay out of the way. He walked across the rocks, watching each step carefully while looking for Sam and to avoid being run over by a bustling fisherman carrying a cage in front of his face, or spinning quickly to grab an item on instinct. Remembering back to the morning, Kane hardly remembered what happened next. He had been in a state of fear and shock. The need for the job set in. There was nowhere else to go for him. He found the captain a few minutes late. Looking back, he could not remember how he identified him. They were both awaiting the other and the invisible attraction must have taken them both, watchful eyes that pull your own toward them from behind a turned back. The broad-shouldered man turned and his face had matched his voice. Kane had clearly been lost and easily caught by the eye of someone looking for a stumbling kid in over his head. He remembered the crew briefly greeting him with instant looks of inspection and indifference. A few, he remembered, looked him over a little longer than others, or maybe that was just the drawn out eye rolls they gave him. They knew as well as he did that he was in over his head. The captain did not shake his hand. Kane couldn't tell if this was rudeness or because his hands were busy. Later, with the knowledge of knowing the man, he concluded it was both. He had a smooth white beard just like the pipe-smoking sailor on the blue pack of cigarettes his dad used to smoke, with crystal blue eyes as if the reflection of the ocean was stained forever on them.

"Kane, yeah?" he asked, checking.

"Yeah. You're Sam then?" Kane replied, and Sam nodded back, taking a second to look him over while the others continued working.

"You've never been on a boat before, right?"

"Like a lobster boat?" Sam was breathing tired, blowing out cold white air with each heavy breath, waiting for Kane to figure out the answer to his own question. In this first ten second exchange, Kane had realized this man would not suffer fools or foolish questions and that he would need to learn everything fast and on his own. "No, I haven't." From the crew, bending over repeatedly, carrying and setting down large cages, a few chuckles and smiles was heard and seen. Kane remembered the flushing feeling of his face going red.

"You see that bench there?" He pointed to a long wooden bench running in front of the wharf's hall, sitting on the concrete shelf above the rocks of the shore, roughly fifty yards away.

"Yes," Kane replied.

"Go and sit there and watch us."

"Okay," Kane said, at a loss to the reasoning behind this. He assumed his potential boss was hoping for someone he could use, and realizing that he couldn't, he had relegated him to the side before telling him to never show his face again. Kane began for the bench before he was called out to one last time that morning.

"And only watch us. Focus on what we are doing, not all this shit around us."

Kane nodded to him with prideful promise this meant he still had a chance.

"When you see us head out, you can leave. We will be in around six o'clock tonight. Be back on that bench at five and when we come in, watch us again. That works?"

"Yes, sir."

And with that, Sam went back to working with the three others on his crew. Kane did as he was told. He watched Sam put in the same effort as the others around him. He watched the largest crew member pick each cage up with stoic ease and put each down without the slightest grimace. At around six-foot-five, he was very obviously the strongest, and witnessing the physicality up close was intimidating. Seeing this towerous presence wince through it made his presence there seem even more foolhardy. The only girl in the group had a stern look and had yet to see speak at all, or even change her facial expression. She could only be about five feet tall, but she carried herself taller than the others did. She had short brown hair and strong arms. The other member was a wiry, teenage-looking kid who was now laughing and talking while the others listened, conscious of him or not, he couldn't tell. He had short hair, unkempt and yellow blonde, both undoubtedly from the salty air. His eyes were black and he seemed to be looking at everything but focusing on nothing. Kane had no idea what they were doing, but he watched. He watched them move their gear to the dock, and then onto their small boat together before moving to the lobster fishing boat. After the few times he had witnessed this great leaving of vessels in the morning, he had never focused on one person or group, and he did feel more aware of the workflow they had together and with those around them. They were a unit, a pod; it was like they could see the other's next move. There was never any instruction that he could see, or pointing, or even waiting for the other. One of them would lift a cage just for the other to take one underneath it, to have another spin from their own task to take the original cage and set it back down. They clicked together like the gears inside of a clock, and they flowed in rhythm like the black notes on a sheet of music. Kane tried to absorb every movement, but felt discouraged by his inability to grasp their intent. The sun was starting to show and he stood up to stretch, ready to dwell on the unease of coming back in eleven hours and face his fears. Brenda had kindly set this up for him and he had now introduced himself. There was no coming back, only failure or success, and he wasn't sure what that word meant to him yet. Their boat was all white with bright red trim and he watched the crew continue to work, wondering if it ever stopped. Kane waited there for them to make their exit before he did the same. Sam must have been under the open roof of the ship, bringing the engines loudly to life, turning into the waves, a bubbling froth building at the tail of the boat from the engine underneath. Kane could read in red script the name of their ship, the ship he might soon call our ship. *Caught in the Pot.*

Kane returned to the same spot on the bench three hours early. There was no way he was going to be late for his second meet up on the same day. When he had gotten home, he had disparagingly glimpsed his sketchbook, realizing then the short time he surely had would have left to draw. If he even found the time, would he find the energy? He promised himself he would. As if to seal the agreement, he brought it back with him and quickly drew everything he could see, finding the beauty in each standing rock, indifferent bird, lonely piece of driftwood, and playful cloud, separated from the rest, exploring the world away from the mass of grey it had escaped from. It was like he was gorging his soul before a great fast. When the *Caught in the Pot* returned, as did every crew, they moved the same but looked wet, and smaller, as if the day had shrivelled them. They wanted to get home, but there was work to be done. It was immediately evident that they would not be saved from anything out here and they moved with that understanding. Sam, even as the boss, helped them unload the boat, the large cages now filled with shuffling lobsters. Kane stood up to watch. Sitting on that bench while so much effort was being put forth felt lazy to him, even if there was nothing he could do to help. If that was the test, he had failed already. With the cages and gear now hauled elsewhere and out of sight, Captain Sam gave his team a talk, gave a quick nod, then walked away, crewmembers dispersing in different directions to finish up the day's last work. The hard part seemed over. Kane wondered if he had been forgotten about entirely. He couldn't stand frozen in awkward unknowing forever, so he took his first steps towards the truck, and to whatever was next.

In the last acts of work for the day, a friendly nature forged organically and casual conversations could be heard echoing above the shores. This is when the first cigarettes off the boat were lit, and toques could be taken off to wipe the sweat off of one's forehead. It was an earned pause before finally finishing, both a regaining of strength and the acknowledgment of another day in the books. Eventually, after a few smiles, waves, and quick chats with crew members from other boats, Sam walked straight towards Kane, looking down at his feet the entire way before stopping several yards away from Kane, still on the rocks, looking up.

"You can sit down," he gestured lightly, almost smiling, probably noticing Kane had been standing for forty-five minutes. Kane sat and listened.

"Do you use?"

"Use what?"

Sam took a slow breath through his nose, pensive and waiting. "Do you do drugs?"

"No."

He said nothing more for a while, just looking, deciphering if he was being lied to or not. He was staring directly back at Kane, measuring his pupils or trying to read his soul.

"In any case, never come to work doped up. Ever. I'll know."

Kane waited for more in the same silence.

"Brenda is an old friend of mine. She said you're a good kid. She also told me you have no experience on a fishing boat.

Normally, I would never let anyone on my boat without years of experience. It's unsafe and frankly, most people underestimate how hard it is. But you seem keen. You showed up. Twice. I lost a crew member a week back and so I am giving you a shot. This week, you will do what you did today. Show up, watch, come back, watch some more. Monday, we will take you out, so ask questions this week. Got it?"

"Yes, sir. Thank you for the opportunity."

"Thank Brenda," Sam said, starting to walk away. "And call me Captain."

And then he was gone. Kane was relieved this week he would have a chance to simply observe. He assumed that meant no pay for a week, but it was worth it. He walked home, texting Tilly to see what she was up to, excited now for the promise of new work and more money. Maybe this was possible after all. He wondered why the nameless crew member had left. It was odd the captain never said that he had quit, or moved, but that he lost him. Kane wondered if, when he inevitably left in six months for greener pastures with Tilly, that would be how the captain would phrase it to other people. "We lost him."

For the remainder of the week, Kane arrived at the wharf at five in the morning and five at night, watching the crew perform the exact same tasks the exact same way. They were like the cogs in a wheel, each task and item used to begin the next. The trucks, to the beach front, to the dock, and to the boats, turning so that it could turn the others, a closed loop of workers used for fishing lobster from the sea. Using his sketchbook now not for drawing but for filing questions, he studied from his spot on the bench. He would have been noticed by others the same if he had been invisible. The captain would answer his questions after every day; some seemed like they would have obvious answers, and some were so specific Kane hoped they would impress. The captain never suggested these questions were either, he never scoffed or laughed at them, nor did he ever say "good question" or take a pause. What do you do with the lobsters when you come in? Where is all of this stored overnight? When do we gas up the boat? How long before you bring the traps up? Over the week, Kane's slow and base level understanding led to deeper questions about the operation. Kane got the impression the captain was taking all his questions and providing answers because this was his one chance to ask. When Monday came and Kane was expected to put the answers he'd received into practice, he imagined there wouldn't be time to ask simple questions, let alone ten. This crew, every crew, was a conveyor belt that never paused, never faulted, and Kane could not affect that. On the Thursday, Kane sat there much later than usual, into the dropping darkness. A few boats seemed to come in here and there after six, so Kane just waited. When they finally arrived, around ten at night, the captain had just looked at him as he had each time and asked what questions he had for him. No apologies, no explanations given.

This was not the ocean that Kane knew. The first two weeks he was actually out on the water was his antagonistic re-acquaintance with her. For the first time in his life, he was getting sea sick. The physical exhaustion, relentlessly cold air spitting against the glaring sun, the heavy weight of heavy rubber Grundéns waders, constant slamming of relentless waves, and the constant smell of fish and lobster and guts and shit. It got so bad, Kane would only bring soup to eat because it was easier to puke up.

"Over the side!" was all he could hear. If this amount of throw up was dangerous or abnormal, the crew never seemed concerned. But he had learned all he could from sitting on that bench, the captain saying, "See you Monday morning," and handing him the rubber uniform with the advice to wear layers. He was sick to his stomach, and with each command from a crewmember, he felt equally as nervous to ask a question as he was of making a mistake and fucking a machine up for the day, or worse. He was shown how to tie several knots, the anchor hitch, of course, for the anchor. He learned the half hitch when ropes needed to be extended to other ropes, which was rare, but he needed to know it because these were often used in case of emergency. If you didn't extend the rope fast enough with a half hitch, a trap might be lost to the bottom of the ocean, along with the day's profits. After being shown once the reef knot, the clove hitch, and the bowline, he feared he might confuse one for the other. He would be fairly sure he had tied the anchor correctly, but when dropping it, his heart would drop with it, terrified they would lose the anchor entirely. He did his best to watch others tying their knots. This was how he felt about everything, from where things belonged on the ship to setting a trap correctly. He watched the others move to learn, but also to see if they still had that worry on their own faces. Did they ever have it? Would it ever leave him? He had made a few mistakes along the way. He got a rope twisted in the wench and it took them five minutes to untangle it and set it free again. Kane just waited while he was scowled at like he had sunk the ship. A few times, he had been pushed aside without a word. Deep down, he must have known it would be that way, but living it was more than waiting for it. Every shift, he thought he was going to be let go, and even though he needed this, he wanted to be. He couldn't quit, but he was always embarrassed and afraid, and even worse was the physical toll on his body. He could barely move in the morning. The pain would wake him up at night, making for restless sleeps, compounding the problem. The fear was what kept his eyes open out on the water. Every turn of his body was so rigidly tight, he waited for the moment his bicep or Achilles tendon would just give up --" Nope, you just pushed me too hard Kane," and *snap*, recoil like an elastic band into his shoulder or his knee. He was in so much pain already, he wondered if he would even know. One morning in the early days, it took him several minutes and a fairly comical roll over method without using his arms just to sit up enough to leverage himself out of the bed. His body would need time to adjust, to stretch, and grow stronger. Kane was still waiting.

Now, the crew left him alone. The smiles and eye rolls had seemed to stop. They all kept to themselves anyway, except for Kirk. Kirk never explicitly spoke to him, but rather, he spoke to everyone or everything. Sporadic thoughts and phrases struck from him like lightning, whether someone was listening or not. They were always casual observations that led to an anecdote that steered into a tangent completely unrelated until there was no remembering where the train left the station and no guess to its destination. He was quiet when work needed to be done; Kane imagined he'd learned quickly after a few awkward "shut up "early on. Kirk's good-natured ramblings in Kane's early days had meant he was really the only kind one, even if slightly overwhelming. He really appreciated him for that. He was very funny, and it didn't matter that the crew barely laughed or spoke back; Kirk was a needed presence on the ship, to outwardly express their unspoken camaraderie. At nineteen, Kirk was the youngest on the ship. Wiry and gaunt, it was amazing his lanky limbs could withstand the abuse of the work. He once saw Kirk have a full conversation with Brad that seemed back and forth, but Brad had managed to reply with "uh-huh" four or five times. Not that any of the other crew members would have gotten any words in themselves, but Brad was especially quiet. Besides the captain, Brad was the oldest on the ship; Kane assumed he was forty years old, but judging the weathered and broken faces and bodies of fishermen proved impossible sometimes. He was large and bald with handsome features, light stubble and soft expressions that made him always seem content, pondering an answer that could be found somewhere else other than where he was. Jenn was the tough one. There was no patience in her for Kane's failings as a fisherman; she undoubtedly thought it ridiculous he was even given the chance, and Kane couldn't blame her. She had probably been on this ship for years earning her spot. Annoyance was all she showed for Kane, and indifference was what she showed to everyone else. Anytime something was going wrong, or needed to be done quickly, she was the first there and doing it. She was the best and hardest working crew member on the ship. She appeared to be Kane's age, with her facial features always arranged in a stern manner, always at the ready to fix a mistake, or to jump into action. A few times, Kane had caught her lips curling into a smile during one of Kirk's long-winded stories, and, noticing her risk of being caught by someone, and maybe even feeling embarrassed about catching herself, she turned her face and attention away, killing her brief lapse in martyr-like stoicism.

Kane was still learning, still struggling, and still terrified, but he felt the momentum of understanding building. The knots were by no means instinctual like it clearly was with the others, but he knew when to differentiate them. He knew when the time was to scrub off the deck without being told. He learned that each boat had a distinct lighting scheme that would light up, visible only really at night. Kane had seen these lights on the water, but never thought they might have a practical function. *Caught in the Pot* had patterned lights of red, white, red, and could be seen on the roof of their boat, as well as in the entire aesthetic of the boat. It was in the trim of the hull, the steering wheel, and in the cleats and the sidelights. This pattern was also on each of the twenty or so buoys they had in the water as a way to prove ownership.

"What happens when boats just take lobsters from buoys that aren't theirs?" Kane asked, expecting the captain to answer, but he didn't even turn around. The crew, now annoyed, pretended not to hear him until Kirk finally answered him simply with, "They wouldn't."

By way of immersion, Kane was learning an entirely new language of fishing jargon, that lobster traps were referred to as pots. The name of the boat was a rhyming, fun way of saying caught in the trap. At learning this, Kane felt a fondness for the name of their boat. He could relate.

The only task on the boat that was Kane's and his alone was the role of the visibility lookout. It was the simplest of tasks that took only a matter of seconds, but a misinterpretation could mean disaster, or so he had been told when shown his sole responsibility. The day would be called off for almost nothing. There were blistering days in the summer where your skin would burn in under an hour from the bouncing sun off of the water, and the scorching metal buoys could sear it the second it touched flesh. Heat stroke and dehydration signs were often seen and often ignored. He was told of times the boat would depart the cove into deeper water, met with the last remnants of a night storm, wind and waves both attacking the boat in sheets of rain. The only threat feared with a high enough risk to all boats was not one of attack, but of deception: fog. Fog is what Kane had to look for, and more accurately, be able to look through. Fog was inconsistent and unpredictable. It could reach around a corner suddenly or quickly descend from the heavens above and blind a crew, leaving them helpless to rocks and the world below. If that did happen, there was no telling how thick the white may be, as not all fog was the same. This unknowing scared most boats off, and rightfully so, but some saw it as a financial risk to be weighed on the Libra scale of their desperation. On one side was the cash and lobsters they could make -- or miss out on -- and the other side of the scale was a boat easily parting the fog's blanket -- or being enveloped and sinking the boat in the rocky shallow. The *Caught in the Pot* would never, under any circumstances, take a risk in the fog. The captain was so adamant about this, he wondered if he had made a mistake in the past, succumbing to the luring promise beyond the white, or if this was common practice. When the captain showed him how he would check every morning, something in his eye told Kane it was the former. It seemed archaic in nature and highly inaccurate, borderline voodoo wisdom, but it was Kane's duty and he took it seriously. Within five minutes of leaving the dock in the skiff loaded with all of the traps and gear, on their way to *Caught in the Pot*, Kane would retrieve a pair of binoculars from the side mesh pocket on the boat to look for the three hash markings that scarred a tree. Roughly two hundred yards from where the beach stopped and the tree line began, turning right and opening into the cove, was a large tree, a few feet into the woods. When he'd first learned, Kane had known to look just right of the groupings of four large rocks and between the bushes separated by a creek, but now he looked straight for it in memory. He could find it in seconds now and took a quiet pride in that. It was a tree like any other, high reaching with healthy, green pine needles blending into the pine of other trees surrounding it, but this tree had three slashes carved into the bark, wooden scars revealing the yellow flesh underneath. Their purpose was an indicator of how the fog was behaving on a particular day. The first was at the base of the trunk, the second was ten feet above that, and the third mark was thirty feet, the highest it could be before disappearing into the canopy of needles. They must have been put there by an axe, possibly even by the captain. How one had climbed so high, Kane had no clue. Since the day he had started, Kane would peer through cupped hands and say, "three marks" to the crew and that was it. There had been one day that he couldn't see the highest one.

"I only see two today."

"Which two, Kane?" the captain said annoyed, explaining in his simple three-word question that in the future, Kane was to specify.

"The bottom two are visible, Captain."

They proceeded on as if it were nothing, and Kane placed the binoculars away and did not question it. Later on, the captain explained to him that seeing all three hash marks was obviously a full green light to fish. If only the top one was missing, he would know to be aware of sudden changes in temperature and barometric pressure and to stay ahead of the fog. If the bottom hash could not be seen, it meant a heavy, thick fog and there would be no fishing. If all three were out of sight, they were to turn around immediately, but if it was ever that thick, it would be a surprise they made it that far already. The most dangerous one of all was if only the middle mark was visible to Kane. This meant unpredictability, and people were known to do stupid things. They would never be one of those boats, and Kane had said he understood. The fog always seemed to be haunting Sachem, a careless spirit with unfinished business, roaming the streets of the old town it once called home. But out here, on the water, the presence was a malevolent one. Over years and generations, nothing had taken more lives than the fog. It was named "The White Death". Fog meant no wind, and that meant silence. The idea of losing someone to the abyss, even in silence where a whimpered "please help me" could be heard from far away, terrified Kane. Your eyes played tricks on your mind out on the water in the fog, and played on one's fears as well. On the day with two tree marks visible, Kane had thought he heard a splash behind him and he quickly turned, the hairs on the back of his neck standing up. It was mid-day, but all he could see was this thick, grey cloud and a few hundred feet of murky ocean surface surrounding the boat. Turning, he had the same feeling he'd had as a child after turning the light off in the basement after playing, then walking up the stairs, running up in fear with a quick glance back to meet his doom, and only seeing a pitch black world beyond the door frame. That day on the water, just like his blackened basement, there was nothing behind him. There were no spirits or devils ready to grab him, and surely there was nothing that had caused a splash in the water. But there was a swirl of bubbles now, in an eddy, moving past and away from the boat. Kane knew this was nothing but the superstition of the coastal marine layer sea of fog was trying to grip his nerves. Kane was rational and let a deep breath out, feeling silly with himself, taking a few steps back still from the edge of the boat, away from the water that held his undivided gaze a few moments longer.

Tilly arrived when Kane was tucking the corners of his freshly washed sheets under the mattress. This was the best possible timing, and her seeing it once would have the effect that this was habit. It's who he was really, anyway. They kissed each other before they even spoke, having sex on his unfinished bed, half covered in sheet and the other half exposed blue mattress. When they were done, they laid there together, contorted and naked, breathing hard and sweaty, Kane now feeling the pain in his muscles he had easily ignored before. She told him she missed him, and he told her he missed her back. She asked how work was and she kissed him when he said it was hard but worth it. Tilly slid up to kiss him deeper, rubbing his cheek with her thumb.

"You look tired," she told him.

He looked at her unfinished tattoo and touched the lines to see how it had healed.

"I have to finish this soon."

"Yes, you do."

Seeing Tilly, Kane felt revived in body and spirit. Two hours ago, he could barely get up. He hadn't kissed her in so long, or touched her, or heard her voice. He hadn't really smiled since he had. Now he wanted to live, to get up, draw with her, experience Sachem together like they used to.

"Want to go to your place tomorrow?" Kane asked her, knowing this would make her happy. "And I can look at the car a little bit."

"I was thinking the same thing," she said with the smile he was hoping for.

Kane felt a worry that it was the Oxy pill he just remembered taking that was inspiring him. It worried him that he'd forgotten he'd taken it, and he worried that he couldn't tell the difference. But he kissed Tilly, thinking and hoping it didn't matter. That little pill was designed to take pain away and that is it. It did its job. This happiness was real and he felt it because the burden of pain was gone. His slowing heartbeat skipped faster now as he sat up on one arm, running a hand through his hair and looking into Tilly's adoring eyes.

"I love you, Tilly," he said, for the first time.

She grabbed his neck and kissed him again, both of their eyes closing to enjoy what they had missed and the three words just spoken.

"I love you too, weirdo," she said back, smile fading, kissing harder, both of them slipping all at once further into the other and themselves.

CHAPTER 12

During Kane's first few weeks, in the nights unloading the boat, Kirk rambled incessantly, back and forth from the dock to the work trucks across the rocks and small pools of still and stagnant water. Kirk had apparently been tasked with talking him through the first days of work without helping. The captain had one member who was guarded, one who was quiet, and one who talked non-stop, so it was a no brainer. The talk was never really about the *why* or the *how*, however, and the reasons Kirk was chosen were the reasons Kane found him difficult to follow. He was still new and Kirk was kind, so Kane listened to the stories, waiting for the sparing moments he could inject a "yeah?" to throw friendly gasoline into the crackling fire of his stories. The others would leave most of the work for the two of them so that Kane could fully grasp what would be asked of him when they were a working unit. It was better for him to take his time and learn it, especially not on anyone else's time, except for Kirk, who never once complained about it. Kane appreciated the lack of resentment that Kirk never seemed to have toward him.

They would be alone, soaked and sore, Kirk grabbing the bulky boxes and cages, expecting Kane to do the same. Sometimes, surprised by the weight, his arms would give out in the first few inches picking it up, crushing his fingers between the wood. He would quickly slide them out from the pinching pressure, leaving them throbbing, often with tiny wooden slivers in his nail beds. He always found just enough strength to avoid the embarrassment of Kirk -- already loading the truck a hundred yards away -- seeing him, still on the dock, cursing himself. So, Kane would heave it onto himself, sometimes letting the sharp edges dig dangerously deep into his biceps just to give his hands a break. He would let it rest an inch higher or lower, easing the stress on other parts of his body, but leaving bruises and cuts down his wrists and at his elbows. He hoped that it was temporary and that his body would adapt. Kirk spoke loudly enough for Kane to hear him, maneuvering across the rocks like a spider on its web, never tripping up and never looking down. Kane's feet would slip and thud on slippery rocks, wiggly rocks, and spots where there was no rock at all, and with each misstep, he felt the weight of his load grow in his tightening arms. Kirk would yell about his cousins and how many were first and second and the different ways they seemed like successes and failures, even though he didn't much keep up with them. He yelled and asked about movies before admitting he knew nothing about them, and then continued to speak about them at length with the passion of a critic.

Another day, the hot sun had managed to soak the shores between the cold clouds, drenching the two of them in heated sweat underneath their clothes meant for sub-zero air and rain. Kane's thoughts felt melted from the heat, drying his throat out and uncomfortably raising the beats of his overworked heart. Kirk just smiled and whistled, slamming the back of the truck closed and wiping the beads of sweat from his face with the thin fingers of his bony hand.

"I might have to get a margarita after this," Kirk told him, letting his tongue hang out like a dog in a hot car.

"You don't strike me as the margarita drinking type."

"I am when it's this hot out."

"It sounds pretty nice actually."

"I reckon I would suck a guy's dick for a margarita if it got hot enough."

Kane looked up at him, caught off guard. Kirk just smiled jokingly and Kane did the same in return.

"Like, if the cum was a margarita I mean."

They both laughed out loud. Kane remembered thinking that this was a pretty off-colour joke, but he laughed at the surprise of it all. He laughed at the relief of what a smile and not a frown could mean from a co-worker. He laughed because, for a moment, his body forgot about the cramping and spasming that was beginning in their rest. He laughed because he thought it was funny.

"And the sweaty balls are right there for you, perfectly salty," Kane added. Both of them laughed even harder.

On the fourth night of that first week, the Thursday, Kane had to stop and interrupt Kirk. He stopped because he could not continue, and he interrupted Kirk to tell him just that.

"You okay over there?"

"I don't know how you keep going and going," Kane said with a chuckle, but defeated and out of breath, not quite yet off the dock with the cage now on the ground.

Kirk set his own down beside it. "Wish I could tell you it gets easier."

Kane just closed his eyes, said "fuck," and fell onto his elbows when his two hands could no longer support his shoulders. From here, he slunk lower even into a pathetically sprawled fetal position across the slatted wooden boards of the deck. The loud footsteps of others' boots stomped beside him. The world outside of his closed eyes was a blur that he could not care about in that point of failure. Sounds came and went, trailing away as they passed and growing louder as they neared. A couple grunted swear words were muttered as voices passed by. Kane wasn't in the way, but he was certainly bringing shame to that spot on the dock. The vibrating sound of motors rippled through the water from below, and the silence could be heard when one was turned off. Kane needed to get up. It had been long enough. He opened his eyes to the brightness of the white above, squinting at the bright sheet of grey sky, slowly standing up to face the disappointment in Kirk. He felt afraid of what he might tell the others, or the way in which other boat crews would describe what they had witnessed. He slowly stood up to find Kirk was no longer there, and neither were the three large cages that still had to be loaded into the truck. Folding his coverall straps over his shoulders and taking off his sweat-soaked shirt to cool off, Kane saw Kirk standing at the truck smoking a cigarette and looking at his phone, waiting. The cages were stacked neatly in the bed. Empty-handed with a sheepish shuffle, Kane never had the chance to apologize in disgrace to Kirk who patiently waited with an understanding look of a young man who had once been there, but now had nowhere to be.

"Fuck!" Kirk blurted out, exhaling smoke and clearly looking over Kane's torso. "I had no idea you were so covered in tattoos!" Kane was taken aback. He expected to be made fun of, or insulted, or at the very least, be scolded for his pitiful conduct out on the dock. Kirk seemed excited and impressed, and Kane didn't know what to say; he just looked down at his own tattoos, images he had seen countless times before.

Sitting in the bar now, paying for their drinks and getting ready to leave, Kirk still seemed interested in Kane's tattoos.

"Are your tattoos all done by the same artist?" he asked. "They look like they're all done by the same artist." He was right, but he didn't wait for an actual answer from Kane. "I only have a few. Just a couple stupid shitty ones. Hard when you never really go into the city."

"What do you have?"

Kirk rolled up his sleeves to show him an anchor and a lobster on his wrist. He did the same with the legs of his pants to show in cursive "Caught in the Pot" in cursive on his calf. He was right -- they were shitty, but they weren't stupid. Kane liked them and he told him so.

"So are they?" Kirk asked.

"Are they what?"

"All the same artist?"

"Yeah, mostly me actually."

"You did these!?"

"Yeah," Kane said smiling, comforted by the extraordinary kindness Kirk was showing him.

"Would you give me one?" Kirk asked him bluntly.

"Yeah, of course I would."

"How much do you charge?"

"Not much. I wouldn't charge you anyway"

"What?" Kirk asked with alarm, as if insulted. "Why wouldn't you? I have a few friends who get wasted drunk at parties, or at least used to, and even *they* charge people. I mean, it's usually in beer or something, but still. Their work isn't even close to this good."

As they walked out of the bar that was filling up faster now, Kane politely listened to Kirk who continued to tell nearly incomprehensible stories of how Drew accidentally spelt Jason's dog's name wrong, but Jason got him back a week later when he drunkenly gave Drew a stick and poke dick when he had actually asked for lettering that he doesn't even remember anymore. Kirk finally finished and Kane thought of a way to answer the question that had begun this tangent, wondering if Kirk even remembered where he had started.

"Well, I'm not going to charge you. You have helped me all week, especially today."

Kane's voice trailed off and he was back to feeling guilty over it, addressing it almost so that Kirk would do the same. The moment was a tense one. Kirk looked him over, thinking and saying nothing, an odd rarity.

"This job is hard as fuck. You are doing fine. People act tough because the work makes you that way, and for most of these guys, this is what their lives have been. They forget or have never really known what it's like to start this work. You'll get it. People don't get these first chances, so you never see people like you."

Kane nodded, listening. He understood. His body was weakening still, but every doubt he had had washed away to the sea, making the recollection of the crashing sea a peaceful sound instead of a threatening one. He remained self-conscious, embarrassed, and worried, but he accepted it.

"Okay. Thanks."

Kirk slapped him hard on the back and smiled. "I'll take you up on the free tattoo though!"

Kane smiled, and listened to Kirk describe in detail all of the different ideas he might want to do, and he knew to retreat and let these ideas crash and orbit chaotically like the formation of a solar system, as all ideas of Kirk's and thoughts were, until his ideas were formed and aligned together, however grand and impossible they might seem to be. Kane would say "I can do that," calmly to every question, allowing Kirk's thoughts to carry on. Kirk was enjoying talking about this new project and friendship, and Kane owed him that, no matter how drained he felt.

Kirk's mind must have slowed to a halt as he shut the door to his work truck, releasing Kane and allowing him to breathe and leave. The window of the work truck rolled down and Kirk called out one last time to say goodbye. Kane waved goodbye back.

"And you asked me how I do this," Kirk added, with the clunk of the truck going from park to drive and the tires slowly pinching new cement. "We'll talk about it during the tattoo." Kane nodded, waving goodbye once again.

Two weeks later, Kane took the folded piece of paper from his back pocket and showed Kirk the gaping, grey jawbone of a great white shark, complete with two connecting rows of razor-sharp pointed teeth, an isolated outline of a lethal bite. Kane had thought it seemed like the perfect representation of Kirk's personality. Sharks ate only meat. They had no grinding teeth in their mouth. Every tooth was designed like a dagger to cut and rip apart flesh. It had taken him an hour to sketch in fine pencil, and another hour to perfect. Kirk had asked for anything Kane wanted to do, and above the back door to the General Store, the large mandible hung like a moose head might over a fireplace back home. It was a stunning piece of art and he had been wanting to draw it since he had first laid eyes on it. Kirk loved it when he showed it to him, presenting the skin on his upper back, wondering if Kane could do it there. He could. Kane had known Kirk would love the image; it was badass, Kirk worked on the water, and the great white is the apex predator. Really, Kane mostly felt it fit Kirk's personality perfectly because the only real weapon a shark possessed was its mouth.

The two of them sat side by side on his couch. Kane prepared for the tattoo with his open tattoo bag on the table. Words and opinions sputtered in all directions from Kirk's mouth like a rusted over spout. He spoke about the origin myths of the mermaid and why they could be found on almost every lobster fisherman's skin drawn in ink. They were beautiful and they were sirens, something to be terrified of because the dangers were never known until it was too late, and the last you would see as your boat disappeared amongst the rocks, was not the beauty of a saddened mermaid, but her true self, grotesque and wicked. Kane focused harder on his ink and needle, knowing this was a tap that couldn't be tightened shut. Kirk brought out a spoon, a small bottle of pills, a lighter, and his red bank card, all in a line, as if to begin his own ritual. Kane didn't really think much of it. The blatant nature of the way he carried on so casually implied it was a harmless act, nothing to hide or to concern Kane with. That was, until he took one of the small pills out of the bottle, green and innocent, like a piece of candy, and started to heat up the back of the spoon. Seeing the flame hit the metal alarmed Kane and he stopped what he was doing. He only ever saw things like this in movies, and it was the behaviour of junkies and addicts.

"What are you doing?" Kane asked.

With that, Kirk looked up and let out a laugh, realizing this might look odd, but of course, was absolutely harmless.

"I'm not shooting up or anything like that. I just prefer to heat the spoon when I bust the pill up. It busts up better. Easier."

"Okay." Kane had more concerns, more questions. Luckily, with Kirk, further explanation was soon to come. The flame disappeared and the air smelt of wet ink and butane. The metal of the spoon was browned and Kane thought he could smell that too. Kirk's eyes looked down excitedly, white buildup in foamed edges on the ends of his lips, a duo of constant talking and lack of hygiene that made Kane feel a little sick.

"I'm going to snort this," Kirk said, now pressing the hot round back of the spoon into the pill, breaking it into unequal fragments, and then pressing in a turning motion making smaller pieces. He pressed more, into even smaller pieces, grinding harder, forcing further, until only a fine powder lay in a small mound, scraped into lines by Kirk's bank card. Kane just waited, uneasy. He had never seen anyone snort anything before. Kirk rolled up some denomination of paper money, hunched over the two green lines of unknown powder, but pausing on his way down to look at Kane, one finger already pressing to close his right nostril. "Do you want any?"

Kane didn't know what he was answering for, but he knew his answer all the same. "No, thanks."

Kirk, unaffected, bent his head down and took two quick swipes with his head, snorting hard and quickly. In the movies, cool characters always did so with a slow deliberation, as if sipping a fine scotch, sexy and luxurious. Here, Kirk's head jerked upward with an aggressive snort, his eyes wide and looking up, feeling the drugs splash into his blood, his fingers rubbing his nose like the twitching legs of a dead spider.

"What was that?"

"Just Oxy."

Just Oxy. He let the words float away, light like the matter in which Kirk clearly treated a drug Kane had always thought of as very serious. Kirk began talking again, with the same rate of verbal detonations he always inflicted on listening company. Kane didn't hear a word he said, not that Kirk would notice anyway. Kane was frozen by the immediate questions he wanted to ask, grabbing him by his inability to elect where to begin. The mound of powder that had just been built was now gone and up Kirk's nose. He was a few minutes away from tattooing him.

"This isn't really going to hurt that much," Kane said.

Kirk replied, looking up. "I know. I didn't really think it would."

"Are you ready?" Kane asked, looking up at Kirk.

"Yes, sir!"

The needle and ink entered his skin.

Thirty minutes into the tattoo, Kane stood up to get a glass of water from the kitchen. Without putting his shirt back on and covering his half-finished tattoo, Kirk stepped into the frigid outdoors to light a cigarette. Once Kane was alone, he fell onto his butt on his bed. He never took a break, especially during a short session like this. He didn't really need a glass of water. His arms and his back just needed the break and, still in his first week, he didn't exactly feel comfortable showing Kirk how destroyed he was. Kirk came back in with the smell of freshly-stale tobacco smoke now stained onto his clothes. Smoke smelled so good off of a cigarette but was vile once it attached itself to the fibres of cotton or wool. Sitting down, closer to the smell that lurched his stomach, he also winced in pain.

"You didn't grab a glass of water," Kirk said, noticing Kane's struggle to sit.

"Right," Kane hesitated. "I'll just grab it after. I'm almost done."

Kirk twisted on the couch, sitting on his side, allowing Kane full access to work on his back. Kirk spoke to the idea of Kane behind him, and Kane spoke to the back of Kirk's head.

"You know how they always say the first week is the hardest? It isn't. The last week is the hardest. Your body will get stronger, but you will push yourself harder. Out there, that isn't what fucks you up anyway. It isn't the soreness you feel from muscles you don't have yet. It's your joints and your tendons pulling further apart from one another that never have the time to heal."

These were the rolling opinions Kane had heard consistently from Kirk since he'd first met him, but what he was saying resonated. It was like Kirk had become accustomed to throwing his thoughts at everyone, like sharpie graffiti on a bathroom stall wall, and now he felt Kane's attention. He was painting a mural, and one that Kane was eager to admire.

"Five or six days in a row and you get one or two to heal. No way. It isn't happening. You just have to endure it. The pain will keep you up at night, no matter how tired you are. You ever slept on thighs with charley horses in 'em? Vibrating and tweakin' and shit all night? Because you will. Then you'll wake up tired, making you depressed, hurtin' your body more out of carelessness, until you get hurt or die, and if you're lucky enough, maybe make some workers comp at a quarter of what you make."

Kane listened intently to Kirk, stunned by the fragility of his anger, this kid who seemed so unfazed by everything around him. This was built up over time and he could almost feel the resentment coming off of him. He paused his hand, letting his palm rest on Kirk's back, holding the needle above the unattached jaw of the shark. He had to stop; Kirk was now trembling.

"I wasn't taking that shit for this tattoo. It's for the job. You'll need it too. I can tell. You can barely walk."

"I can figure it out. Tylenol. Something. I don't need Oxy."

"Everybody has their cure out there Kane."

"No way that every fisherman takes Oxy just to do the job."

"Everybody, Kane."

Kane thanked him for the information. He was appreciative of it. But it was also stupid advice that he didn't need. Kirk snorted Oxy because it was a cheat in the drug, originally made for slow release throughout the day. When it went up the nose, it was instant and strong. Kirk told him that everyone found their cure, and with that, he switched his tone as fast as he switched to a new subject. Kane wondered if oxy was Kirk's only cure. No way would he ever get hooked on oxy for some job, especially one he planned to leave soon. He felt sorry for Kirk, feeling so helpless, so weak in his mind to think others would be just as weak as him. If everyone needed a cure, what would his own be? Hot baths and stretching? He had tried that. No, his cure would be Tilly. He thought of her round cheeks that grew smoother with her smile, just before she would stick her tongue out affectionately at him. He thought of laying on a long couch that they both owned and taking in her face before kissing her as she fell asleep on his chest. He was in pain but he missed her in a way that laughed at his inflamed knees and his searing muscles. And his love for her was its own drug, not the kind that erased the pain, but let you feel it without caring about it at all, much like Oxycontin.

"I'll leave you a couple pills," Kirk said, over his shoulder. "You'll need them, I promise."

"Thanks, but I'm good man."

Kane completed the finishing touches in these last few seconds, worried that Kirk was thinking he felt above him for turning down the drugs. In reality, Kirk probably just thought he was being naive. And maybe he was, but he would quit before that. The jaw of the shark was sharp and menacing, but his dark and pointed shading made it more of a relic of an animal from long ago, one to be in awe of and not feared. Kirk twisted around to see it for himself in the mirror, thanked him over and over, saying how much he loved it. Kane refused any sort of payment again, and Kirk thanked him even more. Kane was exhausted and he felt the entire world vanish when Kirk left. He collapsed onto the cushions of the couch, feeling momentary agony in the fall and the landing. He texted Tilly to tell her how it went, happy with himself and happy for his love for her. Smiling, he put his phone on his leg and closed his eyes, waiting for her reply. He waited for the flood of excitement. He waited for the vibration of his phone that carried her incoming text. He wanted to hear about her day. He wanted to tell her about his own. He wanted to ask her what she wanted for Christmas and when the next time they could draw would be. He wanted to say a teasing dirty thing to her before she went to sleep. He felt excited and he felt stronger. She was his cure. His phone vibrated and he quickly flipped it to view the screen. It was a text from Kirk.

"Left u sumthing its by ur toothpaste".

Any hopes in healing with hearing about Tilly's day sunk slowly like a descending shadow into the couch, away from him as he stood up and away from it. Why the fuck would Kirk do that? He knew what it was and it made him furious. It made him afraid. It was one thing to bring drugs into his home, but then to do them? And then to speak to him like some junkie brother without an ounce of will, like he was some small-town fisherman with nowhere to go. Kirk could never understand. He took doomed strides into the bathroom and felt his heart beating quickly as he opened the bathroom drawer where he would normally find nothing but a twisted tube of toothpaste. No little baggie, no plastic bottle, just three innocent-looking green pills staring at him, unmoving. Kane shuddered at their nature, and he felt like they could see him. He didn't throw the pills into the garbage or toilet; he simply pushed the drawer closed, still staring down, feeling their presence inhabiting his home and his mind. He wondered if taking one would heal everything. They felt close to him, and he felt an intimacy with them. Superman's body would weaken whenever he got close to kryptonite, but Kane was already weakened. So was this destined to be his kryptonite *and* his cure? No, when he returned to the bathroom next, he would toss them. He should have done that in the first place and texted Kirk back to fuck off. Tilly was his cure. He had been too tired to do it right now. Tilly was his cure.

CHAPTER 13

Just like that, Kane was back on the water, or he was grimacing on the walk home, starving and sore, feeling each snapping shard of his splintering back. Or his eyes were opening to the sound of his alarm that he could have sworn he'd set just five minutes ago. He used to drift to sleep peacefully in the dark and quiet of the night, often with a few goodnight texts back and forth with Tilly. The passage through dreams and time was made obvious to him when he woke to the familiar lights and sounds of a Sachem morning, both near and far, of the town awakening. Now he was oblivious to it and his sleep pattern was similar to flicking a light switch suddenly off and then on again, instantly spilling him from sleep and into work again. Each day's next was identical to the ones now passed, and eventually, without any way to distinguish one from the next, days were no longer chapters of memory, but simply dates on a calendar. Tilly had said she loved him back just two days ago and that was possibly the happiest he had been in his entire life, giving all of this meaning, but what did it matter, if, once he was back on the boat, those sweet memories of only a few days ago were lost adrift in the sea of days that was growing vaster with each day? Yesterday, he had spent the afternoon at her place with her mom, just lying around and drawing a bit and taking a dive into the engine of the Chevy to see if he should order anything or start researching an unknown issue he found, but could not fix. Ten minutes after opening the hood, he had closed it, exhausted. His body was so sore. His arms were tired. Thinking and caring about this mundane task that had no end in sight sucked all of the energy from him, energy he desperately needed to save to find motivation to head back on the water day after day. It was one thing to be quietly lazy with Tilly, but Jessica had noticed a change in Kane. He half expected it, and he could read it on her face. She would ask him how the car looked today, but she wasn't really asking about the car. He was clearly unenthused about it and she was worried for him. Kane too easily told harmless lies about the need to bring a few tools he required but didn't have. Before leaving to find Tilly, Kane gave Jessica a reassuring smile that yes, he was exhausted and in a tough situation, but that he would be okay and to trust him. She didn't press further on the car, the bags under his eyes, or how this new job was going.

Now, he was just caught floating through space as time passed elsewhere. When Tilly was waking up, he was at work. When she had her days off, he was ducked into the wind, hanging from a metal rail just to stay upright as the boat smashed into another wave, sending him sideways. He missed her, and he resented his situation even more because this job was not only taking away his time from her, but his ability to think of the times they had. He had been doing this for only a month and was already calculating the amount of days he had worked multiplied by the rate his happiness was dropping. It was conceivable that he could be doing this a year from now, and it both inspired him to find a way through it, especially given the amount he would earn, and dejected him, knowing this despair was his only path. Christmas was only a couple weeks away. He would look forward to that. Maybe his life would just be these incremental chapters of joy filled with spending saved time looking forward to better days. He would need to remember to call his parents and tell them he wasn't coming home again.

It was Tuesday and over a week since he had last seen Tilly, or really had any interaction with someone who didn't call themselves a fisherman. No fog in the area, but Kane wished that there had been. He might have lied and said the three marks couldn't be seen, but fear forced the truth. There was no fog anyway. Like blowing cigarette smoke out of the window of a speeding car, fog could never last long in this. The weather was as severe as any he had experienced yet. He couldn't tell if it was raining, or if the wind was so hateful it was picking up water from the ocean surface and whipping it at the boat as waves erupted from each side with each crash. Gargantuan crests of water were rolling under the powerless ship, the belly of an indifferent, breathing giant. The enormity of it terrified Kane and it would have paralyzed him if the others didn't seem so confident, and also if he didn't need to throw up so often. To these expert fishermen, this wasn't dangerous work, it only made things slower. This was an inconvenience.

They had pulled four traps in five hours. They would normally have reeled in and set at least ten traps by then. They had not even taken a break for lunch yet, nor would they, it seemed. In weather like this, who would have the stomach for it anyway? But the chaos above did not not affect the world below and there were lobsters to catch. The buoys bobbed along the water, a fraction out of sync with the boat, making them nearly impossible to retrieve. Luck and time and the ability to withstand salt water spitting into your open eyes was all they had on their side. To grab the buoy's rope underneath and sync it to reel the trap was like threading a frayed wool end through the eye of a needle while speeding down a waterslide. Kane wanted to scream at the top of his lungs in defeated agony but withheld, and had been feeling that restraint for over an hour before Jenn screamed a drawn out "fuck," a disturbing, high-pitched cry from someone who hid most emotions. Kane felt a relief of his own after hearing it, a collective yell the entire crew shared. They should have joined her, howling at the elements in defiance or defeat or both, like raging wolves at the moon, or after a kill. Her face was fighting, gasping to stay tough and determined in this wretchedness, but fatigue was overcoming her, something Kane had never seen happen. He could see her expressions fade, and her face become soft, and she looked quite young. He saw her as an innocent young woman wishing she was somewhere else in the world and under better circumstances. Jenn would harden herself over and over again, gritting her teeth and plunging into the work, fighting not just her own weakness, but a vulnerability she clearly did not want the others to know she had inside. It wouldn't matter to Kane, or the other members of the crew, if they even noticed this tug of war anyway. The rest of them had given in to this exhaustion from the start, and they had no appearances to keep up, self-imposed or not. Jenn would see it as a personal failure.

The *Caught in the Pot* was on her way to the next trap. Any day, but especially today, Kane could never guess how much time they had from trap to trap. He didn't know if the others ever knew either. Maybe it became instinctual, becoming ingrained with each trip. Maybe it became instinctual to never think about it. Maybe the captain, the only one who could really know, kept the information from them. It would make sense, because they always needed to be ready; this unknowing made them clean and prepare immediately after a trap was reset so that they could be ready for the next. If they knew it was an hour away, it might seem like cause to lollygag.

Sometimes there were ten minutes between, and other times it was an hour. Today, they moved slower. It wasn't because they were over the day, even though they were, but because each condition made the next more difficult, adding each minute up until one more minute was two and two more was fifteen. Visibility was worse, even from a few feet in front of your face. The winds screamed angrily into their ears and smashing water made sweeping blasts all around them like howling bullets in the rain. They were forced to yell and point just to acknowledge each other. The deck was slippery, ropes were heavier, and their muscles were finished. Hanging onto beams and bars for dear life in between hauling three-hundred-pound lobster pots from the depths of the ocean weakened them all so evenly, they didn't even notice they had slowed. The fighting boat slackened as they did, only gently whirring now, quieting itself, fragile and open to the elements that battled all around them. When the motor ran, you felt connected to the machine that was your haven. It was your safety. It protected you from drowning and from death. When it stopped, leaving them helpless to the will of the water, it made Kane feel small and fearful. The captain stayed at the wheel of the boat, monitoring every rolling wave that prowled stealthily all around the ship. Brad immediately got himself ready to anchor the ship, which was needed for extra support to stay as still as possible. Kirk was sitting on the side, frantically looking around at the scene unfolding, clearly his mind at a loss now that his thoughts can't spill out of his mouth and onto everyone around him. He was a full kettle, boiling and steaming from the ears. Kirk met Kane's gaze with weary but bulging eyes and smiled a little. In that moment Kirk could not ramble and he seemed so kind, Kane wished that it was quiet so that he could speak. Jenn, who could now begin her approach to the buoy, waiting for the right time to rein it in and find the rope to the trap underneath so that Kane would do his best to haul up, hopefully with the help of Brad. Of course, on the boat, there were very important rules and safety guidelines. They knew where the donuts were to throw in if someone went overboard. There was no reaching over the edge for any reason without a spotter. When the wench was pulling up rope, everyone essentially needed to stop and watch, in case it got snagged, or a gust of wind caused it to whip around, snapping off or smashing into someone. The job was dangerous as it was, and each rule was implemented not just so accidents would never happen, but so everyone would know exactly what had happened. They were there so people could be saved. The one rule that he was told repeatedly, and the most adamantly, the rule that Jenn was now failing to follow, was under no circumstances for even a single second should there be any loose rope of any kind on the deck of the ship.

Most injuries were concussions from slamming your head on the railing, or slipping on a wet deck covered in fish and lobster slime. Losing fingers under the weight of a lobster pot with faulty wiring sounded horrific sounding, but quite quick and relatively painless, or so Kane was told, and to do this job for more than ten years would mean losing a finger or two along the way. The captain had not lost any. Rope was different. Rope was easy to make, easy to use, and easy to manipulate. Rope built the pyramids. It built civilizations. Rope was used in medieval forms of capital punishment and torture. To have loose rope on deck was like walking into a minefield. Maybe the other end of the line was tied to something and about to stretch, taut with tension in a single second. This happened multiple times a day and was normal and safe because all rope was kept off deck or coiled on designated hooks. A bundle of rope could pinch a person and yank them straight into the ocean in less than a second, possibly ripping clear through their legs, fingers, limbs, or even neck, before going in, shattering the bones like hollow jars, killing in an instant or sending them paralyzed and defenseless into the water. Kane wondered if any of these stories were exaggerated, but they were told with such vigor, he could see the importance of the rule, even if they were tall tales. A person could have a leg in the hole of a looped rope only to have the anchor dropped. When that anchor fell and the rope ripped tight, a leg was a stalk of hay and the rope a scythe, but the rope was not sharp. It was a fibrous weave and, although it would be quick, the tear would ravage the flesh. A loose rope caught on the side of the ship, tangled with the crates above would raise the rope and see it pin someone to the side, slowly getting tighter and tighter, and if you couldn't get out in time, the only way to stop it would be to stop the boat and reverse, adding slack to the rope. No boat could stop that fast. And here, Kane was looking at Jenn, leaning with both hands on the railing, waiting for the chance to grab the long hook and attach to the buoy, a coil of rope near her feet. Kane couldn't see either hand of the rope, only the figure eight pattern it made, with Jenn's two feet on either side. She was in a dangerous position already but if she moved her feet at all she could be in serious trouble. Kane didn't know what to do. Jenn wouldn't be told she had fucked up, especially not by him. And if the odd loose rope happened, he hadn't seen it yet, but if he said anything, would he seem green? Kane worried he would look stupid and remind everyone he was still the new idiot. This dilemma was decided on before Kane even had a chance to truly think of either outcome or the following ramifications from it. He didn't care; he was doing the right thing.

"Jenn," he said loudly over the storm. She didn't look back at him. She didn't hear him. If she did not care, she would have at least looked over.

"Jenn!" Now she looked back at him, and in her movement, Kane saw the movement of the rope.

The rope flickered slightly in first life. Kane didn't have the wits to determine how long he had, or why it was moving, but the look on his face caused Jenn to freeze. His panic at the call of her name shocked her, and now he was staring at the ground with wide eyes, allowing precious milliseconds to pass that felt like paused hours. With both of their eyes frozen on different happenings, Brad was the now-involved third party capable of assessing the situation. Brad sprinted, mindful of the rope below, ready to whip at any split of a second, took a handful of Jenn's sleeve and ripped her toward him, him stumbling backward and hitting the side, catching himself, Jenn tumbling to her knees. This action broke the hypnotic state Kane was under and he looked at Brad, breathing heavily, and looking afraid. Jenn was slowly standing up. The captain was turned now, looking confused, angry but not certain where yet to direct it yet. Kirk was standing, energy ready but with nothing left to do. Jenn looked embarrassed, angry at herself and looking at Kane, angry at him as well, whether it was intentional or not, Kane couldn't tell. A few seconds passed by, all of them granting themselves a few breaths so the jolt of the incident could wear off. This was a mistake, there was a fall, the new kid had noticed it -- they all knew this would be awkward as soon as this wore off.

"What just happened?" the captain asked the entire crew, taking a few steps out of the cabin. As he stood there, waiting for his explanation, in a startling instant, the rope cracked at eye level with astonishing speed, hovering at eye level, extending to the railing, and broken at a perfectly straight ninety-degree angle into the water. The rope was so tight you could hang from it and it would not bend an inch. The tight sound of the rope twisting taut, slowly this way, and then slowly that way. It was the only sound, as if the crack had broken the sound barrier, blocking out the storm and waters around them. They all stood in an eerie awe, an acceptance that they now stood safe, when the difference of four seconds may have meant a shocked, horrified silence, rather than the startled one they shared instead. The silence of a crew watching a young girl being told everything was going to be okay by Sam, her captain. The boat would not have been racing to the shore. They were so far from land, there would have been nothing any of them could do. Kane pictured vividly the scene of blood, pooling and trailing, dripping off the sides of the ship, falling into the ocean to be consumed vampirically. Not just the ocean, but the nature and danger of what they did became wholly real to Kane. Chills rippled through his bones and congealed his cold blood. He would think of that image often, this horrid memory that had never even happened.

They all stood in a circle on the uneven shore, as they never did, to see each other off for the night. They were all waiting for the scolding from the captain. Kane hoped that Brad being the savior meant that he was free of any resentment Jenn might have toward him. The sooner they got this over and done with the sooner he could get home. The night would rid the crew of any stiff grudges. It had been a hard day and they all wanted it to be over. Kane needed a hot shower. He needed to sleep. His skin felt soggy, his hair was matted and greasy underneath his hat, and the muscles around his ribs felt crushed from leaning and hanging onto railings against the roaring winds. His irritability from the day and the growing physical pains he could not ignore made him repeatedly visualize, in excitement, the fifteen-minute walk home, moving through the door, and reaching into the black bag just ten feet away on the table where he would find his Oxy pills.

"Tough day today," the captain said, matter of factly. Nobody acknowledged the words, waiting in shame and waiting for more from the captain. No berating came. The captain just told them to get some rest and that he would see them tomorrow. He walked away with nothing more.

"Fuck, nice!" Kirk said with the surprised grin of someone who did not fully understand the weight of the captain's words. "I thought we were in deep shit." If nothing had happened and the captain had seen the loose rope, they all would have gotten in serious shit, but he knew they learned the hard way. Surely he had had many close calls during his years on the water, and all of them surely still haunted him. Their lesson was learned. Allowing them to dwell and learn from it was the only way; if they were to be yelled at for it, it would become a regrettable mistake and not an ominous close call, always a present reminder of what could have been.

It wasn't that the crew wasn't close. Kane was new, but he could tell they all trusted each other, even if they rarely talked about personal things, except for Kirk who talked about everything. That was why Kane felt he might never be truly included. He might never be good enough or trustworthy enough to be fully accepted, and that was completely okay with him. He was planning to leave. It was just the way things were. So, to stand there together, unmoving, like they were back from the battle and shell shocked, was completely out of character. It was like each person was trying to find the right words to express how they felt and how to relay it to the other. Saying "I am sorry" admitted guilt; saying "it was an honest mistake" was pointing a finger; saying "that could have been really bad" was reliving the moment uselessly. The moment was now stuttering, like sitting on a bus that had yet to leave, following a tearful goodbye. Eventually, Brad said the only thing that was appropriate, standing on the rocks at the wharf, looking at their shoes as the crews from other boats worked around them, packing their gear, and slamming their truck beds before starting the ignition to head home: "Let's get out of here then."

Those words broke the link of the chain that bound them there. Beginning with a collective tired mumble, they took steps onto new rocks and in different directions. Brad threw his backpack over his shoulder, fishing his keys from his pocket. Jenn walked smaller at his side; Brad often drove her most of the way to her house. Kirk frantically dug through his backpack, undoubtedly looking for his first cigarette in too long. Where Kane might usually check his phone for the messages from Tilly that he loved receiving -- mostly random thoughts and ideas she had had throughout the day that he could address one by one -- today he just walked, reeling over the accident, allowing it to anchor fully in his mind, letting him feel it for what it was.

"Kane," a voice called out just before he was off the rock bed and onto the sidewalk. It was Jenn looking back at him, now walking forward, with an indication he should go to meet her in the middle. He had been worried about this. The captain had decided not to furiously light them up, but she was about to do him in. Dreading the possibilities of everything she might say to him on this ten second walk to her, his heart pounded. He shouldn't have said anything. Brad would have caught it -- and he was experienced, so he was allowed to. Or he should have kept his fucking mouth shut and ran over to clean the rope up without making a big scene of it. Brad had stopped, waiting for Jenn and looking over at them with cautious curiosity. Kirk was lighting his cigarette and frowning in confusion, nothing to say now, only watching. They both stopped, Kane looking like the guilty party who was tired of the trial, and Jenn looking conflicted, likely wondering which insult to throw first.

"That was stupid of me," she said.

Kane didn't know how to react, opening his mouth to find words that wouldn't come, only saying "uhh" in return. Jenn didn't seem to mind.

"I think I left the rope out," Jenn said.

"It could have been me too. Or anyone," Kane said back to her.

Jenn smiled back earnestly and held it, unafraid, appreciating Kane's attempt at sharing her shame.

"Anyway, thank you."

"You're welcome."

"See you tomorrow," she said, half waving and catching up with Brad who stood stone-faced. Kirk, on the other hand, had a sweeping grin on his face.

"What?" asked Kane, even smiling himself.

"I've just never seen that from her before."

"Seen her say thank you?"

"Seen her smile."

Still rattled from the close call earlier that day, Kane couldn't help but feel grateful for it. It had forced a connection between himself and the others, most of all, his toughest test in Jenn. He was not just absorbing into the dynamic of the crew, but creating something entirely new, a chemical reaction had taken place in them when he had called out her name. All five of them had seen new sides of each other and in themselves. Kirk had asked him moments after Brad and Jenn left if he wanted to grab a beer with him at The Thirst Trap. At this job, or any other, he would have normally said no in some polite but awkward manner, making up some half-assed lie about wishing he could. Today, he said sure, and he didn't even really know why. Kirk, taking determinedly firm drags off his cigarette, had asked him because this new kinship seemed to be enveloping them, and to share a post-shift beer would seal it. Kane checked the time: 7:13 p.m. He told himself one beer and forty-five minutes was really not an issue to worry about. They were all always far too tired to make this a recurring question. Kane was probably too tired now, which was why he simply said yes. It was the hardest day he had had so far on the *Caught in the Pot*, and he remembered the times when he thought scallop diving was the furthest his body could be tested. He felt strong. The two of them walked down the street toward the bar as cars and trucks drove past in a careful familiarity. Kirk was talking in fast forward now, jumping topics and answering his own questions. Kane wished Brad and Jenn had been asked to join. It would have been nice to share an eye roll at Kirk's stories, or get to know them, making time on the boat less nerve-wracking. This was probably for the best anyway, Kane thought to himself, half ignoring Kirk. He was going to leave soon with Tilly and he couldn't tell them because they would hate him for it, and probably get rid of him on the spot. Making friends wasn't really something he should be doing. Kirk hadn't been able to be heard in the howling of the storm today, but Kane was happy to listen to him now. Kane didn't put much thought into why he had said yes to the beer with Kirk. Truthfully, he was justifying it so far back in the recesses of his mind that he was not aware of his denial in the slightest. They continued walking side by side with the sounds of the bar close now. Music spilled from the frequently opened front doors with the loud chatter of patrons above those spilt notes, on break from their glasses and puffing their cigarettes. Kane didn't care about the generic beer waiting for him that would be poured through yellow, uncleaned tap lines, or this clichéd bar filled with small-town drunks passing time. He cared that he had only had three more pills left.

CHAPTER 14

Another week gone by not seeing Tilly. Kane had never been in a long distance relationship, but he imagined this was what they felt like, even though they lived just a few miles apart. They were separated by time and opportunity. There wasn't a word for a relationship separated by time. Measurable land and space being the only things to define a long distance relationship was an illusion. Two people could be separated by ten miles or ten days of time, there really wasn't a difference, except for the knowing that the other was close by. To Kane, this only made it that much harder. Sometimes, when his boat was moving from pot to pot, and he could see the miniature version of far-away Sachem, he couldn't help but think Tilly was just a pocket petite piece inside of it. He would put his thumb against the horizon, covering the entirety of the town. If he could do that, surely he could just as easily pluck her out from it. After they said goodnight to each other, either by phone or by text, he knew how happy he could make himself if he just got up and went to her house, if only just to kiss her goodnight. More importantly, he knew how happy it would make her. To make himself happier, and her, and in return reward himself even more, seemed so simple and so right. He could be there in an hour, but he never went. He could barely even take his clothes off at the end of the night.

Kane lay awake in the dark in pain, dreading and waiting for the alarm on his phone to sound, ordering him to wake up. It should be any second. When he'd last checked, it was fifteen minutes before time to wake up. When it did go off, he would have another ten minutes before he actually had to stand. The moment of standing was the reminder of the pain and the promise of hell to come. The hell of more misery, the hell of a fear of making embarrassing or tragic mistakes, the fear deep within that today's quarter pill might not seem like quite enough. The nagging sound of his alarm erupted in the dark. His ten minutes began. He was doing the math of mere minutes, deciding how long he could savour his time away from the thought of it all. Christmas break starts tomorrow and that was enough. No matter how tough today might be, he would not have to come back to it. Four days off. It would feel like forever and a day, enough time to kiss Tilly and know it was not one of goodbye, but one of indulgence. It would be a much-needed break for his body, and for that same reason, a break from taking anything for it. He wouldn't have to numb himself to walk, to smile, to sleep, to truly feel her.

Kane brushed his teeth, opening the drawer where the pills no longer were.

Kane sat on his couch, checking his phone for the time, doing and thinking nothing, waiting until the last second before he would need to leave for work.

Kane hauled the lobster traps across the beach, used to this old pain that was once new.

Kane peered at the nearer world through the binoculars. Three marks. All clear.

Tension was lost on the boat today. Maybe it was everyone's shared reprieve of the upcoming days off. Sitting on the boat, casually scanning the waters for their next trap, Kane felt it was actually a tension within himself that had eased. The others were acting normally; the captain stood straight and tall at the helm, Jenn was wrapping rope around her arm in a bundle, Kirk was sitting slumped with his arm over the side, speaking to an unconcerned and disinterested Brad with an array of facial activity that could not be heard over the wind, the roar of the engine, nor the cutting water crushing in from all sides of the boat. Kane was always terrified of each lobster trap. Each was another opportunity to fuck up entirely, and the relief when he didn't was always short lived as they headed to the next one. The fear of repeating or worsening a situation was even stronger when he did screw up, which was less and less now. But today, because of how he'd handled last week, and how the others had treated him, he felt an allowance, a slack in his metaphorical rope because he had literally seen just that. If he screwed up now, he would hope they would be more willing to help, or to forgive. And if they didn't, he didn't care. He'd earned it. But seeing their softened faces now, allowing him to sit without a glance in his direction, or stomp their feet in front of his face to finish something he should have started, led him to believe he had earned that benefit in what was once understandable doubts. He sat nervous still, but with a shimmer of confidence that was new to him during his time on board the *Caught in the Pot.*

Just under three miles was how far a person could see when out on the ocean, the long line that surrounded you on all sides where the sky met the water. The captain had told him that when talking about fog, and the way three nautical miles can quickly become three metres. On a clear and calm day, that meant you were in the middle of a six-mile gap of sight on all sides. Today, as Kane looked for their next red and white beacon of a buoy, he could see the life in the scene, and the fury and stillness that waged in the weather above that line. Tilly would have loved to be there, taking all of it in, and depicting with poetic translation this demonstration of God and nature on paper. The sky was a grey ceiling, but far enough out there, breaks in the cloud allowed a shy light to shine through. Kane hadn't seen bright sun since before even the first snowfalls. The sun's rays poured through in just two spots, both far away, but enough to tell it made the water it touched seem kinder, and put a filter on the grey caliginous matter directly behind. Scattered showers were rolling in slowly, a deadly, menacing strength of mother nature to be caught in the swells and violent arms of it, but from so far away, Kane could admire it's harmonious hovering, a gentle, sleeping beast. From far away, everything was beautiful, he thought. It was only when you got so close to something that you could no longer see it for what it truly was. Tilly was far away. The future in which they were living better lives elsewhere, together, doing something they were excited about felt far away to him too. The boat slowed, snapping him out of his admiration that he had unwillingly turned into a provoking melancholy. He would find happiness in the closeness of life. There was nothing for him to worry about. He had to keep going, allowing that booming, black cloud to pass him by, and he would travel further and live in those rays that healed the sky.

To the surprise of everyone on the boat, they were headed in early. Every shift Kane had worked, they were in by five, no earlier and often much later. When told, most of the crew looked pleased with the decision while maintaining an order to their emotions, withholding smiles and exuberant yells of glee at one another. They didn't want it to seem like work was so arduous that to be free of it meant pure joy. Of course, it wasn't long before Kirk started loudly celebrating, allowing each spouted word to stain the boat deck with a clumsy lack of grace. The captain smirked to himself, fully aware of their concealed happiness, and quite pleased with himself that he could offer it to them. It was a side of him Kane had never seen before. In that smirk, standing at the wheel, relishing in the unlikely accord, he was more of a Sam than he was a Captain. His skin was rough and tan like a browned leather, forged by salt and water and wind for decades. His wrinkles were proof of a hard-earned life and it gave his face a handsome character.

"This just means we have to work that much harder when we get back," The captain yelled over the rush of the elements. "That works for everyone?" he said, allowing for a larger smile to show through his beard. The crew all replied enthusiastically, his pledge for a tough day of setting every single trap was now a pact that they could enjoy this half day. Jenn yelled back at him, "Aye Aye, Captain!" Brad gave a tired, but very grateful thumbs up into the wind. Kirk just spoke a little louder about how great the news was. Kane agreed in silence, smiling, letting the harsh sounds of waves and winds crash around him harmlessly, for he now had a shield of relief. His day was almost over and he would have four in a row off, and so did Tilly. He sat at peace and squinted slightly as the sun shone barely through the near impenetrable wall of grey as the boat rushed through the waters. From the corner of his eye, he saw the captain looking at him from his own corner, probably checking in on the only person without a reply. Their gaze held and the captain broke it to check something on his dash, flicking a switch and grabbing his radio, holding it now to his mouth. Kane couldn't hear it. It was too loud. The captain, or Sam, was still smiling. He must have seen Kane's face and gotten his answer.

Loading up the traps for the day, and the week, was strange during mid-afternoon. There was a calm to it, no rush to leave and no rush of others. It was only them. The tide was in and that meant there was less space for their gear, but also made trips from the dock to the truck shorter, and in effect, easier. They smiled at each other as one walked this way with a pot and the other walked that way to grab another one. They only had a small haul of lobsters from the day, emptying out the traps that were set and setting no extras. They couldn't leave their profit sitting in the cages for five days and Kane figured this helped the break even. All of the lobsters were eventually gathered and loaded into one large container as they always were, waiting amongst one another before the captain took them in to be weighed and sold. Kirk was usually tasked with this job, allowing the captain to leave a little earlier, but not today.

"Get out of here and enjoy your Christmas," said the captain.

"We can finish up here," said Brad, but the captain gently shook his head, a thankful refusal.

Kirk yelled toward the captain as he picked up the first haul of the lobster containers. "You sure are in a good mood today, Cap." The captain didn't look back nor did he slow down. He quietly called back, a trailing voice carried by an excited yearning, "Very shortly, I'll be seeing my family for four long days." And he walked away.

The four of them looked back at one another. They always started before the town was awake and finished as they were going to bed. It was strange for them to be there, like they had never seen this version of Sachem before now, like they did not belong. They all felt it, even Kane. They stood afraid, as if the town would not accept them. Businesses across the street had their open signs in the windows, and customers walked in and out of them. The occasional car drove slowly by. They saw this town in the dark, and when they did in the light of the day, it was in the sleepy hours of the weekend. Their work was complete and they were happy to be done, but it didn't seem right. They weren't very good at small talk, and even Kirk was quietly smoking his cigarette. A couple appeared suddenly, and they parted to allow them through. The middle-aged man and woman seemed to be out for an afternoon stroll, friendly and with no agenda. It was the type of thing normal people did. Kane found it hard to recall. They slowed down and peeked in on the other half of the day's collection of lobsters the captain had not returned for yet.

"Are those fresh?" the man asked, both of them looking up, awaiting the answer like oblivious children. Neither Brad, Kane, Kirk, or Jenn answered him. They quickly looked at one another from the sides of their eyes, smiling, and laughter building and filling them like a tank until one of them burst, leading all of them to explode with laughter. The couple allowed a single confused chuckle, unaware of the humor in this inside joke they couldn't have been a part of. They walked away without an answer. When the captain returned for the last of the lobsters, they were all still laughing, although now dying down.

"What's so funny?" the captain asked.

"Nothing really," Jenn said, still smiling.

"Hey, Captain," Kirk began, "would you say these alive and energetic lobsters in this cage still smelling of salt water are fairly fresh?" They laughed again, even harder.

The captain looked at them like they had all escaped from an institution. "Merry Christmas," he said, rolling his eyes. They continued to laugh as he walked away, smiling at their silliness. Their laughter leveled to smiles, a quiet appreciation for the question asked by what must have just been two out of towners visiting their loved ones for their own Christmas holidays. They hadn't meant to be jerks and he didn't think it had been taken that way. Regardless, it was worth it for the crew. They would leave each other once again with a tightened bond, coming back stronger than they had been before. Strength meant things would come easier, and he hoped for that, and not that they had hit their limit and would now see only a weakening in it. Kane wondered what they all had planned for their days off. It made him aware, and care, for the first time, of how little he knew about these people. To know someone from the way they acted on the ship was far too simple. One could guess how long a lobster fisherman had been on the water by their skill level and demeanour, and that maybe that could lead him to educated assumptions about their time spent in Sachem, but that was it. Kane knew nothing of their situations, their personal struggles, or their lives on land. He had never cared about this at any other job in the other towns he called home, but here, he did. He cared because in the past, he had always had one foot planted on the next bus. Here, he felt stuck, without options and hoping for a better life, carrying a fear that this was going to be everything he would ever be. Laughing together, he connected with them and realized all that they shared. In this town, saying, "Have a great Christmas," could be a trigger, a sad reminder that they surely would not and never have had had, a great Christmas.

"I'll see you in a few days then," Kane said. The others left with the same smile, nodding in agreement and splitting off in separate ways, like fine, cracking ice.

"Should I bring anything tomorrow?" Kane texted Tilly. Walking home, he wished he had somewhere to be. It was barely two in the afternoon. He felt rejuvenated, his mind more than his body, but with the knowledge his body had no more burden to bear. The town was resuscitated and he felt the same. He wished Tilly was at the shop so that he could surprise her with a coffee, but she had taken the day off to clean and help her mom with some baking, undoubtedly doing nothing but eating bits of raw dough and chocolate. He would see her over the next four days and he felt like giving her space anyway. It would give him an opportunity to take some space of his own. Not from her, of course -- he missed her so bad he felt pulled to her now like a magnetic force -- but space from his doubts and the panic he had gotten used to suppressing. Kane was out of practice being happy and he wanted to test it out on himself first. He wanted to explore his mind, shaking loose what had molded over and rusted, stuck like the grime in the molds of the engine he was meaning to repair. He needed to think and create, do something he was truly good at. He needed to draw. He had not yet gotten Jessica or Tilly a card for Christmas, and the notion excited him so much that his walk home was now a jog.

Jessica had been easy to buy a gift for. The red Chevy desperately needed many fixes, but one Kane was sure of, and knew how to properly install, was the battery. Tomorrow, two days before Christmas, he planned to work on the car and detect any other hurdles he would need to jump over before this car could start. Driving would be an entirely new set of challenges, as the tires needed replacing, fresh gas would need to be added, and he hadn't even checked the brakes yet. He wrapped it classically, now looking like a small and colorful green cube with a red bow on top. Kane hoped that the car battery would be a funny moment under the tree, as it weighed about fifty pounds. Walking it to their place was going to be a pain, but it was necessary and worth it. He felt happy to do it. The long walk up to their home would have been impossible today, but hopefully a day's rest would give him the strength, plus the weight of a battery in his backpack. He felt a buzz in his pocket.

"No, weirdo," she texted him back. Kane smiled, deciding he would bring a bottle of wine and some cheese anyway.

Arriving at home, Kane quickly changed out of his damp and loosened work clothes, fetid from over a week of hard work. He shoved them straight into the open mouth of his washing machine. He dumped soap over them and shut the lid, turning it on without looking for other dirty clothes. It was all he wore anyway. He had to, they disgusted him. It was excess skin, rotted off of him as he slithered out from it. Standing naked in the hallway, he felt changed, newer with every second that passed and every step away from the *Caught in the Pot*. He couldn't have recognized how deep into the job he had gotten. He had even begun to enjoy it. He hadn't been able to smell himself. This was a metamorphosis, a break in a curse, or just a sudden realization that he would need to peel these layers over top of his skin again, transforming back in just five days. Kane turned on the shower, losing no time now to wash the residue of that life off of his skin, the invisible film, sticky and thick, sent spiralling down the drain. Kane felt himself becoming clean, becoming himself again. His muscles ached but the work was long ago in a distant past, the promise of tomorrow repressing and burying what was. He placed his head directly into the hard stream of warm water, drowning out every thought other than when he went back to work, he could never forget to never lose himself like that again.

Kane gathered his papers and pencils and set them on the coffee table that now saw ink blots and streaks stained on it, a living room Rorschach test. His coffee sat cooling, steam dancing in its escape. He wanted to hunker down for a few hours and take his time with this, getting up for nothing. He opened his phone for reference and ran his fingers through his still-damp hair, taking a deep breath, excited to focus and create. It had been too long. Looking at the bare walls of his apartment, and every flat surface, every table or countertop was a slatted space with nothing, no personality, utterly boring. He wanted to see art on his walls. He wanted to hang her art on them. He wanted plants to give the space life. He wanted to enjoy it with her. He knew he would not care in a week when he spent little time in this room. This was not his home to decorate. This was not his home at all. He felt happy to feel this way, a relief to know he still could. She was his home and he would be there soon. The small tattoo kit was shoved out of the way to make space and Kane could feel the contents like an electrical charge in his fingers. It wasn't the ink, the needle, or the lighter that sparked inside of his mind; it was the makeshift baggy, knotted in twisted plastic wrap that held the fourteen blue pills of Oxy that Kirk had given him for two hundred dollars. He didn't need to take any. He shouldn't even need one per day while he was working, but a couple a week helped to control the avalanche of pain instead of allowing it to become catastrophic and unpredictable. He worked a half day today. He had the next four days off. He was in a natural recovery. Oxy made him feel better, but it also helped him sleep and seemed to cool his mind. This was a prescription drug. He only had to be cautious not to abuse it. Of course, he knew it could be highly damaging and addictive if he were to do so, but Kane would never. Sometimes he wondered if, when he quit this job and had no use for it anymore, there would be a small withdrawal period. He was sure there would be. He could handle it and he was sure of that too. Kirk had told him to never use more than one a day, and he said he wouldn't because it was the truth. Kane didn't need these pills every day, and Kirk had told him when he sold him this bag that it would be the last time he could get him any. After that, it would be up to Kane to find his own. As far as Kane was concerned, these were not to feel better in the morning, nor were they to help him sleep. These were emergency pills only for pain. He would be away for a few days from this bag of pills that called out to him so vociferously. He was back to himself. He felt clean. He was still tired; his foggy mind would show only one or two hash marks right now. His legs were stiff and his arms were sore. He just wanted to be himself again. He wanted to be his best self for Tilly, for both of them. He unwrapped the bag of pills, allowing two to fall onto the table, now tempted to swallow both. Kane had never taken that high of a dose. He had never needed to. He didn't need to now. His mind wandered, staring at the capsules, imagining how incredible they would make him feel. It wouldn't just repair him. It would empower him. He would arrive, knocking and smiling, excited and appreciative to be invited over for the holidays. He shook his head and put one back, still pinching one of the round pills in his fingers, examining it, an internal wrestling of what he knew he needed, what he knew he wanted, what he didn't quite know yet, and what he was choosing to ignore. There were already graphite stains on his fingertips. He looked at the paper and how little he had accomplished before discovering the Oxy, derailing his drawings that he had been so enthusiastic about only moments ago. The black marks on his skin reminded him of the first time Tilly had drawn with him. Kane had accidentally rubbed some onto his lower lip, leaving her giggling at him.

"What?" he had said. He'd touched his face to rub off what she was apparently laughing at, only to smear more black across his cheek. She just smiled and scooted toward him, licking her thumb and gliding it gently and slowly across his lips and his cheek. She did so again, looking at him thoughtfully until the black dust was now on her fingers and not his face, but her hand stayed, holding his cheek. "Did you get it?"

"Not yet," she answered softly, leaning in and kissing his lips with a tender patience that Kane returned. The kiss stayed soft for a long time. Their eyes were closed. Their pictures had fallen carelessly to the ground at their feet. When they stopped, both of their eyes stayed closed just a little longer, but opening slowly with a second to spare to see each other's warming smiles. It had been the first time they had kissed.

Inspired by her, he let a fist full of papers scatter across the floor, crouching over a single sheet. Kane pressed the brunt charcoal tip until it broke apart, small streaks coming to life below the broken bits of black. He was curious to know what the finality would look like, even though he could see it perfectly in his mind, and as he drew, he smiled. He blew the charcoal dust from the paper, and pressed down again, the bitter taste of the Oxy pill still coating his mouth.

CHAPTER 15

Kane hadn't spent a Christmas at home with his own family since he was seventeen. When you're seventeen, Christmas was still the excitement of unwrapping presents and seeing sad, deflated stockings filled by Santa in the middle of the night. The belief turned to a laughable joke that had become a sincere way for his mom to avoid taking all of the credit for the small and thoughtful gifts she must have been stockpiling throughout the entire year. That was what he missed the most during the holidays, seeing her accumulated kindness, proof pulled one by one from an oversized red sock. Being in this house now, he felt guilty. He missed his family and now that he was, in a way, settled, his choice to not be at home was not one of necessity, but betrayal. He had enough money to go back. He had the time off to see them. He hadn't been home for several years, but here he was, sitting in Tilly's living room on the couch as she opened an old cardboard box marked "ornaments." He'd texted with his mom a few weeks prior saying he was sure he wouldn't be able to visit again this year. He didn't need to conceive a lie because she never asked; she'd sent her words of understanding over somber text, facing her own comfortability with his indifference. He would call them on Christmas morning and he would lie about where he was, and they would believe him, and they would miss him. What he would not say was that next year, he would plan it out better and make it home even if he didn't have the money or if he had to quit his job to do so. He had said it for the past three Christmas mornings and saying it once more would be insulting, a widening of the divide that he could already feel growing between them. Love was easy, and to try and to care and to make an effort should also be easy, but Kane was failing at that too.

"Get over here and help me," Tilly called over from the floor. Kane smiled and set down his coffee, clouded with cream and thinned with Irish whiskey. Jessica had asked and then insisted, surely just creating a welcoming, jolly Christmas spirit and to let him know she was a cool mom. These were the holidays and a little booze at 10 a.m. was allowed. Truthfully, Kane just wanted the coffee, but to say no might have said the opposite, a confession to her that he still didn't feel comfortable enough in her home to feel that kind of free spirited abandon, even if it was Christmas Eve. So, he smiled at her wink and her "Merry Christmas" and took a grateful sip. Tilly was already drinking her own, laying each ornament one by one on the carpet. The tree stood six feet tall, loveable and scraggly, standing in the corner, awaiting its makeover. In an effort of goodwill, the local logging companies would save a few hundred smaller trees for the townsfolk to take at no cost. Jessica noted her appreciation in the generosity and tradition, as did the town as far as Kane could tell, seeing the delighted lines of bouncing children waiting to pick a tree of their own. Kane knew the logging companies chopped down hundreds of thousands of trees just like it throughout the year, simply because they were in the way. He had never decorated a Christmas tree before and Tilly looked so lovingly keen to finish it with him. One by one, Tilly would grab an ornament and examine it, smiling. Every small globe, or silver bulb, Santa's face, or reindeer stuffed toy forever held a connection to her memory of past years. Each new item from the box, clutched in her hand and set on the floor brought a different smile and a different story. Kane heard each one, knowing that he now would be forever connected to this moment every Christmas. He felt lucky, as he always did, with her because she was always surprising him. They sat there together, her confiding in him not her secrets or her goals, but her memories, pieces of herself, explaining her nostalgia so that he could better understand her heart. It made him want to share his own and it made him worried that he never could.

Later in the day, Jessica had laid out a colossal spread of food, a festive cornucopia of cheeses, meats, veggies, and dips that was far too much for three people to eat. Kane hadn't eaten well in months and he thanked her for it. She told him she was just excited to show off. They ate cheese and crackers, large shrimp from the wharf, cased sausages that the butcher shop had brought in for the holidays. There was bread and dips and spreads and Kane ate so much he worried he would get sick. Jessica and Tilly just watched him in a delighted awe, smiling at each other every time he filled his plate full. They sipped on the wine he had brought, which Jessica said she liked.

"Oh, Chilean," said Jessica, eyeing the label. Kane shrugged and Tilly smiled. Jessica poured. Tilly's cheeks turned rosy when she drank wine. She was adorable. He wondered if his own face was red and became embarrassed, blushing and only making so anyway. They played cards for a long time. They drank more and laughed together. Jessica never brought any stockings out to be filled and he was glad for it. That would be his own thing, his own time capsule of fond recollections, taken out one by one, accompanied by his own smiles and his own stories, and she would smile back at him and be connected to it forever. Next year, he would buy her a stocking of her own and fill it, picking up things throughout the year, just like his mom had done for him. Tonight had been one of the best nights of his life. Tilly was not just a respite from his torment, she was all his favorite reasons to be happy. She was not the only thing that mattered, but all other things mattered more because of her. He would always love tattooing and drawing. He loved to cook and he missed doing it. He loved going back to bed on a Sunday after a trip for coffee and getting groceries for a late lunch. He loved to learn step by step how to accomplish a goal, like with the red Chevy out front he now wished he had looked at earlier. He loved travelling and the search for more. No, she was not all there was, but she made all things better shared. He felt like he was walking in the darkened hallways of the unknown and his past, mysterious rooms yet explored or forgotten long ago. Some he loved and some he didn't. Many of these rooms he hadn't been inside yet, and others he felt he could never leave, locked inside and looking for the key. She was the love of his life to keep him company, to show him other rooms, to carry the flame and allow him to see the spaces he wasn't able to before.

They were all lying on the couch now, watching an old black and white Christmas movie, black and grey colors lighting up the living room with the sound low, almost muted. Jessica was reading from her book, digesting and content, in silent admiration of young love before her and a Christmas that now belonged to three. Tilly was nodding off, her head resting on Kane's chest. He didn't even know yet where he was assigned to sleep. It didn't matter to him. He hoped it would be right there on the couch with her sleeping body across his own. He'd spent last Christmas inside a movie theatre with a six pack of cold beer he'd snuck in. He'd been bored and nothing else had been open. This was better. Time was moving too fast. He would be back on the boat soon. He closed his eyes, trying not to sleep, trying to feel every second, focusing so intently on the time in hopes it might just stop completely.

He woke up on the couch alone. Someone in the kitchen was moving a pot, closing a cupboard, and turning on a gas burner, clicking quickly until the flame burst. Kane could hear all of this but he didn't open his eyes for a few moments. He was still dressed, and a little embarrassed for a reason he couldn't place. Without the chance of collecting himself, he felt disarmed. Water started to boil. The sounds from the kitchen paused as footsteps now entered the living room. They must have been very close to him. Maybe Jessica was about to turn on the TV, and he would have to sheepishly pretend to wake up. Then, a pair of lips kissed his cheek. He rolled over, eyes closed in the first glare of morning, and kissed her back.

"Merry Christmas." She smiled down at him. "I'm making breakfast. Come help. She hopped joyfully into the kitchen. He was happy to wake up and join her.

It was ten in the morning. He hadn't slept that long in months. He was still full from yesterday, but she couldn't be resisted. Tilly was doing a tiny dance for herself, leaning over the stovetop, wearing loose fitted pink socks, short yellow shorts and a baby blue hoodie. She noticed him admiring her from the couch, smiled, and continued on. He was so in love with her. It was morning and he was hard and he very badly wanted to have sex with her, there in the kitchen, burning the eggs and laughing about it after. It was just another small daydream about what he hoped would soon be real.

Christmas day was here. It should have meant only happiness. He shouldn't be thinking this way, he knew that. The harder he tried to stay in the moment, the closer the dread seemed. He was exactly where he wanted to be, and sitting in the living room with the two of them, he listened and laughed, but that nagging feeling buzzed around his head like gnats only he could see, unable to swat them away. He made truces with his own mind to worry about these things later, in a sleepless night or in the privacy of a shower, when he didn't need to split himself in two to do so. Worry made room for nerves when Jessica declared it was time for gifts. Tilly smiled and, with the grace of a startled cat, she pounced out of the room, presumably to grab her presents. He was just as nervous for his reactions receiving his gifts as he was to present his own to both of them, in front of each other. Kane's were already underneath the tree, now fully decorated with strings of lights crisscrossing loose across its needles. He sat waiting in his chair while Jessica stood up, both of them smiling at the unknown weirdness of whatever Tilly was up to.

"Would you like some tea or anything, Kane?"

"No, I'm okay, thanks."

As she walked by him, she put her hand on his shoulder and gently squeezed it with a familiar, motherly affection. She was probably unaware that she had even touched him, but it meant everything. The casual ease of it said more than words could. She accepted him. She approved of him. She saw the way he looked at Tilly. She saw, not how Tilly had changed around him, but how she had stayed exactly herself. Her touch was a promise that family was here too, even if his own was across the country, separated by an unanswered phone call made only an hour earlier.

She called to him from the kitchen. "A glass of wine, maybe?"

Kane answered with a laugh. "You're a maniac."

"What do you mean?!"

Tilly stomped into the room, knowing the drama was in her favour, and her entrance demanded effect. She was carrying two medium sized boxes, crudely covered in a mess of crumpled black and white newspaper and strewn together tape that was already flapping unstuck in several places. Kane smiled, unsurprised, as she set them down, sticking her tongue out at him the way she always did, and splashed onto the couch to stretch, calling out for her mom impatiently despite having just spent ten minutes in her room.

Jessica walked back into the room, bringing her hot mug of tea that she blew softly on the surface to cool. It was as if that warmth flowed directly from her and coated the room. This was Christmas and Kane felt at home. Tilly dropped to her knees and grabbed the first present, shaking it vigorously beside her ear.

"This one is for me!"

"Cut that out, Till!"

She set it on the couch. It must have been from Jessica, because it wasn't his. There were only a handful of gifts sitting with the fallen pine needles on the floor, surely pathetic looking compared to clichéd Christmas cards or large, rich families with gifts for all, including the dog and ones marked "From Santa." Kane loved it this way. There was no question who something was from, or the intent behind it. There was no simple "thanks," only to set it aside and reach with long arms and wide eyes for the next wrapped and forgettable thing. This was an exchange of love and care, a lived in and slow, unfolding intimacy. Like the gift inside, the giver and their intent meant more than the brightly coloured paper.

Tilly handed Kane his first gift, neatly wrapped and from Jessica. Tilly's present from Jessica looked the same. They both opened them as neatly as they were wrapped. Jessica opened her own from Tilly. Kane wondered if they were the same gift, and seeing Tilly pull out a white card was evidence that they were, seeing his own white slip of paper lying at the bottom of the box. The box was a ruse, or a reason to elegantly wrap this innocuous unknown, folded once. Kane grabbed it and read the words as Tilly read the same, only out loud. "One free bus ticket slash one free hotel room slash one free dinner."

"It's there for whenever you want it," Jessica told them both. "For a trip to the big city for a couple nights."

Tilly hugged her mom. "Mom, thank you."

"That is so nice," said Kane. "Thank you." He felt it imperative that she knew the depth of his thanks. He was nervous now to give her the stupid car battery.

"You two have only ever seen each other in Sachem. You deserve a mini vacation."

Kane and Tilly shared a look of excited gratitude. It was an honorary declaration of her trust in Kane and them both to send them off to another city. Their look said "I can't believe she would do that for us." It said, "I can't wait to plan and talk about all the things we will want to do". It said, "I can't wait to have constant sex with you over and over again with nothing else in the way but dinner plans." It said, "I love you and I can't wait to go." Jessica was tossing the crumpled mess of black and white paper to the side, looking at her gift from Tilly, smiling. Kane didn't know what Tilly had gotten for her mom. She wouldn't tell him. Tilly was only half smiling now, clearly self-conscious of her gift after just receiving such a thoughtful one. Jessica smiled and turned to laugh, and so did Tilly in return. They laughed and Jessica handed Kane the plastic-encased package so that he could also see. Tilly had gotten her mom an easy install bidet for her toilet. Kane added to their laughter. A funny gift that was actually fairly practical and worth using. A perfectly Tilly gift.

"Thank you, dear."

Tilly opened hers from Kane now, and the laughter and smiles softened, awaiting the reveal and reactions. To give someone you love a gift felt so personal and to have it shared with a third felt like showing it in front of the world. Tilly's mouth opened in loving surprise and smiled, pulling out a hardcover book from the opened, petalled walls of the unwrappings in her lap. It was a copy of Herman Melville's *Moby Dick*. She had mentioned it on one of their first drawing dates. Kane had asked her when she first got into drawing. She said it was because of *Moby Dick*. Not the book itself -- she had tried to read it three times and completely hated it -- but for the images on the cover. Tilly would have happily ripped the pages from it entirely without a care if they didn't serve as a binder for the spine. It had been in her home since she was little, thick with useless pages to her, but painted with vivid imaginations that told her all of the story she needed to know. There were light blues of water, crashing and turning white. There was a large wooden boat off in the distance with a small, solo figure standing at the helm, as if searching the ocean. In the foreground was an impossibly large whale expanding past the limits of the cover, one large eye of the mammal showing clear through the blue. The one eye was simple and circular, but told the entire thousand-page story of this powerful creature, hunted in bloodthirsty revenge by foolish men. She would try and copy the image with crayons, and then pencil crayons, anything she could find. In her childhood, this visual poem was her training, but was now just a mental relic, a piece of nostalgia she had looked for and never found. Her copy had gotten lost or destroyed or tragically misplaced. It had been a long time ago and she could barely remember the cover she would stare at for hours at a time. This particular printing of *Moby Dick* had turned out to be a rare one, and never appeared in bookstores or online searches. Digging through the past had quickly become sad for Tilly, and she would stop as soon as she started, occupying her mind with other things, present things. It was now a more painful reminder that even the most meaningful memories would soon fade. For her to see it again would be a recapturing of that conceit. Truthfully, Kane wasn't at all confident he had the right version, but the way she had described it to him, with the detail and truth in her words, him learning more about the way she felt about art in those early days, he was cautiously hoping. It was also absurdly hard to find and even harder to acquire, which he'd took for a good sign. If he had chosen correctly, then she was absolutely right. The cover really was beautiful. Her smile at the sight of it was the exhaled relief that he wished for.

"K-Kane…" she stuttered. "Mom, look at this." She held the book out so that Jessica could see. Kane sat, demurred, but pleased. He had started this journey over a month ago and had given her this book in daydreams countless times.

"He found it," said Jessica.

"Open it up," Kane added, guiding her and deflecting the attention back to her.

She despised the words inside. They served little purpose to her. He hadn't ripped the pages from their stitching, but he had made use of the contents for her. It was a project that gave him life during the monotony of work. He could only complete small pieces at a time, perfect for his lethargic, depressed mind, desperate for accomplishment of any kind, for his impulse to make her happy. Tilly opened it and quickly covered her welling eyes with her hand and her quivering lip with a bite on her smile. Kane had carefully used an X-Acto knife to thinly slice slits into the pages, eventually making deep squares. He'd painted the surface of these carved sections with carpenters' glue, hardening them and setting them into place. This hardcover book, with the cover that reminded her of her childhood falling in love of art, was now an artist's palette to fill with paints and pigments. They would harden and crust inside, but would then chip away and break off, allowing her to reuse it and cherish it for as long as it meant something to her, which Kane hoped would be forever. Tilly set the book at her feet and sat up, looking at Kane and forgetting about the book with all her care now on her love for him. She hugged him and kissed his cheek as Jessica sat witness. They rarely touched one another like that in front of others, but any awkwardness they feared from it would be far greater if they left this pure moment to hang on a simple thank you. Tilly sat back down, picking the book up like she was afraid to let it go a second time, feeling the cover and allowing her fingers to trace the lost lines of her memories.

Jessica lightly flicked her fingers forward to Tilly, waiting for her gift, and snapping Tilly back into helper mode. Tilly lugged the car battery over, and dropped it with a surprisingly loud thud that seemed to make every small item in the house jump a millimetre in the air. Confused, she opened the box to find a much more boring, small black box with red and white screws on the top, the positive and negative rods on the battery.

"Is this a car battery?" she asked excitedly. Whether it was genuine or out of politeness he could not tell.

"Yeah," he answered. "It's the main thing it needed, really. Once that's in. I'll be able to tell what is really working and what isn't."

She looked thrilled. "That's so exciting!" Kane believed her. "I can't believe you are really doing it. I honestly never thought that car would ever drive again."

"I'm sure I am in over my head and I just don't know it yet."

"I appreciate it all the same. Thank you, dear."

"You're welcome." He was glad it was over, reassured that his gift had been a good one.

"There's a card too, I almost forgot." On one side of the unwrapped gift was a manila envelope, still taped to the side. He ripped it off and handed it to Jessica, while taking a gift from Tilly, the last present under the tree, her gift for him. He smiled at her and she looked intently back, taking in every movement he made before he opened it. He saw this and started to peel away the newspaper, torturously slow, smirking at her discomfort.

"Oh, just do it already," she said. "Put me out of my misery." Chuckling at her, he obeyed. Inside was all of the necessary contents for a tattoo kit. The lighter, the needle, the ink, the string, all of it.

"I just figured your set could use an upgrade," she said. "But if it's not right, don't feel you need to use it, any of it." She was right, Kane did need a serious upgrade. Looking down at this organized set, he felt overwhelmed by her attention. She had never taken a physical inventory, made a checklist on what he used for tattooing. She never asked him. She just watched him work, and obviously listened with genuine sincerity. He felt odd, seeing how polished and new all of this was. Instead of his plastic Bic with bits of plastic label chipping away, was a stainless steel Zippo that smelled like kerosene. He would miss the old way; they felt like childhood toys to him, and to grow out of them felt like a violation. But he smiled, and thanked her, looking at each object before hugging her in return, squeezing her hard and for a long time. Moving on to better things despite craving the safety of the past, of the status quo, was one of many reasons he was in love with her. She showed him the way, but never pushed him, and in that hug, he hoped he could do the same for her. His internal fight to leave and to move deflated like a balloon that was about to burst, slowly and carefully, until it bounced against the air, up and down, nice and easy, up and down, up and down.

The hug stopped and when Kane returned to his chair, he noticed Jessica was staring at the picture he had made from shards of charcoal two days before. She was smiling, but had two wet trails streaked straight down both cheeks. The tears in her eyes, she had stopped and hid when the embracing couple weren't looking, but her cheeks gave the moment away. There had been a photo Kane had found stashed in a drawer in their basement, discovered accidentally when he was digging aimlessly around the house for a few select tools for the car. He had come across a picture of Jessica when she was much younger, and what must have been a young Tilly, about three years old. The photo was film, decayed over time, blurring badly these figures from a dream, rather than a different time. Their faces no longer had any recognizable features, just their outlines and the suggested details in their clothing. They were standing in the front yard that didn't look much different than it did now, save for the red car in the background now in a different spot, looking alive and spirited even through the dimmed haze that twenty years of exposure light had burned onto the image. The high-reaching bushes that now guarded the house and covered their windows were only small here, showing the walls of the house now hidden. Like every displaced and forgotten picture was, this was a still of youth. Even through the blurring of time, the two in frame could be no one else. Jessica was looking and laughing at her toddler daughter, Tilly, who had her arms up and a white dress on. She was probably humming away as she always was, and leading the way out in front like she always did. Tilly, who now sat across from him, some eighteen years later, looking at him with the loving gratitude she had for someone with the skill to recreate an image like that, and the heart to know to do it and make her mother happy. But Kane hadn't really recreated this old picture with his charcoal pencil; that wasn't how he worked. To see and to capture the nature of a person, the love between family, and of the feeling of lost time being found, was to hand the moment back to them and say, "we can see it too."

The smell of turkey filled the house, a reminder of other chapters of life and family with the promise of new ones. Jessica's wistful smile was not a prideful one, excited for the feast she had prepared, crouching and looking into the oven window. Kane stood at the kitchen island with his back to both of them, mashing hot potatoes. Tilly was pouring herself another glass of red with one hand and picking at the steaming dressing with her other. Jessica noticed this, but allowed it, drinking wine of her own. They were all happy, and had given each other the right to be.

The bitter air was intensified by a wind that cut so strong. Kane would take his gloves off and check his cheeks for blood. He felt wet, but when checking his fingers, he saw no red. It was so loud, the tall waves carrying white caps could barely be heard smashing into all sides of the boat. They all worked without words. They knew what to do anyway. Out here, the wind and salt water dried your skin so much that even tears made little difference when any moisture was gone, leaving eyes dry like sandpaper, stinging with each blink. It wasn't always this cold. It wasn't always this windy. It wasn't always this wet. Today, it was all three. The ocean was reminding them what it was capable of, punishing them for forgetting. Kane fell forward, carried by the weight of the lobster trap he dropped, muscles screaming and fingers failing in the penetrating pain or numbness. He couldn't tell anymore. Nobody noticed; they were swimming in their own struggles. This was the ocean Kane remembered and the life he feared every moment he wasn't in it. Out here on the water, aboard the *Caught in the Pot,* it never reminded him; it had tricked him. It had tricked him in his days off, thinking he could remember it, go back to it in his mind, remember all of the reasons this was worth it. Day one back of who-could-know-how-many-more just like it. He had blinked once on the water to see Tilly kissing him, and under the tree, and at dinner, and at his house, only to blink again and be right back here. It was as if none of it had ever happened. He didn't hope to remember when he got home and he didn't wonder if he could ever hope for those memories again. He just slammed another lobster pot down, slipping in an accepted, tired pain, and resting only a moment before it was time for the next one. He was here now, singing in the shipwreck. Welcome back.

CHAPTER 16

"What do you mean there's no way you can get any more?"

"I have no way to get more Oxy for you. I told you that when I gave you the last batch."

"I only need one a day, you know that."

"Man, I have nothing. I wish I did, I really do. One a day, one an hour, it doesn't matter. I can't get it for you."

"Fuck. Maybe I ask Jenn or Brad?"

"No fuckin' way man. No point. Bad idea. Trust me on that one, trust me on that one."

"Why would that be a problem?"

"These things only exist if we talk about them, man. Best not to bring that onto our boat."

"They might have extra."

"They won't have anything for you."

"You said everyone does it."

"Not them. Especially not Jenn."

"Why especially not her?"

"She's just not into the stuff man, never would be. It's a pride thing, I guess."

"A pride thing?"

"There's prideful people that still need it. There's tough people that still need it. There's smart people that still fuck around with it. But she's all three, and a lot of it. Doesn't take it, never would."

"Still, you said everybody does it."

"Well, she's not everybody, alright?"

"Well, which one do I not have, Kirk?"

"One of what?"

"Am I missing pride, toughness, or brains?"

"Look man, I'm just talking out of my ass here. You are all three of those things, okay? I think I am all three of those things, maybe not so much the brains, but hey, still. She has seen the dangers of it up close. She was warned and it stuck with her. You haven't been, that's all. But you are all three, so you won't abuse it. I have seen the dangers, but I know not to abuse it. Sometimes I do, but mostly I don't."

"I get it."

"You don't look so good, man. Taking less might not be such a bad idea anyway. You know the job now. It'll be easier. You did what you have to do, now do what you have to do again."

"One pill a day, that's it. I already said that."

"Look, I can probably find you some, but they are going to be so expensive. It will eat up a quarter of your paycheque anyway."

"That's fine."

"That's fine?"

"Yes, Kirk. I won't need this stuff forever, but right now, I do need it. Can you get it for me?"

"I'm sure I can, yeah, if you're willing to pay for it. I'm telling you though, if you are doing one a day I can get you probably a month's worth but it's going to be like over a thousand dollars."

"Like I said --"

"Yeah. That it's fine."

"I'll stretch them out further than I did before, even out the cost."

"And if I *can* make it work this time, it doesn't mean I can make it work next time, so you need to figure out a plan for yourself. Try and get a prescription. Anything. I'm serious."

"Well, how do you make it work?"

"I don't really fuck with Oxy."

"What? Of course you do."

"That last batch was a treat. It's thirty or forty dollars per pill, dude. You could stretch it and get Fentanyl, but then it's sixty, sometimes eighty bucks, just to hit the same place. I can't afford that shit. Almost a hundred a day, five hundred a week just for pills? `Fuck that."

"Again, you said everyone out here does it."

"No Kane, I said everyone has their cure."

"What is your cure then?"

"Same as most everybody else's."

"Which is what?"

"Heroin, man."

CHAPTER 17

The *Caught in the Pot* chugged further along into the gloom of the shift and also in each other's gloom that was impossible to ignore. Like easier days before it when the crew seemed high spirited, Kane viewed them now only as a melancholic, hurting group, bleeding heavy shadows wherever they moved. Nothing had changed, other than what Kane knew. The way Kane saw things now had changed the world around him so forcefully, he wondered if the others could feel his understanding of it. He couldn't believe that heroin coursed through them all, like ice in the captain's veins, or nerves that rattled his own. It wasn't only these new shadows Kane took note of, but the ones under their eyes, or, deeper even, in each of their glances. It was the shadows they cast even in these shadowless days of grey. The shadows followed them not in imitation, but as a sticky haunting of a life destroyed. It was their demonic embodiment made physical, a possession, a life in the somber walk of its own destruction. He would pity them if he didn't fear them so much. It wasn't the dangers of being high at work that put Kane on edge; in fact, that hadn't even crossed his mind. They had found their cure and still showed up every morning, fit and fine, while he ached in waiting for the far-too-expensive Oxy pills from Kirk. It was the normalcy of it all that Kane feared most.

Without Oxy to shield him from the true agonies of the last few months, Kane once again felt the inescapable pains of working on the boat. He felt it in every wire cage that shredded his palms in a tight lock. Hour after hour of fighting the rocking of the boat, purple and pink hip bruises pressed cruelly deeper into his sides as he leaned over the boat. As one knee tore, the other would have to take the workload, stressing his upper thigh, until there was no haven left but to grit your teeth. This pain did not go unnoticed to Kane while on Oxy, but it freed him from the burden of caring. There was a relief in knowing that he was aware enough to know at least it was there, but to feel it once again was excruciating. It slowed time. His vision blurred even more than usual. The harsh, cold winds beating against his temples gave him throbbing headaches so pounding, his jaw ached. He couldn't tell if frostbite was now finally able to set in, or if the bitterness was only exaggerated by the tingling sensation in quick and small waves on his skin, small withdrawal symptoms from a pill he would soon get back at a high price. The pills were already calling him back, and any resistance to them was a feeble attempt against his need to take more.

Kane moved quickly, snatching the cash from the counter that had been waiting eagerly in his mind for days. His fearful anticipation without his fix was now excitement, alleviated and relieving like a river freed, rushing past the dam holding back its rushing waters. He headed out the door. It was Saturday and if it wasn't for the bait of drugs clawing deeper into his mind, almost worse than the pain he was trying to conquer, he wouldn't be able to sit up, let alone travel to meet Kirk. Tilly was at work now. It had been over a week since he had seen her last. He couldn't muster the energy to see her, but when the text had come through from Kirk, there was never a doubt. Kane walked briskly, wincing, sickened with himself over that thought. He wanted to miss Tilly and love her the way she properly deserved, and he couldn't do that until he had his medicine. He would text her shortly after the pills that tasted like chemicals made his tongue go numb before dissolving down his throat. He would take it for her now, and he would take it for her for the tomorrows. She was, and always will be, his cure. He kept telling himself that as his walk turned into a jog, and the cold sweat matted on his forehead turned to one of hot fatigue, and when his clammy palms took the wrapped bag of pills that cost roughly as much as the complete repair of that red Chevy he hadn't touched in months.

Kane took two. Euphoria hit. Pain stopped. This was what it did. Kane took two. It had been a while and two wouldn't hurt anything. He could feel the drug soak through him until it oozed from him, engulfing him. When Kane cleaned his ink needle, he would dip it into a glass filled with water, watching the few drops slowly expand, taking over the water completely and blackening it. He felt like that glass of water. He loved it. He could still feel the stiffness and aches in his joints that prevented him from moving as fluidly as he would like, but it was no longer pain, pain so far from his body and mind, it was as if he'd never felt anything but this bliss. The uncertainty of his future, from missing Tilly, from needing this drug to attain the things he was already so worried about were all also still present in his mind, but the pain they carried had been lifted. Oxy didn't need to be snorted like Kirk had done in this very same place on the couch. That was for junkies. Kane loved the slow release of it, the way Oxy was intended to be taken, the way scientists and the government had worked together to design and manufacture it, the way the ink would keep the water jet black and the Oxy would keep him like this. The first fifteen minutes was always the best. It wasn't at its strongest, but Kane would always forget just how good it felt, and it had been a while. Six days, he thought to himself. Six excruciatingly long days and it felt this good. He would really miss this feeling when the time came for him to stop using it. But maybe he wouldn't, because by then he wouldn't need it. By then, he would have the life he wanted. All he needed was Tilly. She was the real cure. Kane sat in silence on the couch, relishing in the expansion of his euphoria before picking up his phone to text Tilly. He missed her so much he could almost cry if he didn't feel so damn good.

Tilly would be there tomorrow. Kane, now unburdened by the impatience for his pills and the physical pain they mended, could now feel an excited impatience to see her. He smiled into the mirror of his under lit, lifeless bathroom mirror. There was no mat on the floor, no pictures hanging above the toilet, no hand towels folded over the bar, and no candles, lotions, or colorful containers of hair gel sitting by the sink. It was like he had never moved in, and in a way, he hadn't. The only artwork was the hundreds of black tattoos covering his naked body. He still had not finished her lighthouse tattoo. He hoped he would tomorrow. She wanted to try a painting project she had been thinking about for a while, but was keeping it a surprise. She loved to do that. The reflection that looked back at him was a broken one, a lie and a truth between himself. Strange, to reflect on a reflection. To look long enough to see your own face as an outsider would, as everyone else did, was to begin to see new things. Kane didn't have to look long enough to feel alarmed at what he saw staring back. His hair was matted and unkempt, his face now sunken into deep purple bags under his eyes and red, spotted cheeks where the wind and cold and salt had gnashed hungrily at his skin. He looked tired and he looked sad. He forced a smile into the mirror, thinking it was just a bad moment, but his smile felt unnatural because it was, and the way it looked upset him. A fake smile was snakelike, a lurking trick disguised by friendliness, or was it profoundly sad, an unconvincing mask to preserve yourself in the world you felt was unkind? To see it on his own face forced him to look away, unable to look himself in the mirror. He thought that was just a clichéd saying. It didn't take long for the feeling of Tilly being there tomorrow and the feeling of the two Oxy pills to rearrange his thoughts to happy ones. Tilly hadn't been sure if he would be available to her tonight and had promised her mom she would be over for dinner. She had asked him to go, but he told her tomorrow would be fine. She had sighed on the phone and he wished he had gone, but now looking at his eyes, pulling down the skin underneath to reveal the whites and his dilated pupils that blacked out any colour, just like the ink in the water and the Oxy in his brain, he knew it was best to wait to see her.

Kane twisted the shower handle, a high, piercing squeak of the rusted metal on metal with every turn. He touched only the left handle, his hand testing the water. It was scorching hot and he barely felt it. Steam was already filling the room and fogging the mirror, hiding himself from himself like a scared child in a room alone, hiding under the covers. The air was thick and humid now. He took a deep breath before stepping into the scorching stream. He felt layered with a putrid stink, stagnant skin that was decaying his flesh. He showered as often as he washed his clothes, about once a week now. Tilly had never truly seen that side of him, even though this cleaned version was the disguise now. He wanted the water to burn, hot enough to feel clean. He would acid wash himself if he could, whatever it took. He knew normal water and soap would work all the same. It didn't hurt. It barely even registered. The Oxy numbed every inch of him, even in this. He was always unbearably cold at all hours of the day. He spent his nights waiting for the warmth to reach his center. His colorful pills were a guard against the cold then, and a guard against the heat now. Steam filled the room entirely now, thick and growing like the building fog he watched for on the sea. "Three marks, sir." "Two marks today, Captain." His skin was red from the water, but his head did not move, his face rested in it, the sound rushing over his ears and drowning everything else away, an orchestra of drums, a feeling of numb indifference. Pain didn't exist here. Problems didn't exist: Tilly didn't exist, neither did the red Chevy he needed to fix, all of it a mirage of a future that was floating in the distance like a heat-haze, teasing in front of him always; *he* didn't even exist here and he liked it. He kept his head steady and his body unmoving. He waited to feel it.

Kane took three of his fingers, wide like a claw, and placed them on the fogged out mirror. He scraped three lines down the middle, three distinct lines through the vaporous air, like the hash marks on the tree telling him it was safe to venture out. He saw his eyes in the top line and held his gaze with himself, wondering if he could trust that notion. He wiped them all away with one big and blurred streak of his towel, and then left the bathroom.

Kane met Tilly at the Sachem Sunday Farmers' Market in the middle of town, just off the water, on a street shut down for vendors of seafood and fresh vegetables and craft-made candles and specialty meats and artisanal honeys. It was a slice of summer life in the dreary marathon of winter. She had always wanted to go with him and he was happy to have the day off to go with her. They were to explore and grab items to cook for dinner. He was now on a full day's rest, his body felt refreshed, and his mind was skimming along happy and easily on just half a pill, enough to keep it that way and not so much that Tilly would take notice. Together they explored every vendor, talked to each person about their unique product, Tilly asking the questions and skipping ahead in front to the next one. They didn't really have a plan for what they wanted to make. Tilly had told him, "if we buy the most interesting things along the way, we will only be able to make something great," and he had smiled. Who could ever argue against something like that?

On the way home, Kane carrying both bags, one in each arm, Tilly reached in and grabbed the raspberries that had come loose in a small cardboard tray. She ate a few, turning her lips wet and red. It made Kane want to carelessly drop the bags, spilling their contents all over the street, and grab her and kiss her.

"We have to go to my place for this?" he asked her. "No picnic?"

"I think it might work better inside," she replied. "Plus, we have to actually cook this food, dork."

"You're right," he smiled.

"And it's freezing outside." Kane couldn't really tell.

She tossed a berry into the air above her face, only to have it miss and hit her cheek, bouncing clumsily off. They both laughed at her silly inability. She smirked devilishly and softly tossed one underhand at Kane's face, where he caught it with a cool ease, and even though it was luck, he played it off as such, chewing the raspberry with a smile and a wink. Tilly looked on impressed, but now determined to knock him down a level, to match her goofiness with his. So she tossed another, this one higher and harder to catch. Caught again.

"I don't miss," he said. She tossed another, harder again, and again, he caught another in his mouth, still chewing on the first couple, laughing now. He had no defense with his arms tired and carrying the bags. She threw two in the air now, both smacking him in the face, with his eyes closed and his mouth gaping open, and that was it. His cool guy persona was now the bumbling fool. He laughed at her and she laughed at him as she walked up to him, kissed him softly, then placing one raspberry nicely in his mouth and a second in her own, and kissed him hard and long in the middle of the quiet street on the way home, away from the market, grocery bags at either side of them with the sweet taste of raspberries on both their lips.

"I want us to draw each other," she told him. She took her Christmas gift from Kane out of her bag. She opened it up, showing it was now filled with different colors of acrylic paints. "I haven't used this yet. I haven't seen you in so long. I think it'll be fun."

"Okay, weirdo. Good idea."

She hugged him, placing her head on his chest, and he rested his chin on her head, squeezing her tightly back, engulfing her as much as he could. She gave his cheek a kiss and looked longingly at him.

"You're looking tired, my dear," she said with care and not malice.

"Just a long week," he said, matching her care in his own tone and smile. They touched lips, building a kiss harder and more intense every second before she smiled and broke it.

"Help me in the kitchen with whatever we are going to create and then we can draw and eat," she told him.

He agreed with one more kiss.

They laid on the carpet of his living room, both backs against the walls across from each other, legs splayed out before them, occasionally eating from their bowls of cooked and fresh vegetables in a sort of mustard, curry, honey medley. Tilly had made it and Kane had helped. He found it delicious and he wasn't sure if it was expected or a surprise, much like all moments with her were. Funny or sincere, goofy or genuine, she was always an expected surprise, and looking at her, waiting to draw her, he knew any image he drew would fall short of the nature of who she was. Being an artist, he had always known that about her beauty, but to know her was to know better of the impossibility of the task. Like looking at your own reflection, to intensely observe the face of a loved one was to try and understand what words, or even thoughts, could not. He always felt this way, but now he must translate it. It was both why he found her so beautiful and the reason he loved to draw. They had sat and settled, gotten themselves comfortable, shifted their paints and brushes and pencils and paper, and now just looked at each other, a pause of intimacy like young lovers about to take the others' virginity. To ask the other if they were ready, a question of consent, would have felt appropriate. Instead Tilly just smiled to break the tension, not because it was uncomfortable, but because it was the only way to start.

"Make me look pretty now," she said. "No pressure."

Kane just stuck his tongue out at her and began to do his best at capturing the love of his life in streaks and smudges of black graphite.

Staring at her, he didn't think about the drugs he was on. He didn't think about wanting to take more. He didn't think about the brutality of the work he dreaded. He only thought of her, and what she was thinking about him.

TILLY

She wanted to draw him the way that she saw him and the way that she loved him. But this person she loved sitting across from her did not look like that person. She was okay with that. Work on the fishing boats was clearly destroying him; she could already tell that by the sound of his voice on the phone, a flat lined copy of his charming self. When he hugged her, she felt his love. She felt it in the way they kissed, had sex, walked around and joked with each other. All of this happened less and less of course, but they were still them. It was obvious to her that he was miserable when he wasn't around her, and that wasn't fair. She decided when they finished their drawings, they wouldn't show each other, not for a while anyway. It might be nice to see the states that they were in, and, even more interesting, how they saw each other during this time. And after they were finished, she would tell Kane everything. Tilly was afraid he might get too excited, or terrified, or develop delusions about what that might mean for the two of them. She loved Kane with all that she was and she wanted to be with him forever, but she still didn't know what she wanted to do, or where, or when. Kane just wanted to be with her. He would support her decision, and even offer insights and have thoughtful, unselfish advice for her. He loved her and she knew that. It all just felt like too much pressure. But hearing him the past few weeks, and seeing him like this on the floor, she had to tell him.

His face was gaunt. The reactions in his emotions were slowed, his eyes trailing behind the rest of his expressions. His eyelids weighed heavy, and his frequent smiles that had once erupted in a second, lighting up and exposing her own, were now a forced rarity. He had dark and short stubble, and his hair was slightly longer than it usually was. He was still so handsome, but not his type of handsome. An unhealthy clone that sat slumped, a frail confidence she was happy to conjure from him, but worried about the times she was not around. She knew about the drug problem in Sachem, especially on the boats. She knew that Kane knew. If they hadn't talked about it before he'd started, which they had, he would surely have discovered it on his own.

She knew Kane would never fall into that. She knew that he listened to her and wouldn't keep that from her or ever succumb to doing that to himself. She knew other people that had fallen into the trap. She knew that most users lied to themselves first and everyone else second, but there were always lies. Most of her knew it was the result of exhaustion, but the small part of her that suspected, and deeply wanted to reject the idea it could be anything but that, was the scariest. To be in love was to expect the truth and always tell it, so again, she needed to tell him everything. Her mother was indeed planning on moving away from Sachem, a possibility that had become more certain over the past weeks and even months. It was everything he wanted and what he was working toward, even if he never said it. Of course he didn't; it wouldn't be fair to. But the truth was, it is what she wanted too, and she knew he knew that. Tilly just had no idea what to do with that freedom. Tilly had drawn the outline of Kane, and the shading on the wall behind him. His posture was portrayed in outline only, this boy she loved so much doing the same across from her. His drawing would surely be a charred black, focused rendering of exactly as he saw her, and he saw her so magnificently. She loved being seen that way. She loved seeing it in his art. The little detail in his work only freed the one looking at it from focusing on too many things. He trapped feelings in his art. He looked up and smiled at her, an authentic, unlaboured smile, a peek at the man she truly loved. She hoped he would do that enough times that she could capture that version of himself, her version, the version she didn't feel the need to rescue. Truth in love was more complicated than simply telling it. She was learning that she was swimming in quicksand; only small movements would save her; if she did too much, she would sink faster, but to do nothing meant sinking completely. She would kiss him and tell him to save his drawings as a capsule of each other. And then they would talk about the trip from her mother they had not gone on yet because life was too busy and too stressful right now, but it wouldn't always be. She would tell him about her mom's plans and, for the first time, talk about their plans together. He would accept her decision to take it slow, not for them, but for her. And she could discuss her wariness of his job. That also wasn't entirely fair, and she knew that. She replayed these conversations in her mind as she gave detail to Kane's likeness. She still had no idea if she would ever need to tell him, or if it was too early, or too much all at once, that she was now two weeks late for her period.

JUNK

His tattoo kit waited innocuously on the coffee table, the same bag that had once held everything he needed to make a tattoo and the same coffee table with the same stains of ink, all reminders of what he once did and once loved. Fuck Kirk for not being able to get him more Oxy. There were no new black marks on the table and the contents of the bag were now replaced. The living room smelled artificial, the disinfectant spray fumigating and filling the air. Funny, to so carefully prepare and sanitize the table surface in order to accomplish something so dirty and so harmful. A little safety was better than none. Small steps that kept you from rock bottom, delusions surely. They were the same delusions that there was high quality, healthy versions of this unpurified muck, this perilous prescription of the past. The word was like any other pharmaceutical nickname like it, only this one was now better to be feared, one that had been contorted and manipulated by governments and dealers and lawmakers and addicts so that the inviting, slightly bitter powder was now brown and thick like old molasses, hardened by time. If this was the devil itself or presented by him, it didn't matter anymore. It was here.

He took the new contents from the bag just as he used to with the tattoo tools it once held, and, with the same strategic foresight, lined them in order of when he would need to use them. He sat there waiting, helpless, ashamed of how excited he was for it. That was a feeling many would never know. There was an anticipation in life people felt when exciting occasions were on the horizon of time. Maybe to see a friend they hadn't spoken to in a while, or the date of their departing airplane closing in, or the morning of the date of a girl they really liked but hadn't had sex with yet. It was strange to feel that delighted buzz, but to derive nothing but shame from it, because what was coming was nothing but shameful. He was helpless to it. Fuck that pharmacist who said he had no reason to prescribe any more than two a week of the weak shit. The kettle on the stove started screaming its whistle as it boiled, and he rose to bring a small cup of water back so that he could begin. He did so by adding the smallest amount of heated water to a large spoon, mixing it with a light shake of the brown powder and stirred it slowly to blackened sludge. The next item in line he picked up, his lighter, the same one he used to use to disinfect, he now used to heat and stir further. The silver spoon held this murky liquid like a small metal cauldron, the liquid bubbling and changing. The lighter underneath moved in small circles, slowly rotating the black liquid itself. He could no longer see the bottom of the spoon. Nothing escaped the depths of the heroin; it emanated no light, reflected nothing, and swallowed everything inside of it, like the depths of the ocean, the reason he was sitting here on his couch heating up a spoon with a micro amount of heroin. Taking a very small cotton ball from the table, he placed it onto the spoon and it immediately turned brown. He watched the white disappear, thinking of his red blood turning the same shade of brown as soon as it also made contact with the same contents. This was always the step for him that evenly balanced the two harmonious two sides of hating himself and an intense joy. He used to stick a sharp, clean, simple but effective sewing needle into black ink to create imagery and art. Fuck the captain and the boat and the lobsters and the crew for not warning him against just how awful it got. He grabbed the hypodermic needle that he had bought from the local pharmacy. They were well stocked. The needle had no shine to it, no interpretation of purpose. It was coloured and numbered and used for one thing and he did just that. He pressed the tip of the needle into the crudely soaked fibres of cotton and he raised the back, allowing all of the thickened, vile brown heroin to draw slowly into the needle. The spoon was now empty and the needle full. It was filled with black tar. It was filled with despair. It was filled with heroin. It was filled with the reason the girl he loved had left. It was the reason why he was now so close with Kirk. It was the reason he could function at work. It was filled with heaven. With a few flicks, the air bubbles were gone. In his first month using, now three months ago, he would tie his arm off using a tourniquet that he had also bought from the pharmacy. They were very well stocked. Now, he could find the vein on his own. He could find the scars of previous use. The needles he used to inject his skin with ink would be crafted with precise pokes, artful and imaginative, careful but instinctual. He would do so over and over again until what was in his mind had begun to form on himself. Images would materialize as if out of his control and the deeper he fell into it, the easier it became. Now, he simply injected the long needle into his arm, pushed the heroin into his vein, leaking both gloom and elation into his veins. Entering his blood now, a magnet slowly pulling the flesh from his bones, the life from his soul; the drug quickly reaches his heart, pumping repeatedly, cycling through himself until a new person remains. He dropped the needle on the floor as he always did. He would get it later. The first rush was the best and it was to be enjoyed. If he had to do heroin to live, he would enjoy it in the short windows where he wasn't going through withdrawals and cravings for more. He sunk deeper into the couch, and into himself, forgetting about every pain he had ever felt and would feel. The *Caught in the Pot* never existed and it never would exist. Neither did the pains of his body. Neither did Tilly. His skin became flushed and his fingers weighed down heavily at his sides. His mouth dried itself out, but he laid content because it didn't matter because he also didn't exist. Soon, although he did not know it, the world would exist again, and the work would demand him back in the morning. He would need to take advantage of his fucked up, foggy mind and drowsy body just to fall asleep before Tilly also returned into existence, the spirit inside her and her love he was, not long ago, lucky enough to have shared.

CHAPTER 19

Sachem had always seemed frozen in time to Kane,
preserved the same way it had been for thousands of years. The trees
that surrounded the town, a few inches higher every year. The rocky
shores and cliff faces worn away and smoothed over centuries of an
endless inhalation and exhalation of waves. The town was new, but
erected quickly and out of necessity and had stayed unchanged for
over a century. Sachem wasn't a pristine relic because the people
saw each other change. Kane saw himself change in it. He saw all
the opportunities that awaited him here and then he met Tilly, a
reason to embrace it and stay. She'd opened his eyes further to art
and love and family and what it meant to tell the truth, especially to
yourself. He wished she hadn't taught him all of that. They were the
things that hurt the most. If he'd left, he would have left her, but to
stay was to suffer and quit unless he could adapt to the path with
more of her, and now he had nothing left. Sachem was a dead fossil,
a reminder of life hardened in death.

Kane had no good days as a lobster fisherman without drugs.
It was impossible. The work was excruciating and the recovery
process proved worse. He spent his few hours at home trying to aid
the pain. He was caught in a mental loop of justifying the work to
himself while the real pain reminded him that it could not be done.
Maybe Tilly had never been his cure like he had always told himself.
Maybe she was the reason a cure mattered at all. The drugs were his
cure the entire time, through all of it. Those were the days the Oxy
treated him exactly as they were supposed to.

Calmed moments in his mind always seemed to ease the fury
of the elements. The sun was almost set, casting the filtered twilight
of magic hour on the world underneath. The *Caught in the Pot* cut
through the water like a zipper passing through the churn, in the
same hellish waters that always greeted them with so much loathing.
The crew members all sat in tired peace, relishing in another day
gone and revelling in the same peace as Kane. Brad sat next to Jenn
on the other side of the boat. Brad kept one hand effortlessly on his

toque so that the wind could not rip it from his head that hung over the edge. He let the final seconds of the sun kiss his face with closed eyes, relaxed and tired. Jenn had her elbows on her knees and face in her hands. To show any relief would be an admittance that the day had been a difficult one. She had too much pride even for that. Kane still knew she was enjoying the moment. How could you not lose yourself in it? Even Kirk did not speak unnecessary words to disrupt the rare tranquil moment on an otherwise turbulent deck. The captain simply stared ahead, focused on the open waters and home ahead, leaving behind the rushing white wake of waters and decades of days just like this.

It was possible Kane felt this way because this was a week he, at no point, had felt unnecessarily nervous. He knew what he was doing now. If he made a mistake, it was a mistake by his fault and not his ignorance. The others seemed to accept him. There was no resentment. There was no bothered helping. They allowed him to work and it made his days waking up and going to sleep less terrified. It was possible it was because the darkness of night coming from the land behind them crashed into the sunlight of the other side of the world, extending past the lines of the ocean. The waters that raged were now still. The voices that yelled were now quiet. The frenzy of ships and hands racing one another and the clock to get in seemed unconcerned. They passed by boats that moved slower than they, and were passed by faster ones. There were a few waves, some smiles and a wave from others. Most just finished their work or sat in the same omnipresent peace that shrouded Sachem and possibly the world. Were they the lucky ones now on Earth to have the eye of the storm pass over them, or was this an opening in time that everyone could feel? Nobody could ever know, even if one were to bring it up, which they wouldn't.

Kane let the soothing sounds of swirling waters engulf him. He hoped every time he set foot on this boat, it would feel like this, but he knew it could not. Looking around, he felt a sadness he couldn't share this feeling. Like his love for Tilly, the beauty in his thoughts filled his heart and made him weak knowing words would fail, stuttering from his lips, trying to explain how good he felt. It was like explaining why a song meant so much to you. You could outline the reasons, but no one could ever feel it. Kane could only try and truly appreciate it and forget his inability to express how impossibly awe-inspired he felt. Blue and yellow lights turned on across the water, the identifier lights of another fishing boat. White and yellow lights, farther even and closer to the shore, turned on seconds after. Then green lights. Then purple, red, and yellow lights. Countless boats with their different sets of lights turned on and from different distances, with the black ocean between them and invading night sky, they were like arriving fireflies. The treed hills were black in shadow now, showing no detail, lining the dusk sky that was now a darkened navy. It looked exactly like a stencil. He wished he could draw it now. This was a scene for Tilly's eye and he wished she was here to draw it.

The lights of Sachem that had only been a small cluster in the distance were now a wide and crowded mass. It was only minutes until the work would begin again and he didn't care. He let this feeling dig its hooked barbs into his mind and anchor as long as his attention would allow. If he could understand what was so special about today, then maybe he could bottle it. Maybe his cure was really just a simple understanding away. Maybe it was all his outlook. Maybe this was a just rare peace of his internal and external worlds that was utterly out of his control anyway. Maybe this was simply getting easier. Then he remembered today was the first time he'd taken an Oxy pill on the boat at lunch and let that realization numb from his mind like the muscles under his skin.

He took drugs because he felt he needed them. He did. He had developed the tendency, formed a habit, and became an addict. He was still lying to himself that Tilly was his cure and all of this shit was a healthy solution that he had under control. It is amazing what a desperate person could talk themselves into. Now that Tilly was gone, and he injected heroin into his veins every night, the illusion was gone with her. The sheet of denial had been pulled off of his face showing a vulnerable, drained young man who no longer had the energy to care. The good days on drugs had provided him turned into bad days, changing Kane, destroying him little by little as time passed. The bad days just got worse. Oxy became too expensive and defeated the purpose of why he was doing it. Bad days were soon all he would have. He had been warned by so many. He'd seen the signs.

His heart pounded in his chest. The work today on the beach before they set out was as it always was: backbreaking. Lifting the heavy cages and boxes in monotonous routine, in silence, surrounded by countless others preparing for their own hellish days on their own boats with unique names and colours. Crouching down, lifting from the legs when he could, and using his back when they gave in. His heart pounded faster and faster. He knew the pain was there and he could feel it, but it bothered him none. The human heart pounded in your chest from the second you were born until the moment you died. It was rarely felt until times like this reminded you. The blood that rushed through its connected ventricles and veins and arteries was never felt, except for times like those. He felt his blood cooling his pain, numbing everything like Novocaine in the gums. The Oxy numbed his body and it numbed his mind. He'd taken it two hours ago and it would slowly release for another ten. Perfect timing. He felt his pupils grow larger. He felt the rush of his blood. He felt the Oxy that soaked it. It was hard to feel the pain. It was hard to feel anything.

A loud crash of dropped metal on nearby rocks made a few crews look over their shoulders. Like a trash can tilted by the wind, nets, a toolbox, cutters, bands, and more spilt from the chest now on its side. The young man who had dropped it was quickly getting to his feet, picking the items from the nooks of the stones. He looked like he had hurt his ankle, keeping weight off of it and grimacing through the embarrassment of his mistake. Brad took one large step to help before being stopped by the arm of the captain. A large man carrying his own heavy cage with both arms and elbows out rolled his eyes, but put it down to help. They must have been part of the same crew. He leaned deep, one hand on the cage, reaching for a green mesh net, and, as he reached, the sleeve of his wool sweater slid up his arm, revealing deeply purple skin. Kane saw only a few inches of his arm, but the purple was unmistakably leading to the black pores of an infected heroin arm, swollen and full of open sores. Brad saw it too and took his step back. The captain's arm came down. He must have known. Kane felt disgusted by them now. Oxy healed him perfectly and to succumb to the calls of heroin was more than a need and he couldn't help but feel superior. They all got back to work as the crew beside them picked up their mess.

"Even their captain is hooked," said the captain. The crew looked up at him, at attention. "Everyone gets lost in it. You lose yourself or lose others. I've lost people to it. I've lost pieces of myself because of it."

They all worked slower now. Jenn stopped completely, still holding a cage that remained on the ground. She looked away from the rest of the crew.

The captain kept talking. "I just saw it early enough. But that was the cost. It gets you one way or another. There's a hundred crews out here. Probably five hundred souls on this beach. How many arms look like that one?" In the silence, the hundreds of near and travelled voices were all likely potential examples of his point. What had been the familiar sounds of work was now a choir of contrition. The dropped scatter had been picked up and the other crew continued on, barking and laughing, forgetting what had happened and ignoring what they never noticed anyway. "We are doing good work here," he said, talking about the morning, but really about who they were at all times. "Let's keep it up," he added, again, speaking to more than just the task at hand. He was confiding in his crew his worries and sadness to what the nature of the job has created. He was saying he was proud of his crew.

"Aye aye, Captain," Kirk yelled. Jenn picked up the box she was still holding tightly and lifted it into her chest. She walked it toward the dock and never looked back. She never did look at the crew or the captain as he spoke. Brad picked his own cage up with easy strength and followed her. Kane remained scrubbing hardened green algae crusted on the edges of a pot with a wire brush. He wished he had a cage to carry and leave with. He felt ashamed. He had looked down on that man for using drugs and was now being praised for being clean. It takes a wallop of a feeling, physical or emotional, to feel something on a three milligram dose of Oxy. He felt the shame now.

"How's Tilly, Kane?" the captain asked.

"She's great," he replied.

There had been no breakup, but that was over a month ago now and they still hadn't spoken. She undoubtedly hated him for lying to her and, of course, for using. Kane never called or texted her. He just let her hate him in his own cowardly way. He had seen her a few more times since then, on a couple Saturdays when he knew she would be at work. He would walk quickly by her work, slouching and out of view. He just wanted to see her. He kept seeing his own frantic reflection in the window of her store, but on two miraculous occasions, he'd caught a glimpse of her, one in a fortuitously timed open door and the other because she was standing close enough to the glass that it hid the rest of the reflected world behind her. He took in his fleeting seconds of her and looked away. He feared she would see him and he feared that if he looked any longer he may never be able to look away. That afternoon at his home had been the last time Tilly had seen him, had spoken to him, and for all Kane knew, it was the last time she had thought of him. He knew that wasn't true. He just wished that it was. He knew how much he had broken her heart. He knew that her heartbreak would also break Jessica's. Their hearts were worth so much more than his own and it released him to self-harm with drugs and without the burden of one day needing to quit. Saving himself didn't matter anymore because he deserved this. His memories were Polaroids taken with the confidence they could be looked at any time and cherished forever. Now, they were just sad reminders of better times that he wished he'd never taken. Maybe time could change his mind, and maybe slow the spiral of depression caused by losing Tilly, but he couldn't know. He doubted it. Nothing changed here in this fossilized, lost idea of a town waiting on the edge of the shore to be finally breathed in and washed away forever.

CHAPTER 20

Kane and Kirk both left the yard together, as they often did lately. The other crew members may have just thought of it as a new friendship, but likely they knew the real reason. Maybe they even cared. Heroin consumed all interests and therefore forged friendships. Two users who had time for nothing else would now have the most important part of their lives in common. To consume everything was to devour it. The two of them had that in each other now. One of them could now get the drugs they could use together. They could keep one another closer to humanity. They would be there to guard the other from a deathly overdose. They walked in the direction of their high, as if hand in hand, with dilated pupils. It was the only thing that mattered. Work was now over and behind them and, therefore, barely existed. Kane had spent so many hours wishing the day was finished, he'd finally gotten used to that inevitable moment when it was over. He knew it would end at some point and then he could go home and swallow the cure. Work was just skipping time. The heroin allowed him to continue to do so while savouring it and letting his bank account stack money that he never spent or cared about anymore anyway. He was time traveling through his life, impatiently skipping and rushing through the moments inside the highs. Street Fentanyl or small baggies of heroin, comparable to Oxy and his salary, was a free high. He spent only a few hundred bucks a week, with the only real cost being every single other thing in his life.

"Are you still good to finally give me that tattoo we talked about?"

"Yeah, man."

"Awesome. Can't wait. Mermaid, yeah?"

"If that's what you still want."

"Definitely. Make her hot as fuck for me. Should we get high before or after? I guess I could do it and you just do it after you're finished with it, but maybe that would be weird -- me going up, then you going up as I am coming down. So I will just wait and we can get high after."

"Okay."

Kirk sat on Kane's couch, his old tattoo chair, talking non-stop and doing little bumps of the smack because work was over and he just couldn't wait. They were only small, barely enough to make one feel anything, but the craving was strong. To be finished with work and in your home and have it so nearby, waiting was an impossibility, especially for Kirk. Kane waited only because despite his addiction, he still took his tattooing seriously. The short, ugly snorts were off-putting and extremely annoying for Kane because he needed to focus, and also he wished he could take part. Kirk was getting him high tonight as payment for the tattoo, so he said nothing about it. He had never drawn or tattooed a mermaid before and he was enjoying himself, even if to think of a beautiful figure and face was to think of Tilly. Kirk's skin seems thinner than tissue paper and it was so clear it made Kane wonder if it was. He wondered if it was possible to stay so damp for so long that maybe it was now see-through, like looking through a soaked through sheet. The skin was not tan, or pale, but a sickly, translucent blue, a minnow lying folded in a net, puckering its lips for life. Kane half expected the ink he punctured into his skin to run and bleed out, causing ink blotches where a single point should have been. Would he be able to see the brown junkie elixir coursing through his veins? The thought made him shudder and look at his own skin, a surprisingly similar shade of sickness. He noticed the sour smell they both shared and he took a quick break before he wretched, standing to search for any other air to fill his nostrils.

"Finished?" Kirk asked.

"Almost done, just have a few touch ups."

"How does it look?"

"Hot as fuck."

Kirk stepped outside for a quick cigarette. Kane stood in the kitchen, standing and staring directly at nothing, feeling hollowed out, waiting and wanting to cry, but utterly unable to remember how.

Kane's movements slowed, adding each final perfectionist touch on his mermaid. He took his time still, surveying the skin in this last audit, slowly and methodically, now with more studying than working. It had been the longest he had gone without giving a tattoo since he was a teenager, on another person or himself. He wanted to cherish all of it. He quietly promised himself he would not go this long again even if he had to tattoo himself, but he also knew the control he had over these things was slipping deeper than his ink-covered fingers could reach. It would easily be the best tattoo Kirk had on his skin, to the point that Kane thought a worse tattoo might actually look better, but Kirk would love it all the same. Kane felt an overwhelming pride for the first time in a long time. He had learned to tune out much of what Kirk said, out but he still heard the rhythm in what he was saying and it was obvious Kirk was becoming impatient. He wanted the drugs. The tattoo was now a hurdle, an obstacle of time before he could get his drugs. Kane didn't care and felt assured he still had enough of himself to take his time as he always did, up to the last dot of ink to the beautiful mermaid's right eye that stared back at his own.

With the same dedicated intent Kane had just finished this tattoo with, Kirk assembled the pieces to shoot up together. He had barely even looked at his new tattoo before reaching for the needle. He said he loved it with a smile, and maybe he did, but Kane knew the energetic excitement that had taken hold of him now was anticipatory and not for the fresh tattoo. Kane didn't really care anyway. This tattoo was more for him than it was for Kirk. It took Kirk about five minutes from heat up to injection. Kane waited, sitting beside, unhelping, for this was Kirk's passion and Kane allowed Kirk his moment to relish in it. Kirk rambled the entire time and Kane didn't mind. He liked him. In the rapid pace of his speech, there would be moments of slowed clarity, an opening up in the chaotic sky where Kirk's truth was exposed and was a further shedding of light on just how much everything else in Kirk's life and mind was a cover. He spoke because in silence, there was truth and in truth, there was remembering and for Kirk, he remembered only sadness, or maybe just the disappointing ignorance of having nothing worth remembering anyway. Authentic or disguised, Kane thought the friendship to be genuine. They would never know each other if it wasn't for the work and they would never hang out outside of that if it wasn't for the drugs. Kane didn't have to come to terms with that, and certainly neither did Kirk, because they did work together and they did do drugs. The heavily one-sided conversation of the evening died down like the sunlight outside the window and the quiet and darkness fell over the room for the first time as the heroin began its journey through Kirk's arm. Kirk closed his eyes, letting the last of the sober air in his lungs escape like a soft spirit, feeling the rush of the high, just as Kane was about to as he found his own vein, injected himself, and descended into communal oblivion on the couch in his living room, so deeply that he would miss the text alert in his pocket from Tilly.

They both woke up as they often did lately. Heroin hungover, nauseous but rested and pain free. Kirk would often snort a little extra for the day. Kane would often not. Today, he chose not to. Both of their phones were dead. Kane would think about the possibility of a text or call from Tilly all day, although he knew it would not come. The green digital numbers of the microwave read 4:54 and meant they might be late for work, but only slightly, enough for an awkward first twenty minutes and that was all. Kane drank cold, stale coffee from a black-stained pot, loose grounds floating and falling like sediment in a puddle. Kane took four plastic-wrapped burritos from the freezer and handed two to Kirk. Their unwashed work clothes were left messily in two piles and at the ready to be put right back on. At 5:03 a.m., they were out the door and Kirk was already talking about the cold, when they might need to clean the ship next, the captain's temperament, and the validity of whether boiling a lobster alive might in fact harm the meat inside. It was in these early mornings, stuck with Kirk, walking to another torturously mindless day of work, without the craving for heroin but still the shame of doing it, that Kane truly did want to disappear and wished that Tilly wasn't the one who had.

Arriving together was an announcement to the rest of the crew the reason for their partnered arrival, and their tardiness was an explanation of the severity to it. Brad didn't pay much notice and never did. Jenn showed only a brief glance of contempt that lasted much longer than her attention. They were only ten minutes late, but the trucks were already unloaded onto the rocks. Jenn certainly worked faster than her already-efficient pace to make it as uncomfortably clear as possible. Kane couldn't blame her and, in his shame, he watched Jenn, hoping to catch her eyes just once more to show his apology. She would never allow that. She grabbed a trap and hauled it to the dock. Brad did the same behind her. Kirk fell into rank and did the same, Kane waiting his turn behind before seeing the captain walking down the rocks from his truck, looking unaffected. His punishment was knowing what you did and knowing what you were. The captain would let them live in it for the day, and tomorrow, when Kane arrived ten minutes early in good faith, he would be forced into it again when they all perceived why and saw through it.

"That stuff will drown you faster than the water out there will," the captain said, staring not at the water or Kane, but down at his shoes. It was the first time Kane had heard him mention anything about it, this plague that rotted out the souls of most fishermen, this shameful addiction of the weak. It had been an invisible curse until these words and the captain did not wait for the reply that Kane couldn't form anyway. Kane picked up a lobster cage and headed for the docks just as Jenn passed him, looking only forward and never at him.

Kane hoped to see zero marks on the tree. He wanted the day to end. He wanted this to stop. Kirk talked obliviously over the awkwardness that might not even still be there, but for Kane, it was as thick as this hellacious fog. The normally-contained red and white identification lights on the roof of the ship were now an outward haze, with no lines, beginning or end. Kane raised the binoculars to his eyes, hoping to see nothing but white. The fog-streaked lights beyond nested the boat in whisps and swirls. It emulsified the ocean and the trees and town in a white sheet, but still he saw the marks on the tree. He saw this mystery often. If there was another boat fifty feet away, he doubted he could have seen it, but the tree refused to hide its marks. Kane wanted to question this rudimentary system. He wanted to lie and say he saw nothing. Nobody would double check his work. They never did. This was his call to make, even if the captain could see through the lie as Kane saw through the fog. He watched in silence for longer than usual, hoping a wave of fog might wander past and grant him the day's freedom. The fog moved like a flag underwater, just as deep as the ocean below and stretching across the sky above it. The tree with the slashes across its trunk stood tall, unmoving, watching him back, waiting, surrounded in the sea of white film.

"Three marks," he said.

Kane landed on his couch, exhausted from the day. His phone was plugged into the wall across the room. He felt relieved Kirk wasn't there tonight. He needed the headspace. He didn't do heroin every day and he wouldn't today. If Kirk was there, he certainly would. The captain's words repeated in his ears. Jenn's glares flashed in his head like a dimmed but crackling lightbulb. Did Brad not care because he understood, or did it make him more upset? He dissected each shamed worry, one by one, but he failed because his depression now closed every way out, holding him in this struggling Möbius strip he used to find a way to think through. This couldn't be his life now. Was this the start of something or the end? Kane had no attachment to his life anymore and each doubt and worry and promise of disappointment flooded all over him all at once in this rare moment of stillness. He was too weak to keep treading above it and felt closer than ever to accepting the drowning. Maybe he couldn't stop even if he felt like he could, which, right now, he didn't feel like he could. His charged phone lit up now, quickly going black again. It lit up again with a missed notification. He stood up to look at it, trying to think of anything else to replace these thoughts. The idea it could be Tilly had been buried beneath his hopelessness. It was likely just Kirk again.

It wasn't. Seeing her name on his screen made his heart jump. It didn't matter what she'd sent him. She'd messaged him. He existed. Swiping right, his confusion matched the thrill of seeing her words and the promise of seeing her again, whatever the reason, likely some sort of closure for her.

"we need to talk when works for you?"

He texted her back immediately without even considering his answer.

"Anytime."

CHAPTER 21

Eleven days. Kane had had eleven days to prepare himself to see Tilly again, the first time he had done so in months. Eleven days from the time of her text to the day he would walk into the inevitable oblivion of everything he was holding on to, every figment of a reality where he might be with Tilly again. In the first four of those eleven days, he'd texted her four more times asking her if she was okay, that he still loved her, what she needed to tell him, and to say sorry for everything. She replied only to one, saying simply that they would speak when she saw him. How could he make things right? He tried to think of every reason she might need to see him. Not one came to mind, other than hopeful imaginations of delusion. He had eleven days to slowly wean his heroin usage so that he wouldn't need to be on it just to face her, a strung out, pathetic facsimile of someone she was embarrassed to have once loved. Today was eleven days later. In the end, all he could really do was stay away from the junk and not make things worse. As if they could get worse. They were to meet at the only coffee shop in Sachem, a public place they could sit and talk and be unbothered by others. Either of their houses would make it too private, too intimate, reminding them what it was like to be alone and how distant that now was, echoes of conversations and the other's touch.

Kane was using heroin every day. He could probably ween himself down to four days and still feel right, but he more easily could have done it twice a day. Before seeing Tilly, he stopped using until every reminder of why he was using rushed back and he used again, two short days later. It felt incredible. It felt right. He then went another two days and, weighed down by the guilt of such a poor effort, made it another day without using, even though his body was in the worst shape it had ever been in. His soreness snuck back inside of him after what was a particularly difficult start to the week on the boat, with the frigid air biting sharply at his fingers and face even long after arriving at home. At night, his muscles spasmed and locked in the night in moving knots like snakes in his legs and arms both. Freezing chills were made worse by the flop sweat that coated him like the cold morning dew on a window pane. In the middle of the shivering night, he'd run painfully to the toilet in the dark. He wiped the streak of diarrhea from his lower leg. He sat hunched over, realizing this was not just the pains of the boat, but the pains of coming off heroin. He snorted some that night, making it three days since using. He had another week to try, but the morning was no better. He had to call in sick to work, something he had never done before. It was something nobody ever did. They would all surely know why and say nothing more, which they did not, save for a casual "Feeling better?" from the captain and a long-winded story from Kirk about puking over the side of the ship during a flu and having the wind blow it all back into his face. On that day off, Kane had spent the day spinning on the floor, either hugging the cold porcelain of the toilet close to his skin or crouched overtop of it, spitting bile. He'd tossed and rolled in his bed, agitated, doing anything to try and ease the cramping in his guts. His bed was soaked. He'd even thrown up on the floor, lurching, his abdomen cramping even worse before relenting to the call of the heroin. Even addicted, it felt absurd this would make him feel healthy, but it did, and almost instantly. A person rarely died in the throes of withdrawal, but who could tell the difference between anguish in death and anguish in healing? Three days was apparently his limit, so the week leading to see Tilly, he perfectly planned his rate of using. He used three times more but at half the dose, levelling him off. Kane was not kicking the habit. He was tricking her. Kane certainly did not understand the grasp this would take over himself. What he found was that every lie he told himself and every truth he chose to ignore, meant nothing anymore. He was in a new reality that to stop using heroin was going to be the hardest thing he would ever do, but maybe Tilly's news would be worthy of trying, another misguided lie he decided to convince himself of. It took two weeks for heroin to be completely out of your system and to lose its dependency on it. Fourteen short days. Almost enough time for Kane to have been able to clean up before seeing the love of his life. It was certainly enough time to have cleaned up four times since she last found out. For every single user of heroin in the world, to every sister, brother, homeless man or millionaire woman, teenager or senior, veteran or criminal, employee or manager, teacher or student, friend or foe, injured or depressed, college recruit or drug dealer --

two weeks was enough time to beat the physical addiction. The intensity of the withdrawal symptoms would vary, but those fourteen days would not. Heroin had wide arms, holding you in its lap like the mother you missed or the one you never had. It could kiss your cheek softly or pick you up when you couldn't bear to get up. Heroin looked you in the eyes and whispered that it was possible. It understood your pain and smiled with you, kissing it better, never leaving you, and telling you it would be okay. That was the dependency that stretched long past those two weeks. Quitting was a choice and withdrawals were brutal, but the fear was missing that care. The fear was living without the high when life came back, because after everything that mattered left, which it always did, heroin's care stayed. Kane used to fix himself and he'd developed an addiction. It had become the only thing that mattered. Now, heroin's loving arms were strangling his neck and grabbing his intestines and twisting them while it whispered in his ear, "You are nothing without me." Kane was losing, but Tilly wanted to talk to him and that meant there was more in his life that mattered to him than the junk in the spoon. He wished love was the stronger force, but the truth was, it just wasn't. Love didn't really conquer all. Love allowed. Love filled, like the air in your lungs or the sound of laughter in a room. Narcotics conquered all. They deceived and tricked, an abusive lover promising warmth only to tease it and hold it like a carrot in front of your face. *I am death, destroyer of worlds. I am heroin, destroyer of love.*

Kane sat at the coffee shop, waiting for her. He wanted to get there first because to be late would be another nail in his coffin. He wanted to seem eager. He wanted to pick the most private spot and wait for it if he had to, in the corner by the front window. He was nervous it might be too busy and any conversation they might have had would be guarded against it, holding in truths that needed to be said in privacy. It was shortly after three o'clock now. He had been there almost an hour. There were two other people inside, chatting to themselves, conversation covered by the banging of mugs and loud hissing of the espresso machine. If she asked, he would say he just got there. He watched for her through the window, hoping to see her with as much notice as possible. With each minute that passed his heart hit harder against his chest, and to see her before she walked in the door might give him enough time to do his best to settle himself out of a state of shock. He was nervous to see her face. He was nervous to smile at her, or hug her, or to receive the same from her. He was nervous to hear what she had to tell him now, two months later.

He checked his phone again. 3:08. She was probably wondering if it was worth it, whatever it was. Maybe she'd seen him through the window and decided against it. He looked at his phone again, for the time and maybe a missed text from her telling him she couldn't do it. It was still 3:08. He took a deep breath in hopes of slowing each one that came after it, but his rapid heart would not allow for that comfort. He was sweating, and so he wiped his palms on the side of his pants in case she might touch them. He took the first sip of his coffee, now cold, sitting fearful she might notice and realize how long he had been there. Worried apprehension was bubbling over in him, like the feeling when he'd first visited her home, or when they'd kissed at their lighthouse at the edge of the world. He should get her a coffee. It would be the nice thing to do and would mean she wouldn't have to do the awkward five-minute wait at the counter for it like everything was absolutely normal. Her coffee might just sit there and get cold, or he might lose the table. He imagined every possible fractal of the present situation until they melted together, overwhelming him so that he couldn't focus on anything at all. He looked through the window again, breathing in, scanning the street outside and all the corners of the smaller side ones connected to it. The town was a typical overcast grey and she was nowhere in sight. He turned away as the front door of the coffee shop closed and he noticed her face exactly when she noticed his. They were only ten feet apart and it turned them both to statues. He sat and she stood, frozen in a sea of understanding and the inability of saying what they wanted to say but could not and what they wanted to hear and never would.

Time jumped ahead. Tilly sat across from him now. Had he stood up to greet her? He couldn't even remember who had said hello first. How had she pulled her chair out to sit? Had he even been watching? Time slowed to normal and he saw her now. She looked the same and she looked back at him like he didn't, which made her different to him. Kane looked longingly at her with retreating eyes, ashamed with his appearance so near her bloom. She saw this and looked back with sad, pitiful eyes. She was so beautiful. To see her sitting there, quiet, not joking around or holding his hand, waiting for him to speak instead of leading with smiles and jokes as she always had, was to be in a sleeping nightmare he ached to wake from. She wasn't broken, but what they had was. In the depths of her eyes, Kane now saw things he had never seen in them before. He saw pity. He saw anger. He saw fear. But that was not everything. Whatever kind of love it was; he still saw it in her eyes as she looked back at his hopeful but submissive ones. She was here now. It is all that mattered to him. Her eyes pierced through him. He felt their gaze and their hold on his own, like magnets. As if to hide from her, he avoided her stare, looking at his feet or out of the window, until he drew to hers again and again until they were staring at each other. They were preparing for the unknown. She opened her mouth and spoke to him and even though time paused and sound ceased, he heard her. Stunned, he stared back. Had he heard her correctly? Had he asked her to repeat it? All of the sound in their voices, the room, the world, sucked away from their small table. He could barely even see her.

"I said I am pregnant, Kane," she repeated.

"Pregnant?"

"Kane, I'm not saying it again," Tilly said, now frustrated.

"How long have you known?"

"For certain, about three weeks."

Kane sat, processing. Tilly allowed him the time to do so.

"Why didn't you tell me?" he asked.

"I'm telling you now," she answered back quickly. The silence continued. Kane sat staring at the table. Tilly pushed her chair back as if to stand up and leave, making a loud dragging noise.

"I'm going to get a tea," she told him. Kane grabbed her hand, afraid that she might never come back, or afraid the right words might come to him and leave just as soon while she was away. She pulled her hand away from his, but she sat back down.

"What are we going to do?" he asked her.

"*We?*"

"Yes," he restated. "What are we going to do?"

"Are you still using?" she shot back angrily. He had never heard her talk like that. He opened his mouth, but had nothing to say back to it. Her face softened and she continued. "I don't know what I'm going to do about it yet. It seemed wrong not to tell you, that's all. That's really all there is."

"Does your mom know?"

"Not yet."

"Whatever you decide to do, I am on board with it. This is your decision."

"I know it is my decision. And what is that supposed to mean, you are on board with it? Like you will be capable of helping me? If I keep the baby, you will pay child support and that's it. I don't want a junkie hanging around my child. Or maybe you are more on board with me using the trip my mom got us over Christmas to get a hotel in the city so I can get an abortion. Are you on board with that?"

She was right. Kane knew it. He sat wounded, searching for the right thing to say, the thing that could solve this, to make her smile, to make her smile with him, but he could only search with more questions that fell flat out of his mouth, pathetic offerings on the table before her.

"When will you decide?"

"How would I know the answer to a question like that?"

"I mean, when do you have to decide?"

"I have two weeks to decide." She stood up again to leave, tears building in her eyes now. Kane reached once more for her, but was too late and Tilly was more committed to leaving this time then last time.

"I'm sorry, Tilly."

"Okay." She turned to leave.

"Do you still love me?" he asked in desperation. She stopped and turned slightly, not enough to look at him but enough for him to hear, enough that he could see that she was now crying.

"You were the love of my life."

"You were the love of my life too." Kane trembled with tears in his eyes. "You *are* the love of my life."

Tilly wiped her cheeks and closed eyes with her hand. "I just don't know what there is left of you to love." With those parting, killing words, she straightened herself and walked out the front door and down the sidewalk with her head down, quickly, so that nobody could see her blushed, teary-eyed face. She had none of the jovial skip in her step Kane had always known, the skip that made her different, floating above everyone else. He hoped it would come back. He sat alone, unable to leave with his cold and tasteless coffee, knowing in his heart that for her step to come back, he would either need to right the wrongs of his past and get straight, or leave her entirely with the hope his very memory would vanish shortly after, pinching out the last spark of his own soul.

CHAPTER 22

Yesterday, and the day before it, Kane hadn't gotten high. He had spent the rest of that free Sunday before going back to work struggling not to get high for a third sober day. He needed the heroin to function and survive the boats, so in part it was easier, but with nothing but minutes and thoughts in the solitude of his home, it often seemed rather hopeless, a denial and delaying of the inevitable. Kirk was the only person he considered a friend anymore and that would mean doing drugs. Kane thought about opening up his sketchbook and drawing something, anything. It had been so long. He considered giving himself a tattoo. He was even letting the idea of going to the store to make an interesting meal survive in his plans. None of it seemed all that interesting to him anymore. He didn't have the energy to care. For being two days sober, it was the best he had ever felt and he hoped that wouldn't change. It was noon now and if he still felt okay by four, he would go to the store. He sat on the couch waiting for the clock to pick up speed, defeatedly watching the crawling hands prove it impossible. It was the last week, according to Tilly, for her to make a decision on whether she was going to keep the baby or not. His attention never left the screen. He wasn't convinced she was going to tell him what she decided anyway.

On Friday, after work, Kirk and Kane had gone for beers. Kirk picked up an eight ball of heroin; Kane bought only a small amount from Kirk and not the dealer.

"I just still have some left over," Kane lied.

"No worries," Kirk replied. "Easy to get."

They sat at the bar that now served them more as a hub for scoring heroin than a place for beers, and had only one each. Kane didn't particularly care to be there and Kirk very obviously wanted to find a much more appropriate place to use.

"I still can't believe I haven't lost any of my fingers out there," Kirk went on. "Most people lose a few. I guess it is bound to happen to me. Maybe once you lose one, it makes it harder to do the same things, and then you have a better chance of losing more."

"Yeah, that makes sense."

"I reckon I could probably do this job with four fingers left."

Kirk talked to no end about the things you could still do or could not do with nine fingers, and then eight, and seven, holding his fingers out in front and mimicking the action in the air like some demented mime. Kane had nobody to talk to about anything. Disinterested in the topic and unaware where Kirk was at narratively anyhow, he interjected abruptly, interrupting Kirk who changed gears in the conversation, unaffected. "You remember that girl Tilly I was seeing?"

"Yeah, I remember her."

"She's pregnant."

"Fuck, man. That's heavy."

"Yeah." They both lifted their bottles for a drink of beer.

"Is she going to keep it?"

"I don't know yet."

"You don't know?"

"She doesn't know yet."

"Oh."

"Yeah."

"You still love her?"

"I do, yeah."

"What decision do you want her to make?"

"Honestly, I don't know."

"That's the perfect answer."

"How so?"

"You're feeling it, but you're worried about her. You are being supportive."

"It's more complicated than that."

"It always is."

It was the most Kane had ever opened up to Kirk, and it was the least he'd heard Kirk speak. He took it seriously. He was a friend to him. It was what Kane needed in that moment and, although he resented Kirk in so many ways, he appreciated him. Kirk quickly went back to talking about lost fingers and lost limbs, and Kane obliged by finishing his beer as a quiet audience member, learning nothing about his own situation but feeling better for bringing it up.

Three o'clock now and the first far-off rumblings that the storm of withdrawal was coming had arrived. When he was a little kid, his dad would count the seconds between the lightning and the thunder to determine how far away it was and whether it was approaching or passing by. Withdrawal was always coming for him. He could feel it so familiarly now. He could almost sense it coming, like the air thickening and smelling sweet with rain, reactions between the ozone and the earth. The skies in the distance formed their grey, menacing bodies from the blue. It was coming, but there was nothing to fear yet. He felt it in his brain, the beginnings of a headache. A rain cloud would tower above before the rain it brought fell towards the earth until almost all at once, the sky darkened and waves of rain beat down, flashes of lightning streaking through the new dark followed by wall-shaking thunder. Kane took his phone and went to his room, preparing for the thunderstorm that was about to rip through himself. He went under his bed to grab his drugs and set them at the ready on the coffee table, just in case. There were a few days where he was crawling between wretches and blurred vision to get a taste of it. If he was going to succumb, he might as well make it an easier clean up for himself. Kane had no intention of failing today anyway. Two-day weekends were not enough time for anybody to get clean, but it was all he had, and to get high tonight would be a major setback in his decrease in use. Reaching underneath, he pulled out the black bag he was looking for and inadvertently dragged out several pieces of paper he had stored there and forgotten about. They were all of the drawings that he and Tilly had done together, those shared images, each one a duplicate version in subject but entirely different in style and purpose. They had created things that appeared so different and so beautiful from looking at inanimate objects of the world, passed by time and others for centuries, just by looking at them with open hearts and choosing to be there together. Was that knotted and twisting root system at the base of two trees ever looked at before? Were they the first witnesses of this entanglement of nature in the centuries it took to form? Bushes, rocks, birds in flight, a wave, a dock, and, of course, the boat stranded on the shore for cleaning. That boat, the first thing they had ever shared, their perfect first date neither had known they were on. In each drawing on each piece of paper, he saw Tilly, how she was sitting and how she looked at her subject intently with the occasional tongue poked in his direction when she caught him looking at her instead. How could he not? He saw what was and what would never be again, a future world destroyed, a timeline cut short. Seeing them all amassed in a discarded bundle like this, an avalanche of each moment lived and never to be lived, covered him and laid there, weighed down by the enormity of it all, and wept into the withdrawal.

He awoke the next morning with his cheek pressed flat to the sticky linoleum of his bathroom floor. Kane had moved there in the middle of the night on a few occasions to save himself the agonizing treks to and from the bed and the toilet bowl. There had been times he would need to check to see if he had touched the heroin, unsure in the blur of the malady and blending of the days. He didn't need to check this morning. He hadn't touched it and, standing up, shivering when it wasn't cold and nauseous when he had not eaten, he still felt okay enough to know he wouldn't need it before work either. It would be the longest he had gone, about three days, since he had begun this task of trying to cut the habit that was really a disease. Maybe he could get through tonight too, but after a shift, the nights were always the worst. He checked the time on his phone and learned two things. It was time to begin another week of work and Tilly still had not texted him.

Walking on the hard, flat concrete of the road that took him almost directly to the wharf was always strange. He now spent half his waking life either on ground or at sea. He was beginning to become just as comfortable with both, each one taking a little time to get used to. At the end of the length of the street, he could see the work truck. This happened from time to time, a point of chance, but this time stuck out to him. The cab of the truck remained fully loaded with cages and gear, sitting higher than the roof of the truck itself. Three figures stood beside it, unmoving. They weren't speaking to one another. They weren't beginning to unload the back, or even begin their shift at all. It was Jenn, Brad, and Captain Sam. Jenn sat down on the curb, folded beside the back tire, face in between her knees. Was the boat damaged? Did they just learn that a week or more of pay was now in jeopardy because of a faulty engine or broken rudder? A few days of cleaning would have been told to them last week. Kane picked up his pace now, curiosity leading to anxious paranoia. Was he getting fired? Kirk wasn't there yet either; he was often late anyway, but maybe they were both being let go. Kane just wanted to get there to get it over with now, convinced of his impending judgment. As he got closer, all of his calculated guesses were replaced by fears as he saw the severity of the scene on each of the crew member's faces. Jenn wasn't pouting at all. She was crying. Brad was as still as he usually was, giving little away, but radiating a quiet intensity raging as if he was stuck inside himself and about to burst. The captain noticed Kane had almost arrived, and with a sullen look and head hanging, stepped away from the others to meet him in the middle of the street. The rest of the crews worked around them, boats were being loaded up, birds squawked as if nothing was out of the ordinary, and trucks were pulling up, already laughing and barking orders for the day. The captain's cap was in his hands as he plainly explained to Kane the reason for the oddity of the morning.

"It's Kirk," he said. "He's dead."

CHAPTER 23

Time was an unreliable blur, jumping from one hour to the next moment to the next in a halted stop, grounding Kane when he needed to escape, and freeing him when he no longer cared. Three days ago, he had done more heroin than he ever had before following the longest stretch in three months of not touching it. The past two days, he had done more or less the same, with work being cancelled, the women he loved and lost having not texted him the biggest decision of their lives, and, of course, his friend dying in his bedroom, overdosed and alone. In almost every case, heroin overdoses could be saved. The drug was almost always used alone, and always in private, in hiding, in shame. Of course, there would have been no one there to save Kirk, no volunteer paramedics and no loved ones to call them. The days to save were all the other ones, the days where you decided to stay quiet and the days you chose to ignore the signs. Even though Kane used, and used with him, he would regret that forever. Brad surely would too, even if it made them hypocrites. Jenn would. The captain would. Everyone at this funeral would.

The gathering was small, about fifteen people. Kirk had talked about everything, but he had never truly let anyone talk. He hadn't let anyone ask questions. He had never let them in. Kane had no idea who any of these people were, except for the crew of the *Caught in the Pot* and Brenda -- who was more there for him, he imagined. Maybe she was there for Captain Sam too, since they knew each other well. It didn't really matter to Kane. He would never really know any of these people, or who they were. Did he have siblings? Were any of these people his mother or his father, or nearby aunt's or uncle's, cousins close enough to attend? Which branches of his family tree did they hang from? It didn't matter. They sat together, but really, they sat alone. In a series of twisted jokes, the clouds parted from time to time, reminding them all of the sun and what it felt like to squint your eyes and have the warmth hit your cheek. It was a reminder of happiness, a smile in the face of death, a cruel gesture. Kane sensed the same sentiment in the faces of everyone else. "Just let us sit in the grey. Let us feel it." Nobody wore black suits or black dresses, but they all wore their best. Kane wore black jeans, black dress shoes, and a black polo covered by a black zip up jacket. This addition felt too informal even there, but he felt compelled to cover his tattoos. He didn't want any attention. He wanted to leave. He wanted to turn invisible. He wanted to disappear. Tilly wasn't there. She had no reason to know he was even there; no matter how small Sachem was. His world was becoming so fragmented and he was trying to hold all of the pieces from falling on his cracking skull and spilling whatever was left inside to stick and dry on the cemetery grass for the birds and worms. He wanted to just let them all go. Whatever happens, happens. Kane had never been to a funeral before. A few people were crying, but most just sat, numb or resigned as if this is what they had been expecting for some time. So strange to be sitting so close to him, a once hyper-talkative, well-intended young man who craved connection and to entertain so immensely, he could never turn it off. Ten yards away laid the unmoving dead shell he was now. He had not lived a full life. He had not had an entire future to look forward to. Maybe it would be sadder if he had. Kane wondered if the heroin was still sitting stagnant in his blood, aimless with nothing to do, like dead satellites stuck in space. He, himself, had used heroin that very morning, before the funeral of a heroin-overdosed friend. Maybe he should just crawl into the casket and save everybody the trouble. Kirk had been his friend because they were junkies together, but he had been the only one who was there for him through it all, to help him when things were the most difficult. Kane would miss him and hoped to never forget him. Were they going to throw dirt on him when this was finished? Was Kane's final goodbye to Kirk really with needles in both of their arms, fading into feverish reverie? Was it when he walked away from this place? Or was it the last time he would ever think about him? Kane looked around at these strangers, at Brad who crossed his thumbs and stared blankly into his hands. Jenn, the strongest of the group, was gently crying with exhausted tears, on the edge and avoiding sobbing. The captain looked strong, chin up, as he likely felt he had to be. Kane felt the sense the Captain believed he owed it to the boy, felt he had been responsible for him.

This was Kane's community of people now. He had moved to Sachem with nothing and nobody and thought he was happier for it. He had found everything in Tilly: love, home, community, a cure. And now this was it, a few coworkers and some people he would never know, surrounding the dead body of a young man they hadn't cared enough to save.

The captain shook hands with people with regretful smiles and closed eyes, giving his close condolences and paying respects. The now-smaller crew stood waiting for him as they often did, in a murky silence, for the return of their fearless leader. Jenn started shaking like she was freezing and Brad put her arm on her shoulder. She tugged it away in a violent swat.

"Jenn," Brad said. "What's wrong?"

"What's wrong?" she replied. She stared at Brad in offended disbelief. He knew what was wrong. What could know what to say? She looked up, crying in a quiet, red fury, shaking in an anger she knew not what to do with. Kane was terrified and Brad looked the same. Brad's startled arm hung unsettled in the air and Kane's attention waited, hanging on Jenn's words. She spoke with a potent intensity, quietly, but spacing each word to make sure the two of them together would hear her, finally. "Stop. Doing. Drugs."

Jenn's words and tears released together, forcing her to leave the two standing there to look at each other, afraid of her spoken truth. Brad released his arm to his side and sighed.

"She lost her brother to it."

"I didn't know that."

They both paused.

"Kirk's money is just wasted now. Not like he had anyone to take it."

"What money?"

"The life insurance money. Everyone who works on the lobster boats is part of a higher union. We all work together, that's why it works. You didn't know this?"

"I guess I never asked."

"You die out there, your family gets money. Quite a bit of it, actually."

"But he didn't die out there."

"No. He didn't."

Brad left, walking toward Jenn, giving her the space to cry, but following close enough for when she needed him to be there. The captain returned to Kane, standing in the same spot, now alone, his hands in his pockets with nowhere to go. He looked like he was returning from battle, bringing nothing but bad news and the guilt of survival.

"I hate these," he said. "You okay?"

"Yeah," Kane replied, unconvincingly flat.

"The boat won't be the same without that little shit."

Kane smiled. "No, it won't."

"And neither will your life, Kane. But we will continue to do both, won't we? That's how we honour him. And ourselves."

Kane nodded.

"Are you okay? You look like a wrung-out towel."

"I feel like one that's wound tight."

"Kane," he said, stepping closer, forcing him to look him in the eyes. "Don't let this shit kill you too."

Kane nodded again, feeling the sting in his nose of the coming tears beginning to well over his eyes.

"Let's go." And with that, he walked to join the others, and Kane followed closely behind.

Later, that night, following the paltry reception, with an empty needle that had just been inside his arm now laying on the coffee table, Kane received a text. It was from Tilly. She was going to get an abortion. He didn't text her back. Not yet. Selfishly, he wanted her to keep it, in a way, now knowing this was her decision. It would have meant there would always be a connection between the two of them, a possibility of a return to what they were. Now there would be nothing. But this was her choice and so it should be. It was the right one, he thought. Of course, it was. He was sitting there high on heroin. What person would want a junkie for their child's father? What kid would want to know that about their dad? He would have never been a part of their life. How could he take care of anything when he couldn't even take care of himself? The girl he was in love with was pregnant with their child, she was going to get an abortion, and it was the right decision. He missed her so much. He once would have thought a heartbreak like this would have been worth it because it meant feeling that kind of love, but not like this. His love was destroying everything in its path. Depression swallowed him entirely that night. His last thoughts were of death, and how it was now following him wherever he went.

CHAPTER 24

Kane saw a different person staring back at him. His appearance hadn't really changed, and if it had, he had missed the shift. It wasn't like the movies, but then again, he probably didn't use as much as those characters, using heroin like it was crack or meth or both. He half expected to see a monster staring back, with chapped lips and scabby skin. He looked a little skinnier, and definitely more tired than he ought to be, but it was still him, the face of his mother and father. He hated what stared back, of course, but he hated the change inside himself, not the face itself. He wished his face was fucked up. He wished it was different. Maybe then he could hate it as if it were another person. It was just him standing in front of himself. If his parents were to see him now, would they notice? In the years that had passed they would be looking for a change in him. They would surely see it. He wasn't just destroying himself, but what they had created together. Innocence was actually lost twice in your life: when you yourself lost it and when your children lose it. He felt profoundly selfish and sad to have wasted himself. He loved them both. They deserved better. They had no idea what he was now, and maybe it could stay that way, somehow. Kane had spent much of his earnings on drugs, but he had still managed to save some. There was so much of it. He could afford to visit them, at least, but not now. How could he ever see them again? To ask them for help would be to admit to them what he was. Kane was thinking of his parents often these past few days, thinking about his childhood and what it had taken to raise him. It forced him to think about his unborn child and how ill-suited he would have been to raise it. They would have had no chance in this life. Neither did he anymore. Kane remembered records scattered all over the ugly blue and red carpet in an early childhood home, his dad playing them so loud as they unpacked boxes, echoing new sounds of home in this strange, new house. The way the sound had echoed and dimmed behind closed doors and grown as he explored the new rooms, the scattered cover art a mural displayed on the floor of what flowed through the house. It had formed the way he listened to music, what music he would listen to himself, and what his idea of a home was. His mom hadn't read to him as a child, but she had spiritedly asked him to read for her, whatever he wanted. It had given him an excitement for stories, and opinions, and empathy for characters, and people outside the page. Neither had ever really seemed to lecture him on what was right or wrong in the world, they had just guided by example, allowing him to constantly self-discover. Could you be a good son without being a good person? Could you be a good partner? Could you be a good father?

Kane stared into the mirror and watched himself wither. Stalling for time or stuck in thought, it was time to go. Tilly didn't want him around for the abortion. She had gone with her mom to the city; it was the closest clinic, nearly 150 kilometres away. They'd had to ride the bus. Thinking of Jessica, knowing what he was now. Thinking of the car they could have possibly taken. He thought of the baby they could have had. He was sick with himself. He wanted to know that she was okay, so, after pleading with her, she told him when she was ready, she would reach out. He didn't know if she ever would be until a few hours ago when she had texted him that he could go over, if he wasn't high. He wished it didn't need to be said. It did. He wanted it badly. She instructed him to text her when he was walking up her hill so that she could come outside and talk at the car. It was close enough to the safety of her home, but far enough to feel uninviting.

His footsteps sounded the once-familiar crunch of the gravel road up the hill just before her house. He first saw her head and crossed arms, and with each step slightly higher than the one before it, the standing silhouette of her body leaning against the frame of the red Chevy came into view, bit by bit, her waiting face, her tense shoulders, her crossed arms, and finally her legs. She noticed him back before looking away, an instinctual scratching of her neck, trying to look at anything else. She used to stick her tongue out at him, or gallop toward him, arms waving and beaming. Instead, she waited statuesque, unmoving like the car he had never finished fixing. The grass was overgrown again, wrapping around and trapping the frame like it had before. By now, rust was building up again on the metal, and all of the joints and gears he had cleaned and oiled were dried and rigid once more, back to its state of hibernation against its will. He could see the house now. He tried to see Jessica in the windows, but he saw only black and reflections in them. Maybe he just couldn't see her. Maybe she hated the sight of him. Maybe she just wasn't home.

"Hey," Tilly called out, always odd to hear with the "weirdo" attached to it.

"Hey," Kane called back.

"How are you?" she asked, scanning him for signs of drug use.

"I don't really know how to answer that."

"Yeah, well…"

"How are you, though?"

"I'm good," she said. They danced back and forth awkwardly. She was doing this for him. He was going to have to ask her outright.

"How did it go?"

"The abortion?"

"Yes."

"I didn't do it."

"What?" he said, taken aback. "You didn't end up going?"

"No, I went. I just didn't go through with it."

"What happened?"

"Well," she began, pausing once more to gather her own thoughts. "My mom told me it was my choice and that whatever I decided was perfectly fine with her. No matter what, she was going to help me the entire way through. I tried to separate if I was doing this because it was what I wanted or because of my hatred for what you have done to us, and I couldn't. I couldn't make a final decision solely based on what you have done here."

Kane stood there, processing the news and what Tilly had told him. "And your mom is okay with this?"

"Yes. Her plans have obviously changed, but yes. She was kind of thrilled on the way back actually."

Kane realized there was now going to be this life and well of experiences he wasn't going to be a part of. "And what about me?"

"What about you?"

"I mean, I support you no matter what. I want to be in the kid's life."

"You can support him by not being in his life."

"That's unfair."

"No!" she yelled. "Don't talk about fairness to me."

Kane took a breath and so did Tilly. The silence above the ocean was resounding.

"What can I do then?" Kane asked.

"Pay child support. Go to rehab."

"I can do that."

"Can you?"

"I promise."

"I had no dad, Kane. I know what it's like. It's far better than having a junkie one. I will not let my son turn out sad and messed up bec--"

Kane cut her off. "Son?"

Realizing she had let that truth slip she sighed and looked over the ocean.

"They told me at the clinic."

Hearing "child" was one thing to Kane, but hearing the word "son" made it so definitive, so real. His imagination could focus directly on the situation. He instantly thought of himself in another person, a life created from his own. He teared up and, noticing this, taking pity, Tilly softened slightly.

"There are a couple really good rehab centers in the city. I'll text you the names of them."

"How do you know that?" he asked.

"Because I looked into it."

"You looked into something like that?"

She looked at him now like he was a complete idiot. "Kane, of course I did."

"You were the best thing that ever happened to me, Tilly," he said, crying now. "It just came at a time when the worst thing was happening to me."

"I hate you, Kane," she said, crying now too. "I hate you because I am still so in love with you. I am reminded every day by what you are not anymore. You affected my art. You are in everything I do. I still see the beauty in things that you don't anymore. I see this fucking lighthouse on my skin every day and think of you. And I am about to have a hopefully healthy and wonderful baby boy that will also remind me of you every day, and you won't be around for any of it. I will be. I'm the one who is stuck with you."

"Give me another chance."

"You have a chance every single day," she said, shaking her head.

"I'm going to try."

"How did we get like this?"

"I don't know."

"I warned you," she said. "I tried. I know I did. If you need help recovering, tell me. I'm here for that. But whatever this is, I will have no part in it. And neither will your son."

"Okay," Kane said, squeezing tears from his eyes with his thumb and index finger.

"I'm going inside now," she sighed. "I'm very tired."

"Okay." Tilly let her saddened shoulders drop and stepped across her lawn to walk inside.

"Tilly?" She stopped, looked back, and Kane stepped forward, closing the distance between them. He stopped before her to make sure it was okay, and he put his arms slowly around her, feeling her head fall against his chest until she was hugging him back. Whatever they were to each other now, however they felt, whatever they had been through, they needed this. They had been in love, and still were, happy or not. They had made a child together. They held each other like that for a minute longer until Tilly was ready to leave. He would have stayed there forever. Without another word, Tilly fled from him, walked past the red car, across her lawn, up the stairs he had once taken, terrified for the first time to meet her mother, and opened the screen door and went inside, letting it slam loudly against the frame, a final bang of the gavel. She was gone.

Kane started his long walk home, deflated and depressed, knowing that he was already a disappointment to his son before he was even born. There was no point. There was nothing he could do to get better. He was already craving the heroin back home. He craved the piercing feeling of the needle entering his skin because the pinch meant the high. He had lost everything. The love of his life and his unborn son, his only friend left in the world who he barely knew or even liked; the heroin had solved that. He didn't want to quit. He wanted more. Leaving Tilly's house, possibly forever, looking out at the quaint, innocent town with a hidden, rotten core, he had the beginnings of a thought so morbid, he felt repulsed with himself for almost thinking it was an idea.

CHAPTER 25

The longest a trap would sit at the bottom of the ocean was four days. Anything longer than that, the lobsters started starving and attacking one another. They entered the lobster pot hoping to find something they needed to survive. It didn't matter if it was filled with other lobsters clawing and scuttling, trapped in the cage with no way out. They walked straight in. Kane thought of this each time the rope snapped tight on the wench, turning slowly and humming, bringing them up to the surface. Did they know what was happening to them? Survival instinctually took over in each one of them because they sensed the danger, but by then, it was too late. They were out of the water and onto the boat. Kane pulled off the cage door, as he had done thousands of times, and watched them claw and snap violently at nothing. Their bodies were hard shells and their eyes beads of black, but he could still see the fear in them. It could just be his own reflection staring back. Brad took each one carefully with thick, rubber gloves and banded their pincers to protect the fingers of the crew and to stop them from attacking each other in their state of panic. It was not a group of lobsters, but a pathetic mass coming to terms with the certainty of their hopelessness. Kane found it difficult to look at.

He wondered if Tilly was showing yet. She must have been. Did you start showing at four months? He didn't know. He should be learning all of this, asking the questions and reading the books. He wanted to see her pregnant belly. He wanted to pull up her shirt and see her stretched skin, kiss it with his lips, kissing both of them, and place his hand on her and feel his unborn son kick him back. He wanted to look up and see her smiling, looking down at him to ask, "Did you feel that?" as he rose to kiss her mouth with his hand still placed upon her. He wanted to tell her he loved her and hear her say it back. He wanted her to know how proud he was of her. He wanted her to feel excited for the life and lives they were creating together and were about to share. He wanted her to feel safe. He hoped she still did. Kane bent over and picked up the painfully heavy metal wire cage of metal wire, putting it on top of the one before it, that sat on the one before it, that sat on the one before it.

Work was harder now. Nobody seemed to mind. How could you anyway? They were a person short on the crew with the same amount of work to do. If there was even a person that the captain could have replaced him with, he wasn't going to. It didn't feel right. It had only been a month ago. Maybe it would never feel right. Nobody would say it, but his constant chattering was missed the most. They mourned him with each silent minute that went by. Kane wished he could say it was the extra hours on the boat, or the ten extra pots he was now responsible for, that were the reason he was still using, but it wasn't. The real truth was he wanted it. Even if he could afford rehab, which he barely could, he couldn't expect to keep his job. And then what? Leave Sachem and his son? He had called a counselling hotline dedicated to helping individuals with addiction. He'd called out of desperation, for answers he couldn't even think of questions for, a pathway out of this heroin hell. She had a high-pitched, friendly voice and asked him his age and not his name. She asked for the reason he was calling. He told her he was using heroin every day, and that he was depressed because his friend had just died and he now had a kid on the way.

"I see," she said. "I'm sorry for your loss." There was too much to address. "How long have you been using for?"

"About a year, I guess."

"Why do you think you started?"

"To deal with work. In the beginning, anyway."

"Everyone has their reasons, but everyone still has hope, too."

She told him to think of his kid. She asked if he had anyone in his life he could turn to, if he expected long-term change, and what his goals were. He said, "Thank you," before she could finish her next question and hung up. It was a verbal pamphlet from a stranger at the other end of a phone line.

His parents had called him twice, once over his birthday and another time he didn't know what for. He didn't pick up anyway. Kane had no idea what to say to them. Would they even recognize his voice if he answered? He hoped they wouldn't. Nothing was normal about his life anymore, save for his comfortable familiarity with unchanging and unrelenting despair.

He lifted another pot out of the water, digging into his flesh and burning knots into his muscles. Next to him, Jenn helped him do the same. They reset traps, unloaded them, unset them, and banded lobsters, moving from one buoy to the next, never really starting because it never truly ended. The boat carried them through the fog like passengers on the River Styx, the death of overdose and bodies swimming silently below. Waves softly slapped the boat over the chug of the motor and Kane expected to hear Kirk's stories still carried by the air's breath, over the water or in his head. He heard nothing. The fog created myths and legends from scared and drunk stories of fisherman across generations and Kane often feared them, but now, he felt like he was the apparition, a spectral ship stuck in the purgatory of this watery graveyard, punishment for stripping himself of his own spirit. He was helpless to it. He welcomed this fate because it would mean the damage was done, and the hard part was over. It meant Tilly would be free of him, and his son's future would be unburdened by the sins of his father. He could hardly remember what it felt like to kiss her lips, or see her smile, or to feel her hands tighten their grip into his back when they had sex. They would soon land back on shore for the night and that would be the dream, the ocean, his curse of the past now already dead. Life on land was in fragments, forgotten like a dream often was, and he recalled the idea he had while walking from Tilly's home the last time he saw her. He had done his best to banish such thoughts, but resilient they returned, like a hungry beast, each time more desperate and more unpredictable. Sitting on the boat, floating alone, transparent in time, Kane let the beastly idea breathe and roam within himself before killing it once more, but it remained there, a stinking carcass, the rotting remains festered and stinking for days, impossible to ignore.

TILLY

She didn't wipe the wet colours from the tips of her fingers; she let the grace of the breeze and the easy passing seconds dry them onto her skin. In the most uncertain time of her life, Tilly felt at ease. She was terrified, and she was heartbroken, but she was at peace. This new life grew inside her, grew with her, a common miracle that was now hers entirely. She rested her hand on her little belly, barely showing, allowing the hardening reds, blues, greens, and yellows to leave finger painted lines dragged across her skin. The vibrant streaks of colour a ceremonial war paint, the final touches for a woman ready to face the world, but never alone. She had her mother and she would have him. She wished so badly that she had Kane too as a partner, and a helping father, but she had lost hope. When the doctor had told Tilly the news of her pregnancy, Kane had no longer been part of her life. She was in love with him, but every stacked warning she had given him had gone unheeded and when he could no longer hide his habits and addictions, all of his dismissals caught up with him. She was angry, saddened, and healing all at once. The doctor's congratulatory smile had been given and received without a grain of salt from Tilly. Sitting in the abortion clinic, realizing that Kane had never really shared any of this experience with her, she realized it didn't matter that he wouldn't be around. This child would receive so much love. Did she wish that Kane had been holding her hand, smiling and kissing her in the wake of the news? Of course she did, but he wasn't. Sachem was a small town and Tilly had known a few girls that had gotten abortions. Some of the stories were cautionary tales, a girl normalizing the behaviour of a boy who hadn't seemed to mind that she could barely open her eyes because she was so drunk. That boy, of course, taking his worry out on her with directed blame, demanding an abortion she would have wanted anyway, but leaving her with the guilt of what he had caused. Another girl at school had simply taken her birth control wrong and ended up pregnant with her boyfriend who was terrified, but trying his best to be a supportive partner. In every instance, innocuous or insidious, an abortion was no easy thing for any girl, and she knew that in the scars on these girls left by rumors and cast stones, and now in her own journey. Tilly had been committed to the decision and her mom had been there, in the bus seat next to hers, holding her hands as she would have done either way. Kane was gone, and maybe not forever, but it changed nothing about her own place in this new world. If she wasn't ready, she would have terminated it, but she was, and so she decided to have it, on her own, with the support of her mom, and not a possible fear of his addict father, but of the understanding that he was once the most beautiful person she had ever known and been lucky to have fallen in love with. She still loved him. She was still *in* love with him. If that person ever came back, then she might be able to continue to do so, with caution and a trust she was unsure that she possessed. What she would not do was sit idly, waiting by the window for his return.

Tilly's book of lovingly carved pages, now filled with fresh paints poured onto hardened older paints, sat beside her now, a dry paintbrush on top and untouched. Her sheet of canvas was pristine white and would remain that way. She wanted to come out here, to her edge of the world, where she had brought Kane, where she now brought her unborn son, in both cases to share the weight of the overwhelming beauty, to paint it as if trying to decode the vastness of all the complex fascinations of her blissful life. She loved the gift he had given her, and it made her cry to use it, but she would never try and erase the person that he had been. If that person had never existed, then neither would her son. Tilly wanted to find every piece of that person and burn them into her memory forever so that she could one day tell her son about who his father was. His memory was all she had left and all she wanted. She smiled as colorful as the paints on her skin, closing her eyes to her view at the end of the world, looking at the darkness, looking within herself, comforted, knowing that what was within her was a mother's strength and a baby boy.

ROPE

Her memory haunted him and unmade more passed him by uncaringly like eddies in the streams of screams and echoes in the waters he now gazed into. The water was flat today, a glass coffin exposing the untouched whites of new bones. Echoes of those who had cried over them were heard in far-off murmurs and sighs, but far enough away it left the surface of the sea tremor-free and undisturbed. He looked at the others who appeared to hear and see nothing. As if alive, their boney hands outstretched to their boat, slack and hanging jawbones underneath the dry sockets where their eyes used to be. Were they asking for help or calling out to him? He would soon find out. Twisted skeletons in layers spread from the doorsteps of Sachem homes in mounds, covering the shoes and disappearing into the waters and stretching across the ocean floor, a watery and unmarked cellar of graves and places of unrest. Bones scattered and married into themselves, turning skeletons to bones and people to numbers. The bones of his passed friend would be somewhere down there for nobody to look for or find. How many of them were still thought of? How many souls still had names?

The fog was thick. The bow of their skiff cut through it rather than it parting for them. It was what he had been waiting for. Maybe there would have been clarity of his mind had there been a clarity in the day, but the fog wrapped around their boat, covering it and lifting to their ears, filling his mind with the shroud of the day. He did not fear it. The others stood silent beside him, unknowing, but silent for the dead. They waited for him to make his call. He raised the binoculars to his face, and they watched him with the interest for his words was unforeseeable. He saw only white. There were no trees, no hash marks to be seen. There was no sea between or sky above, only skeletons below and his awaiting crew. Tilly was in the beyond, on land beyond the fogs of misery with their son who would soon join her. The world he had once been a part of was now gone and he had only one thing left to do.

"Two hash marks," he lied, setting the binoculars back into their box. He didn't look at the others. It was his job and they had never questioned him. They wouldn't start now. They forged ahead to the *Caught in the Pot* on that foggy day, a day like any other, a day with lobsters waiting in cages and the suffering quiet ones that caught them.

His misery infested himself. It was out of his control and had been for some time. His addiction, his life, and now, his future. He had tried to quit, but couldn't. He had tried to listen, but couldn't. He was incapable of escaping himself, just as every fleshless skeleton below had been unable to. Getting better would solve nothing now, even if he could do it. He was hopeless. His idea was a sole solution, a gesture to those he still loved, the last of himself before withering away to nothing. He was not afraid. His disappearance had already begun, and this was the only good will he could gather before wasting it like he surely would, like so many others did, like Kirk had.

The boat was pulled deeper into the fog. The ocean remained eerily flat. The winds were quiet and the buoys barely bobbed. The red and white lights were near impossible to find. The crew stood worried, hopefully borrowing more time, for if an outcrop of shallow stones were near, they would never know until nothing could be done. The White Death had arrived. The time to act was now. He was not afraid. In waves and wind, they rushed to action, but now there was a stillness to each and every movement. They spoke in whispers and stepped softly, as if they feared to waken the dead in the depths, the ones only he could see. Jenn was at the stern of the ship, moving the heavy anchor slowly to the side for there was no need for it. He reached early for the rope, preparing the only tool he would need for the task, as he had done with the tools when he used to tattoo, to those when he needed to shoot up. The captain held the wheel, waiting for the job to be done, watching the fog like suspicious prey, waiting for movement, for a sign that the danger was coming. The danger wasn't coming. They were already in it. It was here and it was welcome. The rope fell from his hands, landing with a soft thud, and loosening the wheel into a scattered bundle at his feet. He took his firm hold of the buoy and began to pull the cage to the surface, breaking off the debris of bones, a chalky powder surrounding the small, floating pieces before falling to the bottom once again where they would stay forever. Brad was on the other side of a tower of traps, preparing bands and making space for the one Kane would soon resurrect, filled with the live creatures he resented so much. With each pull, he kicked the rope back and forth, over and under his feet, watching the others in case they turned to see. He was tense, but he was not afraid. His feet were lost in the entanglement of rope. He looked into the water and away from the boat, away from the crew, and away from this small world. He closed his eyes to picture Tilly. She was all he wanted to think of, a last gift to himself. He tried to think of what his son might look like and saw nothing, happier even so that it only meant he might not know what his father was in return. This was no sacrifice, but a gift, a gentle parting for the two of them to pass through together. The same life insurance Kirk hadn't received because of his overdose would be theirs soon enough. He would crawl over the side and, in a final splash, sink so fast and so deep, the others would have no chance to pull him up in time. The cold would take his breath away. He would drown within a minute. His tangled body might untangle, leaving him lost in the fog, belonging to the sea, the last sight of him a simple dissolving of bubbles on the surface where they would look, seeing where he had fallen in, assuming accidentally. The fog overhead would be enough cover to make a rescue impossible. The White Death was everywhere. He was not afraid. He was ready to die for them. He was unafraid. The rope in his hands was heavy and strained with tightness, the pulled slack now intertwining around his waist, through his legs, and mixing with the second rope. He shuddered with the sadness of this conclusion to his life and love, the same two he'd ignited and extinguished in under a year, starting the afternoon his bus had stopped in Sachem, the moment he'd seen Tilly's focused gaze, and ended in the first Oxy pill he'd swallowed. He didn't want heroin right now. He wanted his life back. It was so simple to see what mattered in that moment. With no future, there was no fear. The White Death was in his mind and he was not afraid.

The love that had always overwhelmed him, his love for Tilly, assured him of his choice, this apology, this reckoning. He jumped over the edge of the boat and with the violent snap of the slacked ropes and plummeting lobster pot, he was gone.

CHAPTER 27

The empty black, above the waiting voices and eager eyes of clumps of Sachemites that sat restlessly or stood content, making light conversation with their mouths or intimate ones with their eyes and touch, maybe watching impatient children fill their bored minds in the silence before the first pop or laying blankets down across the grass, stayed black a little while longer. Tilly and Kane sat along amongst them, laying on their elbows on the grass, waiting for nothing and indifferent to the rest of it.

"What brought you here?" Tilly asked him.

"Like, into this world?"

"No, weirdo."

"Or to the other side of the country? Or to Sachem?"

"Yeah."

"Or brought me here, lying in the cold and the dark? I'll answer them all."

"Please do."

"My parents brought me into the world. That's one covered."

"No, no. What were you like as a little kid?"

"I think probably a little shit."

"Really? Why do you say that?"

"I came across an old tape once. You know, when you could press the record and play button at the same time on an empty cassette and record yourself? You're probably too young."

"You're three years older than me."

"That's about how long it lasted, I think. Anyway, it was my humorously annoyed dad telling me not to do something and I was being an annoying brat, whining about something for too long. Strange to hear yourself as a little kid. I guess most kids will know that about themselves now. I didn't like it."

"Why?"

"I was being such a shit."

"Every kid is a shit."

"Felt unnatural, I guess."

"I wish I could hear myself as a kid."

"Why?"

"Just curious. I miss being a kid."

"What do you miss?"

"Make believe."

"You still make believe."

"I do?"

"You can see it in your step. The best at making believe never know they're doing it."

"That's a very nice thing to say. If you were a little shit, you aren't anymore."

"That's a very nice thing to say."

"How old were they when they had you?"

"Ummm. My dad was around thirty and my mom twenty-five."

"So you are the same age as your mom was when she had you."

"Yeah, I guess I am. And you're the same age as your mom was."

"I am, yeah."

"I probably still hold things against my parents, when they were just figuring things out."

"Is that why you went to the other side of the country?"

"I guess that's the next point. I don't think so. No. I didn't leave because of them."

"Just decided to leave?"

"Yeah."

"And you chose Sachem?"

"Among other places along the way."

"Doesn't the clichéd runaway story work the other way? Head out west for fame and fortune and sun and ocean?"

"You'd be surprised. Every kid's dream back home is to one day get away from it all and live among the seagulls and scallops."

"You've finally made it then."

"I'll be the hit at my high school reunion."

"Would you go to your high school reunion?"

"I don't think so."

"Why not?"

"I think social media killed the high school reunion. In movies it seemed like people were trying to impress or put on an act to convince everyone they made something of themselves. They created a version of themselves to brag to people they don't know anymore and barely ever did. Social media does that every day."

"Well I am going to mine."

"Yeah?"

"All seventeen of us."

"Makes it easy to organize."

"Maybe I'll be able to head west one day. Work at a coffee shop. See celebrities. Paint a mural on Rodeo Drive. I can be the hit at mine too."

"Is that what you want?"

"No. I mean, not really. I don't know. I know I want to leave. West could mean anywhere for me."

"What's stopping you?"

Light illuminated her face. Her eyes looked up and he stared at her still, even as the loud crack above finished with a sizzling whimper. He saw the white explosion across her inescapable eyes, a calm fury that quickly disappeared as the light dimmed from her face and the sky. People all around them cheered and clapped. The fireworks had started.

"It's just not the right time?"

"When do you hope it will be?"

"I just hope I can tell when it is."

"You will. You're always a step ahead."

"And what about the last point?" She smiled now, and, as if her smile could light up the night sky, loud whip cracks of exploding yellow fireworks exploded to do just that. For an instant, everything in the world Kane could see was yellow and when everything looked the same, she looked beautiful.

"What brought me here to lie around with you on this freezing ground with everyone else?"

"Yes."

"I can't really answer that."

"And why not?"

"Because you asked the wrong question to begin with."

"And what was the right question?"

"What's kept me here?"

The kiss, both of their faces washed in shadow and hues of bright and fading crimson of red passion that should have flashed on them like a warning sign instead bore through them and they thought of nothing and instead felt everything.

CHAPTER 28

The stillness of his unflinching world disappeared when Kane hit the water, hard and in an instant, the ropes seemingly all around him, squeezing and ripping his legs, pulling him under like an octopus. He was being hauled down at a breakneck speed and the frigid waters shocked him as much as his emotions did. He had been a melancholic statue on that boat, really for the past few months, carved from stone, time chipping away at him, covered in bird shit. Now, he was a scared boy, flapping his arms uselessly at the water, doing his best to rise, desperate for air, and desperate for more life, life he didn't really want. It was just instinct. He'd expected this and planned for it. The sky was gone now. It was only black. He was afraid. His airless lungs were bursting and soon he would gasp for breath. He could feel it coming and there was nothing he could do to stop it. When that happened, he wouldn't swallow the air, but breathe it in, filling his lungs. That was the difference between suffocating and drowning. Suffocating would be an immeasurably horrific death. Drowning was supposed to be quite peaceful, once it finally started happening. He waited for it now.

The cage must have hit the bottom because now he floated, suspended in the vacuum of space and time. He could feel the rope all around him, but it was too dark to see. The sea water filled his nostrils and his throat, and soon would enter his lungs. Tilly would hear the news in an hour or two, and his parents shortly after that. He had hardly even thought of them. They would cry for him. He prayed they would be told about their grandson. Kane wondered what Tilly might name him. Thinking of baby names at a time like this. He had been in another world, a fever dream of drugs and depression, of need and loss, of love and death and often both. Sea water was all around him and now it was inside of him. His senses dimmed to the lightless nature of the water. It was becoming him, and he was becoming it, and he would float far away before settling in a peaceful death to join the other forgotten skeletons of people who had let drugs take them down here. He would die down here and never touch heroin again, so in a perverted sense, he had beaten it. This was the only way, but now, in the lucidity of atonement, he wished so resolutely that he had never jumped. His vision started to shrink down to the centers of his eyes, blackness closing in on itself, a shrinking black hole in deep space. He saw stars all around him now, small lights appearing as his brain begged for oxygen. Or maybe it was all the unique lights to every lobster ship out on the water, and from down in the depths, you could see them all at once. Blue ones, purple and red ones, every colour combination imaginable to identify each other. The galactic network of lights, of people and crews that still set sail above the graves and the past, pushing forward because to stop would be defeat, to stop would be to forget. He was filled with many regrets. He wished he had done so many things differently, but right now he wished he had never jumped. He would never see Tilly again and he would never meet his son. There was nothing now. In these last seconds of his life, he wished he could cry. He could feel each one tick by, a final drum beat of each last pump of his heart, and he savoured each one, terrified, thinking of her and his terrible mistakes. Tilly was his cure. Kane faded out of consciousness, knowing she would never know she was his last thought. Nobody would ever know. The world disappeared and shortly, it would be as if he had never been born at all.

The wire frame of the lobster pot was splayed on its side and its corner now, a few dents in the wire framing where it had plunged too quickly onto uneven bedrock. The force had sprung the latch on the trap door, popping open and leaving a small space between the cage door and the sea floor. This lobster pot, their cage, was no longer confining them, but in the harsh force of the landing, they moved slowly, stunned. Instinct always told them to eat, to mate, to survive, and to live. They crawled slowly on top of one another, each in their individual efforts and confusion, attempting to create space. One lobster might push another, and another snapping back caused the one beside it to avoid and snap back and so on and so on until an average lobster near the end of the cage, where the once locked door was now propped wide, was pushed out to the ocean floor, scurrying into newfound freedom. The other fifteen or so lobsters didn't immediately follow; there was no herd empowered by this discovery of opportunity. They simply each found their own way, one by one, slowly. As more were unwittingly pushed through, space was created, and the lobsters simply walked out, finding their own way back to their lives and back to their world.

He returned as if reborn, regurgitated from the black nothing that had swallowed him entirely, blinded by light so bright it encompassed just as the darkness had. He heard only coughing, his own, and the retching of his chest and throat, pushing bile and salt water violently from his lungs, spilling out of his mouth. He was no longer floating, objectless in the cosmos, but heavy on firm ground. He thought he heard someone say his name.

Kane would never once refer to what happened that foolish day as a near-death experience. The months and moments leading up to his final hours was his near-death experience, for that day on the *Caught in the Pot*, surrounded by coworkers that would have listened had he spoken, he had died. Kane now sat in the waiting room of the local Sachem walk-in clinic of the doctor that had tended to him first. Kane couldn't remember her face. It was she who had decided that he must be transported an hour away to the city for care they couldn't adequately provide. Apparently, they had been afraid of pulmonary edema and pleural effusions, or complications following thoracentesis, the process of draining one's lungs too quickly. Kane was only aware of this because he had a copy of his medical examination upon arrival and he had read it over and over and over again, searching each term, astounded he was still alive. She had tended to his wounds on the drive, stitching his legs up where the rope had squeezed and ripped his skin. He had fifty-five stitches in total. The very same volunteer healthcare workers he had seen save that boy in the makeshift ambulance had been asked to take them. Kane owed so much to so many. He remembered none of it. That had only been a week ago. A week ago, he had committed himself to dying and did so, and now, he sat in this well-lit waiting room, the receptionist flashing warm smiles to each new face that walked through the door and the voice on the other end of every ring. Outdated magazines about fish and tourism and celebrity gossip were piled on the coffee table like raked autumn leaves. His dressings needed to be changed and his lungs listened to. He didn't remember ever being in this room, even though he had first been rushed through it, past other waiting people and into the doctor's office before she had called the volunteers to rush over because there had been no time to spare. Kane didn't remember lying on the deck of the boat as the captain cursed the slowing waves while his hand pushed the throttle as far as it would allow. Sam had driven behind the speeding ambulance and slept in the waiting room, waiting for morning, waiting for the moment the emergency room doctors would give him the okay to see Kane. Two crew members in a month. Kane had never thought what that would mean to the captain, what that would do to him. His selfishness was the only thing he had remembered when he woke in that room, surrounded in blue curtains with the captain looking at him from his chair. Kane cried and Sam had stood to hold the back of his head, his palm resting on his neck. Kane had been unconscious in the boat. Brad had pulled off his own shirt and found heated wool blankets from the first aid to wrap the cuts on his legs. Brad's hands were covered in blood. Jenn's entire front was covered in blood. They were the reason he was still alive and he remembered nothing of it. Two boys ran in circles in the waiting room, around the table, through their mother's legs, who barely noticed them, looking at her phone. They must have been brothers. He wondered if his son would ever have a brother, or a sister. It would mean Tilly had found someone else, found love from a better place. He hoped she would. The kids laughed gleefully, with wide, scared eyes in their back and forth chase around the room after one another. He hoped his son would have that. Tilly deserved happiness. She deserved love. The ropes that Kane had cradled himself with were the very thing that had saved him. They had dragged him deeper than any normal person could swim to, and deeper and more tangled than he could escape from, an efficient, believable work-related death, but it also meant a connection to the boat. Jenn had heroically dived in after him. She would have never reached him in time if Brad hadn't been pulling up the ropes, as they did with the traps, jerking Kane closer and closer to Jenn, until she'd slammed into him in the blackness like two bats tumbling in the night sky, and kicked her way up, hanging onto his motionless mass and the pulling rope. They had burst from the tomb Kane had made, her gasping for air, and him limp, with Brad grabbing his arms and tumbling down with him onto the ground, like a heavy sack of ropes, like a dropped lobster pot, like the body of a dead drug addict.

Thinking quickly, Brad had given him CPR, the captain behind the wheel, hoping, willing the boat faster and the boy alive. That was when Kane had coughed water into the air, rolling over, and making room for the first breath of oxygen he'd had in five minutes.

Kane checked his phone. There was a text from Tilly. She had heard what happened to him from her mother, who had been told by Brenda. She had called him a few times, but he'd had no phone; it had been left on the boat. When Brenda had brought him his phone, and checked up on his legs and sobriety no doubt, she'd kissed him on his forehead. She had never done that before, and he'd joked she was getting soft. She'd laughed. He'd called Tilly back just so she knew he was okay. There was no relief in her voice, only worry still. He had caused her nothing but worry and pain these past few months. If she'd thought it hadn't been an accident, she didn't show it. He'd never told her about the life insurance money anyway. Thinking of all the people on that short day that had come to his rescue, to help him, to save him, make sure he was cared for, and made sure that those who cared for him were aware, he realized that this really was his community, the home he had been looking for, and whether Tilly still loved him or not, he had a place in so many peoples' hearts. He would never be able to repay them for what they have given him. They had saved his life that day, and the day he had walked off the bus, they had given him one to appreciate. If he had known that sooner, he would still be with her. He wouldn't be wrapped in bandages in the doctor's waiting room. Kirk might still be alive. But he knew it now. Tilly's text was of an image. He opened it and started to cry tears of great joy where a month ago they might have been of sadness, or unable to exist at all. He would change his life now. He had been in the hospital for three days and they had refused to give him strong painkillers based on his past and his toxicology report. They kept him another three days to monitor his withdrawals. He had been clean for a week. The doctor would check his bandages, redress them, and look into his eyes and ask how he was doing, how he was really doing. She knew about his drug use. He wanted to ask her for help, and for the first time, he was going to do it. Tears filled his eyes faster than he could wipe them away, and they ran down his cheeks. He smeared them away, across his cheeks, pooling on the back of his hands. The photo was the most beautiful thing he had ever seen. It was better than any drawing he, or Tilly, could ever attempt to make. They would never try. This picture was everything. This photo would be his cure.

"Kane?" a voice called. "You can head inside."

TILLY

"And that sound you're hearing now," said the doctor, "that's the heartbeat." Tilly breathed a sigh of relief, and the hand of her mother that held her own loosened its grip. They stared at the black and white screen, and then at each other, and smiled. Her first ultrasound had been at the abortion clinic, and now she was lying on this hospital bed, terrified there might be something wrong.

"Is he healthy?" she asked.

"You already know the sex?"

"Yes," her mother answered for her.

"Well," the doctor continued, unconcerned, looking closely at the screen while gently sliding the probe across the clear jelly smeared on her belly. "He looks very healthy in there to me." She beamed at Tilly, assuring her. Looking back at the screen, the doctor pointed, thoroughly explaining to Tilly and Jessica the wellbeing of her son. "I am checking to make sure all of the vital organs are working fine, the size of the baby... I am assuming you had an initial due date for October?"

"That's right," Tilly answered.

"Okay," she said. "That's still right. Mid October. Let's say October fifteenth!"

Jessica smiled and put her arms over Tilly's neck, forming a loving 'V' across her collarbone. She let her chin touch the top of Tilly's head, comforting her, letting her know she was there and always would be. Jessica was telling her the abortion would have been fine, but this was too. To consider both was the right thing to do. Tilly put her hands on her mother's crossed arms, listening to the unspoken words of support. She heeded each passing wisdom, feeling it with the heartbeat of the parent behind and the child inside her. It was okay to be excited about this. The time in this child's life had come for them to look forward to loving it.

The doctor spoke her findings out loud. "Placenta placement looks good. Amniotic fluid looks normal. There's just..." and she trailed off, cruelly.

"What?" they both asked, alarmed. The doctor stared off, past them, listening to the only sound left in the room now, the hurried "whomp whomp whomp" of the tiny heartbeat. The second hand on the clock stopped. Time had halted itself. Tilly was terrified, an animalistic, built-in evolutionary fear that she couldn't possibly realize in that first instance, but one she would feel for the rest of her life. She wished Kane was there. She didn't need him there. He had let her down more than anyone had ever done so before in her life. Her father had left. Her grandparents on his side had left with him. She had had high school dreams that she'd watched carelessly flutter away like a spring butterfly. Kane had been different. Kane had asked permission to be let into her heart. He had asked for all of this. No, she did not need him there, but she wanted him there. Her baby had been a beautiful idea, the thought of a playful boy, of picking a name, of her mom teaching her about changing a diaper and telling her about her own motherly experiences with her, eventually meeting a girl and falling in love himself, but now, in the dread of her panic, she just wanted Kane there. She wanted him to be holding her hand, in that room, and every time her son needed a father. It made her want him there for the good times, too. Love needed trust and she didn't trust him anymore. But she loved him still, so much. He had almost died last week. She missed him so much, the person he was, the person she hoped he could be again. It had forced her, in those few hours when she didn't know if he was going to live or die, to realize that she had little interest in a world without him. Her heart broke at her son's possible future without him as a dad. They might never be together again, but the love that bound them before they had ever even spoken was now unbreakably linked to this child they would share. Sometimes when the one you love needed help, maybe the faith that you could trust again could be enough. The clock ticked. One second had passed.

"Never mind," the doctor said. "I thought I heard an arrhythmia in the heart beat for a moment there. Sometimes a baby's heart just likes to jump around a little bit. Sorry for the scare." Jessica chuckled her anxiety away and kissed her daughter on her cheek.

"You should take a picture of that," Jessica said about the black and white ultrasound image of Tilly's son. Tilly took her phone out and did so. "And you should send it to him."

Tilly eyed her mom with a playful unease, another comfort from her mom, an allowance to feel whatever way she wanted to feel. Her mom stuck her tongue out at her, playfully, just like Tilly always did at her. It made her laugh. They both did. Tilly unlocked her phone and sent Kane the first picture of their son.

BLOOD

Sterility was the focus. Clean edges, stainless steel surfaces, nothing porous and rigidity in ritual were necessary in his set up. It still felt the same as it used to. The needles were new with a specificity in their design, not the rudimentary tools he had once used out of ignorance and necessity. He had different steel needles, long, designed with care, grooves and slight indents as if formed to his fingers. He had a one round liner, the thinnest you could get. One meant one thin needle for a tip. They went all the way to eight. It took much longer, but was that much more precise. To him, the difference was like trying to draw a rose with thick, highlighter markers rather than taking the time with sharpened pencil crayons. It was worth it. He had shader tips for thick blacks, the only color he used. He knew the taper gradient at the edge of each needle and he had learned how to master the subtleties of each minutely different edge. His was wider than most to allow less trauma to the skin. He knew the needle thickness. He knew the needle was 0.33mm in diameter exactly because a thinner needle meant the ink flowed slower, precise and delicate like a careful creek, whereas a thicker needle would allow the ink to rush quickly into the skin, the mouth of a river pouring into the ocean. His shiny needles, resembling nothing of the discarded sewing needles he had once used for the same purpose, were lined on his table carefully, his very own workstation. He had tape, paper towel, plastic molds of black inks and a white ink, only to dilute the rich blacks into textured greys. There was no need for lighters or bottles of cheap vodka. These were his tools now. He didn't miss any of it. He loved to create again.

It felt much like his new life. He relished in the rules. He welcomed the strict guidelines that were set for him and set by himself. There were no blurred interpretations or porous decisions that could be warped over time, soaking through himself, changing and manipulating every cell. There was an old way of doing things, but circumstances had changed and now there was a better way to do it, a better way to live. He had had a cheap needle and now he had a perfect one. He had had an old, wooden coffee table and now he had a smooth, stainless steel table. He had had a hidden silence, and now he had conversations with others, a ringing phone, and a curated playlist playing over speakers. He had had a basement suite and now he had a tattoo shop. He had had random encounters and now he had a list of appointments. He had had a needle of heroin in his arm and now he had Narcotics Anonymous meetings. He had had a girl he was in love with and now he had a woman trying to learn to trust him again. He had had a yearning for a home and now he had a three-year old-son.

His station was ready and he sat nervously waiting for them to arrive, slightly adjusting each item on his table, or the light above just so, or flattening a wrinkle in the medical paper lining the bed, anything to keep his mind from running away from his nerves. It was good to feel nervous. It was good to feel anything again. She never asked him if he ever missed it. She was probably afraid to. He was glad she never asked because he did miss it, but not enough to ever go back. He had once known in his heart he could never hurt her, but then he did, and knowing you could hurt someone when you've told yourself you never could was a cursed fear that never left you. It had been just under three years now since he'd last used, just slightly longer than when he had died. This was the first time his little boy would see him at work. It was the first time she was getting a tattoo from him in the new shop with the new tools. The last time he had pressed ink permanently into her skin was a half-finished lighthouse, now both a symbol now of a call to home and a warning of dangers below. This rare sunny afternoon in the city, an hour away from where they still lived in Sachem, he would finish the lighthouse.

The money was fine here. It wasn't even half of what he'd been making on the *Caught in the Pot*, but it was his money. It was his because he earned it from passion, never owing pieces of his body or his soul, but replenishing his spirit because he loved doing it. He had forgotten that feeling. He was putting himself back together again. He loved his job. He loved her and she loved him back. He loved that she was going to online school for graphic design. He loved helping with their son. He loved that he was allowed to. He loved watching her be a mother. He loved being alive again. She really was his cure and they really were his home. He looked out the window once more just as the rare bright sunlight bounced off the red paint of the hood of the Chevy as she turned into the lot, the car he had finally finished for her three years ago, the only addition besides a battery and a few minor engine repairs, being the installation of a car seat in the back. When that engine turned on for the first time, Jessica had grabbed his hand and said "Thank you." It wasn't really for the car. His eyes had welled up and he let her hand go to wipe them and because he had felt he didn't deserve it. She just took the rest of him, hugging him and saying "Thank you," once more, and he cried. Tilly was the one who had turned on the car, and she stayed sitting in the front seat. Kane wanted Tilly to love him again like she used to. Maybe she did. Maybe she never could. Maybe this love they had held together by their beautiful past and their destined futures was intact, but would never be the same. After the tattoo, they were going to go for a picnic on the beach, a secluded spot he had searched for months earlier, a perfect place to bring his family where it could just be them. In his pack, he'd brought papers and crayons and markers and he could draw with her again, and they could teach their son and watch him enjoy it too. Their little one could pick something they could draw, something in the sand, or off in the distance, or some arbitrary conjuring of his innocent imagination. Kane would look at her with the eyes he used to have and tell her, "This is what I am now. This is what I am again. I love you." And he would hope she might snuggle closer to him, closer to both of them, sticking a cherry in her mouth and calling him a weirdo like she always used to and now sometimes did forcefully. He just hoped it was what she wanted to hear, because to want to hear it would be an invitation to believe it.

TILLY

Tilly used her entire shoulder as she heaved the lever behind the steering wheel from drive to park. Every time she stopped the engine, it reminded her how this car had hibernated for so long, left for dead before Kane, the father of her son -- and the love of her life -- had fixed it because he said that he would. It had taken him longer than he'd thought, but life had its complications, to say the least. Things took time. Her little one sat excitedly in the back, chanting for his daddy, smiling and bouncing in his seat, waiting to be set free. Kane was finishing her tattoo today and had a surprise lunch planned for after. She got out of the driver's seat, smiling at her son's enthusiasm, one she shared with him. Today would be a good one, one with family and smiles, and kissing, all things that happened more and more now. Kane felt returned to her. She could feel his excitement for their son to see what he did for a living, what he could do with this new lease on life. She hoped her son would share their love of drawing, that he might get his father's ability to see the beauty in simplicity, the need to appreciate an object for exactly what it was, and his mother's attention to capture everything in that same appreciation, for fear of leaving anything behind. She hoped that Kane, her love and her partner, would know it was okay to forgive himself and to love completely. Not for them -- he showed them often -- but for himself. She wished she could grab his head with her hands and kiss him so hard that he could read her thoughts if only for a second, enough time so that he could understand that she knew this was who he was now. That she knew this was who he was again. That she knew that she loved him as much as she ever had.

The cross straps of the car seat belts clicked open and he practically leapt from the seat like a flying squirrel, forcing her to catch him, laughing as she spun to set him down on the ground.

"Just wait now, hun," she said, but he was already wandering off. She shut the door before turning to sternly instruct him to stop and do as she said just as the door of the tattoo shop opened. Her little boy ran, eager for time to propel him into his next destination, ahead of her, just as she had done the exact same way her entire life. Kane stepped out onto the road, smiling and looking around for cars and other dangers, arms wide open, calling his son to him. Their son reached him and Tilly giggled loudly to stop from crying tears of joy, watching their arms engulfing each other, a father that had almost died and a son that almost never was. Her son was loud with joy, the cries of a happy child, and Kane's smile had faded to a quiet embrace, listening to the sounds of his son, feeling him bubble with laughter, and opening his eyes again to look at Tilly, as if to say to her from the distance of five empty parking stalls, "Please, come here."

Kane had her sit in his tattoo chair. He looked at the lighthouse and assessed what he would need to do to finish it. It wouldn't take very long. He could have done this at home, but he wanted her to see him like this, in a real tattoo shop, moving with his unteachable and relearned quiet confidence. Their little one watched carefully, never bored, as his mom waited and his dad worked. This space was Kane's office, his name sprayed in graffiti on the side wall, surrounded by a portfolio of cut out and taped up pictures of his drawings like ancient paintings inside of a cave. He had split himself open and admitted to her that he had succumbed to something larger than himself and it had almost killed him. He'd once told her that he wore his tattoos like a camouflage of his person. She didn't know if he still thought that way, but to her, they were now points of pride, a personification of his very soul, not a guard against it. He was an addict. One might never have the privilege to find that out about a loved one before it was too late, and you could never guess or understand why they had become that way, but this was their reality and they had gotten through it. They were getting through it. This disease would be with him always but he was more than an addict. He was the person she was in love with. He was funny. He was good. He was a great father and a great partner in love and life. Neither of them was defined by his addiction to drugs, but they were redefining themselves every single day they chose to navigate back to this place. Her mom had wanted her to get an abortion when she had wanted one, and her mom had stood behind her when she'd changed her mind. Her mom loved Kane again like she had before. They had both seen the horrors but they had both seen the beauty. If he were to draw a picture of their life it would be simple but strong, with healed corners and timeworn cracks. It would show the weathering but immovability of a beautiful thing. If she were to draw it it would need to be impossibly scaled to fill every detail, a mural reaching so far it would take a lifetime to paint and you would never be able to see the entire thing from one standing place. They were not the sum of their parts, but the sum of those they had affected.

"Is it going to hurt?" their son asked.

"Only a bit," she answered.

"You can hold her hand to make sure she is okay," Kane told his son, who slid carefully from his chair to do just that.

Tilly lay on the tattoo bed, holding her sweet son's small fingers, waiting for the rescued man she loved to finish the tattoo she had asked for after one of the best nights of her life, a tattoo cut short by their insatiable want and need for the other. This was her world entirely. Kane pulled his chair closer to them, and stuck his tongue out at their son, who laughed and stuck his back out in return. With one last look into her eyes before he started, he asked her, the same way he always had, "Are you ready?"

THE END

ACKNOWLEDGEMENTS

I always saw movies and TV shows and commercials and books about people struggling with addiction, and they always came from broken homes and disturbing childhoods. And those stories are real and should be told. But I never really saw any stories about those we lose from good families and happy homes. Or the ones who are hooked because of bad luck, their genetics, or because their job, and therefore life, demands it. I've lost friends that came from a good place. Everyone has. And that's the story I wanted to tell.

ABOUT THE AUTHOR

Hogan Short was born in Edmonton, Alberta in 1990. After living in Australia, he moved to Vancouver to pursue a career in film and writing. After several years involved with the Vancouver International Film Festival, Calgary International Film Festival, Fantasia Film Festival, and more, he became the section editor at Beatroute Magazine for over two years. Writing freelance for various publications since then, he had a story idea for a movie — so he wrote a book.

Manufactured by Amazon.ca
Bolton, ON